WES
MAC

THE GALLOPING GHOST

In Morral City, the sheriff and a ranch boss were trying to pin the blame for two recent murders on an innocent stranger. The three Mesquiteers put a stop to this. Tucson Smith, Lullaby Joslin and Stony Brooke were a high-spirited, sure-shooting trio intent on finding the true killer. They were famous in the West and have adventures including seeing the legendary ghost of a silver-haired girl galloped silently through the darkness of the mountains.

(Allan) William Colt MacDonald was born in Detroit, Michigan in 1891. His formal education concluded after his first three months of high school when he went to work as a lathe operator for Dodge Brothers' Motor Company. His first commercial writing consisted of advertising copy and articles for trade publications. While working in the advertising industry, MacDonald began contributing stories of varying lengths to pulp magazines and his first novel, a Western story, was published by Clayton House in *Ace-high Magazine* in 1925. MacDonald later commented that when this first novel appeared in book form as *Restless Guns* in 1929, 'I quit my job cold.' From the time of that decision on, MacDonald's career became a long string of successes in pulp magazines, hardcover books, films, and eventually original and reprint paperback editions. The Three Mesquiteers, MacDonald's most famous characters, were introduced in 1933 in *Law of the Forty-fives.* His other most famous character creation was Gregory Quist, a railroad detective. Some of MacDonald's finest work occurs outside his series, especially the well researched *Stir Up The Dust* which was published first in a British edition in 1950 and *The Mad Marshal* in 1958. MacDonald's only son, Wallace, recalled how much fun his father had writing Western fiction. It is an apt observation since countless readers have enjoyed his stories now for nearly three quarters of a century.

THE GALLOPING GHOST

William Colt MacDonald

First published by Hodder and Stoughton

This hardback edition 2004
by BBC Audiobooks Ltd
by arrangement with
Golden West Literary Agency

ISBN 0 7540 8256 3

British Library Cataloguing in Publication Data available.

Printed and bound in Great Britain by
Antony Rowe Ltd., Chippenham, Wiltshire

THE GALLOPING GHOST

Contents

1. MURDER!

From the moment he first glimpsed the huddled figure on the earth, there wasn't the least doubt in Daulton's mind that he was viewing a corpse. Something in the awkward position of the dead man precluded any other possibility. A drunk, losing his balance and falling from the saddle, would at least have assumed a more relaxed attitude; a person merely unconscious wouldn't have fallen into such a stiff posture either. Stiff, that was the word for it, Daulton mused; stiff in death. Seated on his horse, several yards away, Daulton couldn't see the dead man's eyes, but he sensed that they were wide open, glassy, perhaps even reflecting the prickly-pear cactus growing nearby. The dead man's hat had fallen off and lay not far distant from the head of brown hair, liberally sprinkled with gray, and stirring somewhat in the soft breeze. The legs of the still figure were spread wide, though the knees were bent as though the man had been running when he was shot down.

Daulton checked himself at that point. Shot down? For all he knew, something else might have brought an end to life. "Just the same," Daulton told himself, "I'm betting he was shot." This was something he sensed rather than actually knew. He had stopped his roan pony several yards from the body upon first seeing it. Now he dropped reins over his mount's head and slowly descended to the earth. For a moment he just stood there, glancing around.

This was rolling land hereabouts, a terrain of low hills and gradual slopes, covered thickly with brush, cactus, sage. There was a great deal of mesquite in view. Here and there the lacy foliage of palo verde trees shone a brighter green against the darker brush, or made a filigreed pattern with the cloudless sky for a background. Jeff Daulton glanced briefly upward and saw three buzzards soaring and dipping on motionless wings, like vagrant bits of newspaper blown by the soft breeze that rippled the tips of desert growth.

"Jeepers," he muttered, "it doesn't take long for those stink birds to spot something like this. Or maybe I'm wrong; maybe this poor cuss has been here quite a spell and they just discovered it lately. Leastwise, I don't see any sign they've come to earth yet. Could be they saw me approaching and decided not to land." And then another thought struck him. "Or maybe they saw somebody else." He craned his head around the landscape, but there was nothing to be seen except the rolling brushlands, with beyond, to the west, the serrated peaks of the Apparition Mountains. Then a movement behind a wide clump of mesquite caught his attention. For a moment he tensed, then relaxed. The movement came from the dead man's pony, which had sought a bit of shade as protection from the blazing southwest sun, which at the present moment had started its wide arc toward the west.

At that moment the riderless pony snorted and trotted off a short way, breaking small branches in its progress through the brush. After a few paces it again paused. Moving casually, Daulton started toward the pony, speaking to it in soothing tones. The horse's ears lay back, as Daulton came closer, but it stood still. Daulton put out one hand and reached the animal's reins. The pony reared back a trifle, then became more quiet under Daulton's calm tones. A moment later Daulton had tethered the horse to a low-flung mesquite limb. He stood a moment studying the pony's saddle; just below the edge of the cantle were some dried spots of blood. He stood back from the horse, eying its hide.

"Pony," Daulton observed softly, "you look like you'd been run sort of hard before you stopped here." After a few minutes he turned back toward the dead man.

The body lay in a sort of pocket, or saucer-like depression, between low hills fringed with brush. There was little growth, however, in the immediate vicinity of the dead man. Here the earth was hard, dry, gravelly. The body lay on its right side, only the wide-flung legs preventing it from rolling over. The right arm was stretched out on the earth, as though the man had been in the act of throwing something; the left was huddled at his side. He was in typical range togs: high-heeled boots, denim shirt, overalls. A holstered six-shooter showed beneath the body.

Daulton studied the dark stain on the back of the shirt, then took in the two bullet holes where death had entered: one was placed just below the short ribs; the other was higher and just under the left shoulder blade.

"Plugged twice. From the rear," Daulton muttered, frowning. "I wonder if he was running away from someone—or if he was dry-gulched." He put out one hand as he stooped down and tentatively touched the dead man's face. "Hmmm," he speculated, "been dead three or four hours anyway, I'd judge." Still in a squatting position, he moved around to get a better look at the dead man's face. He'd been right: the eyes were wide-open, glassy. Quite suddenly Daulton's own eyes widened, his lips tightened as he gazed at the cold, bloodless features. A long, suppressed breath was finally expelled from his lips and he exclaimed, "Good God!"

For the space of a full minute he scarcely moved, then slowly he raised to full length. His voice was quieter now. "I reckon I'd better see what sign's to be picked up," he told himself slowly, his gaze casting about the earth.

He commenced to move in slow ever-widening circles around the corpse, walking in a half-crouching position. Jeff Daulton was nearly thirty years old, but looked younger. He was well-featured, slim-hipped, with tawny hair and gray eyes; a trifle under six feet in height. His muscular jaw tightened grimly as he scrutinized the earth. He might, or might not, have been a cowpuncher, though he looked the part in his roll-brim, battered sombrero, high-heeled riding boots, Levis, and checked woolen shirt; a sun-faded vest covered the shirt. The roll on his saddle carried a coat, blankets, and a few other odds and ends.

There was little to go on, in the near vicinity of the body, Daulton decided, after a few moments. The earth was too hard and parched to leave much sign, but eventually, as he drew farther away, he commenced to detect evidence here and there. Only a genius at tracking would ever have noticed the faint marks left some hours before by moving hoofs—various, slightly curving depressions in the soil, a few strands of horsehair caught in a low-growing clump of prickly pear, a bit of broken rock dislodged from the earth by a flying hoof—and then, where the earth was softer, nearer the fringe of brush, still plainer hoof-marks.

Part of the picture was coming clearer to Daulton now. He'd

found the prints of two horses; one of them had belonged to the dead man. The other rider had arrived somewhat later, followed the man on the earth into this saucer-like depression, but hadn't dismounted. At least, Daulton speculated, there were no footmarks on the earth to show he'd dismounted. Still, hard as the earth was, prints might not show too plainly.

"Looks to me," Daulton muttered grimly, "like this hombre on the other horse did his shooting from a distance"—he was standing near the dead man again, and a closer examination of the bullet holes in the shirt showed no traces of powder burns—"then followed on to here. Why? Maybe to make sure his slugs had done the job. Then the dirty ambushin' bustard took off toward the east. Likely heading for the town that lies in that direction. Morral City? Yeah, that's it. Morral City. Wonder what sort of a burg it is? Anyway, once the killer hit town, it would be practically impossible to track him by hoofprints."

His frown deepened and he did some more surmising. "Doesn't look to me as though this dead man had a chance. His gun isn't even out of its holster. Probably nearly dead when he reached here. Likely figured to make a stand, jumped down from his saddle—or maybe he fell out—took a few steps and dropped." He shook some tobacco from a Durham sack into a brown paper, rolled and lighted a cigarette while he considered his next move.

Flies buzzed crazily about the lifeless form. Irritably Daulton brushed them away, but his movements were useless. The flies returned, more determined than ever. Daulton swore in exasperation. "Reckon I'd better get a blanket off my saddle, cover up this body, and then head for Morral City and find the sheriff. That's likely the best thing to do . . ."

He stiffened suddenly, his right hand going to holster and drawing his six-shooter, but the movement came too late. There were sharp words from the edge of the brush, and swinging around, Daulton saw three riders walking their ponies into the open.

"Hold it, feller!" a voice snapped. "Just drop that hawg-laig and lift your hands high. Move fast!"

There didn't seem to be anything else to do, under the circumstances. Inwardly Daulton cursed himself bitterly for his carelessness. So intent had he been on reading "sign" and speculating as to what had happened, that he'd not heard the slightest sound as the three riders approached. Or perhaps, the thought flashed through Jeff Daulton's mind, the three had approached with unusual stealth. If that were the case, there might be some reason for . . . Further cogitations were cut short by another command in a coarse voice:

"Goddammit! How many times we got to tell you, hombre? Drop that gun and lift 'em high, if you ain't cravin' a lead slug!"

Daulton released the hold on his gun and elevated his arms to clasp his hands on the crown of his sombrero. "Now, look here," he commenced, "don't be hasty——"

"Shut your murderin' trap," one of the men rasped. "We——"

"Hey, you don't think I killed this man——?" Daulton started.

"Shut your trap, I said!"

Daulton's lips tightened. He didn't say anything more for a minute. The cigarette, still between his lips, sent a spiral of blue smoke across his face. After a deep drag on the tobacco, he spat it out and ground the glowing end under one boot toe, while the three men on the horses eyed him a bit uncertainly, he thought, as though making up their minds what to do next.

"Look here——" Daulton commenced.

That was as far as he got. A leaden slug kicked up dust at his feet, and one of the men snapped, "We told you to shut your mouth. My next shot will come closer—mebbe too close for your comfort."

Daulton shut his mouth. One of the other men spoke coldly, "You, Art, you needn't to be so ready with your hawg-laig. Climb down and take a look at that dead hombre."

Art—Daulton learned later he was named Art Branch—"climbed down," and approached the still figure sprawled on the earth. He was a rather slovenly looking individual, in soiled range togs. A holstered six-shooter dangled loosely at his right hip. His lips were tobacco-stained and he hadn't shaved for a couple of weeks. The brim of his faded sombrero was torn and hung down over his eyes, leaving only enough opening between brim and crown for one muddy-colored eye to peer through.

Daulton eyed the other two men, still in saddles. One was a wide-shouldered blond man with sinewy jaws and hard eyes. A sun-bleached mustache decorated his upper lip; the holstered Colt gun at his right hip looked well taken care of, and in good condition, as was everything else about the man. It was he who had ordered Art Branch out of his saddle, and his name was Trax Whitlock.

The third man was paunchy, with thick jowls and little pig eyes. He too needed a shave, and his bulbous nose indicated a certain overindulgence in the cup that cheers. Daulton thought, Lord knows, if I looked like that, I'd feel in need of cheering too. This fat individual wore a rusty black vest over his sweat-stained shirt, on which was pinned a sheriff's star of office.

Now this fat, potbellied person spoke for the first time. His tones were high and squeaky. "Well, Art," he asked testily, "is that hombre dead or not? Take a look. And get that feller's gun before you come back here."

Branch cast a brief glance at the dead man. "He's cooked for good."

Daulton took a chance and spoke again. "You can tell just by looking at the body, eh? Not necessary to make an examination?"

The sheriff swore. "You was told to keep your mouth shut, mister. Seems like you're just achin' for trouble."

Trax Whitlock put in, "Aching for trouble and cocky. Maybe he'd like to get his gun and start something. Go ahead, feller, pick up that gun and let's see how tough you can get."

Daulton shook his head. "Not me! I'm not that crazy——"

"Now, Trax," the sheriff said plaintively in his squeaky voice. "We can't have anything like that. This has got to be all done legal. As sheriff of Carbonero County, I must protest this attitude. It——"

"Cut it short, Ducky," Whitlock sneered. "We don't need a political speech. We admit you're the boss. What're you intending?"

"I already told Art to bring me that gun. Art, is that—that dead hombre anybody we know?"

Moving warily, Branch retrieved the gun from near Daulton's feet and delivered it to the sheriff. Then he slowly climbed back into his saddle. "Yeah, we know him. It's that Folsom hombre—Joe Folsom, what's been hangin' around town. Claimed to be a cowhand lookin' for a job, but I reckon he never looked very hard."

"And so now he's dead and we got his murderer red-handed," Whitlock said coldly. "The next move is up to you, Ducky. This coyote should be bumped off pronto, in my opinion, but you're the boss. What you intending?"

"You already asked that before," the sheriff whined. "I got to have a few minutes to decide."

Daulton threw caution to the winds and again opened his mouth. "*If* you're the sheriff," he said sarcastically, "and *if* you really think I murdered this man, you should do your duty. Arrest me and take me to town for trial."

"Mebbe we'll take you to town for a necktie party," Art Branch said nastily. "Morral City is goin' to be a heap riled up over this killin'. Two killin's in two months is too many. Look, Ducky"—turning to the sheriff—"ten to one this is the hombre who killed Ben Hampton too——"

"Now, now, Art, we mustn't jump to conclusions. No man can ever say that Sheriff Duckman Gebhardt ever made a hasty and ill-timed decision. As I've told my constituents, more than once——"

"All right, Ducky," Whitlock interrupted in weary tones, "we've heard all this before. We agree, you never have done *anything* hasty—but I figure it's about time you started. You move like the dead lice was dropping off of you." He added ominously, "Perhaps Carbonero County could stand a new sheriff come next election time."

"Now, now, Trax," Sheriff Gebhardt said weakly, "I consider that statement unkind. I'm in charge here. I'm attending to——"

"For cripes sake attend to it, then," Whitlock snorted.

The sheriff gulped, cleared his throat, and addressed Daulton: "Well, mister, what you got to say for yourself? Why did you kill Joe Folsom?"

Daulton said scornfully, "Now you're making fool talk, Sheriff. I didn't kill him. I found the body lying here just a short time before you arrived."

"That's your story, feller." Ducky Gebhardt shook his head disapprovingly. "You'd be far better off to tell the truth. Who are you? What are you doing in this part of the country?"

"Name's Daulton—Jefferson Daulton. Cowhand." He mentioned the brands of various outfits for which he'd worked in the past.

Gebhardt pursed his lips. "None of them brands sound familiar to me. They must be a long ways from here."

Daulton conceded the truth of this, and went on, "I'm between jobs. After the Ladder-B was sold and I got laid off I decided to look over the country a mite before I took another job. I've been down into Mexico for a while. When I recrossed the Border I headed in this direction. Figured on getting to Morral City today. I was just riding through when I came on this body. If your man had made a decent examination he'd have learned this man has been dead at least four hours now—or maybe he wouldn't know enough to realize that——"

"Why, you murderin' son——" Art Branch commenced angrily.

"Shut it, Art," Trax Whitlock said sharply. Art "shut it," and Whitlock went on, talking to Daulton. "You say you didn't kill Folsom, and yet when we arrived we found you standing near him, your six-shooter still in your hand."

"Oh, for God's sake," Daulton protested disgustedly, "why don't you use your head? I've told you this man has been dead four hours——"

"You've had plenty of time to clean your gun," Branch put in.

"Someday," Daulton promised angrily, "if I get a chance I'll clean your clock."

"See that, Ducky?" Branch pointed out. "Even when we got him dead to rights, he makes threats. If you ask me, he's a dangerous criminal——"

Daulton cut in, "Even if I had killed this man—four hours ago —what would be my purpose in hanging around here?"

"There's never any figuring what a murderer will do," Whitlock put in. "We don't know why you were hanging around. And we've got only your word this man was killed four hours ago. You still had your gun in your hand when we arrived——"

"In that case," Daulton snapped, "why didn't you hear the shot?" Silence met the question.

Whitlock said after a minute, "Maybe we did. Come to think of it, I thought I heard a shot." He turned to the sheriff. "Ducky, you haven't examined that gun yet."

"That's right, I ain't," the sheriff said. He withdrew Daulton's six-shooter from the waistband of his trousers and examined it. Then, "Five chambers loaded, one empty shell."

"That's normal," Daulton put in. "Hammer resting on an empty shell. Ninety-nine per cent of the men carrying six-shooters do that. You men likely carry your guns that way too——"

"One empty shell," Whitlock said ominously. "That looks bad, Daulton." He completely disregarded Daulton's explanation for the exploded cartridge.

"Check my gun barrel," Daulton said. "You'll find it clean."

"I already done that," the sheriff said plaintively, "but you had plenty of time to clean it before we got here——"

"A few minutes ago," Daulton said angrily, "you were trying to make out I'd shot this man just before you arrived. Can't you make up your mind?"

"My mind's already made up," Sheriff Gebhardt said heavily. "I'm chargin' you with murder, Daulton, and puttin' you under arrest. Now do you aim to come quiet, or——"

"Maybe he'd like to make a fight of it," Branch said evilly, dropping one hand to gun butt.

"No, I'll come quiet," Daulton said grimly. "I haven't yet learned any way to fight stupidity, and it seems to me one murder is enough for today. I've no intention of becoming the second victim."

2. SKULDUGGERY!

That morning a trio of riders had pushed through Coyotero Pass, in the Apparition Mountains, and lined their ponies out along the old stage road that had at one time stretched between Morral City and various points to the west. With the advent of the T.N. & A.S. Railroad, the stagecoach line had moved its activities to less populated parts, farther north, but its old deep-rutted and hoof-chopped route still remained, mute evidence of a swiftly disappearing method of travel in this highly progressive age of steam-car locomotion.

Prickly-pear cactus and greasewood grew along either side of the trail, and often between the worn ruts. There was a great deal of Spanish dagger to be seen, its rigid spikes standing stubbornly and refusing to wilt beneath the blazing sun. Occasional outcroppings of reddish sandstone elbowed the trail to one side. Now and then small horned toads darted frantically from beneath the ponies' moving hoofs. Once, the passing horses aroused a sharp angry hissing from a Gila monster intent on its meal above an ant hole. One of the riders glanced briefly down at the beadwork pattern of the turgid body and drew his pony wide around the poisonous-looking reptile.

All this was an old story to these riders of the mesquite country —the Three Mesquiteers, as they were called. They carried the names of Tucson Smith, Lullaby Joslin, and Stony Brooke. Men had known them by other names, too—the Three Inseparables, the Cactus Cavaliers, were two of these names. Probably the Three Mesquiteers suited them best. Like the famous three musketeers of the immortal Dumas, this trio was, indeed, "one for all and all for one." Their fame had been sung throughout the length and breadth of the western range lands. Lawbreakers hated and feared them for their relentless upholding of justice; those who lived within the law swore by them and were eternally thankful for their help in running to earth the criminals of those early western days. So great was the prestige of the three that from time to time impostors came into being, claiming brazenly to be the Three Mesquiteers, but these had only a brief existence under the keen scrutiny of all who could distinguish the genuine article from the spurious.

Leader of the Mesquiteers, if they could have been said to have a leader, was Tucson Smith, his lean leathered frame moving easily to the rangy buckskin horse beneath his saddle. Tucson Smith possessed steely gray eyes and bright auburn hair into which, near the temples, a slight trace of gray was beginning to steal. He may have been forty, but he looked far younger. His face was long and bony, his nose arched. His mouth was wide, with tiny quirks at the corners. There was something stern and sardonic about Tucson's face, though the small laugh wrinkles near his eyes attested a well-developed sense of humor.

On Tucson's left, astride a long-legged black pony, rode Lullaby Joslin, who was lanky, soft-spoken, with drowsy hazel eyes. His hair was as straight and black as an Apache's. There was something slouchy, indolent, in the man's make-up. His clothing fitted loosely, the shirt sleeves exposing strong bony wrists. His Stetson was cuffed nonchalantly over one ear, and a brown paper cigarette dangled loosely from one corner of his generous mouth.

Stony Brooke, the third man of the trio, was shorter than his companions, but what he lacked in height was compensated by breadth. He possessed a barrel-like torso and carried in his wide shoulders the strength of a young bull. His nose was what is known as "snub," he had innocent-appearing blue eyes and a wide, gargoylish, good-natured grin. There was something deceptively cherubic about Stony Brooke, as more than one lawbuster had learned to his lasting regret. Stony, in the final analysis, always had proved fully as tough, in a pinch, as the chunky chestnut gelding he was now riding with such easy grace.

The three men wore much the same type of range clothing—faded denim overalls cuffed widely at the ankles of high-heeled, spurred riding boots, woolen shirts, blue or red bandannas, and well-worn sombreros. All wore Colt six-shooters in holsters attached to wide leather cartridge belts. A casual observer would doubtless have put them down as three ordinary saddle tramps looking for jobs, rather than as the prosperous owners of the Three-Bar-O Ranch—the Three-Bar-Nothing, as some called it—which was, by now, many weeks' riding to the east. Generally, Tucson was the quietest of the three; Stony and Lullaby were forever wrangling, each trying to make some sort of joke at the other's expense, when nothing more serious occupied their thoughts.

The ponies had negotiated a long slope and had now been pulled to a walk to rest them for a few minutes. Stony removed the Stetson from his blond head, mopped perspiration from his face, then, replacing his hat, began to manufacture a cigarette. It had scarcely been completed when Tucson reached over and with a smiling, "Thanks, pard," deftly plucked the cylinder of tobacco from Stony's fingers, placed it between his own lips, and scratched a match on the pommel of his saddle.

Stony eyed him with a certain exasperation. "Dang you, Tucson," he exclaimed, "that's the third time you've done that today."

"Yeah, I know." Tucson chuckled. "It just seems like you guess when I'm needing a cigarette. You wouldn't begrudge me——"

"Yeah, he would," Lullaby put in scornfully. "Calls himself a pard, but hates to give up three little smokes in one day. Of all the tightwads I ever saw——"

"Aw, aw, you can both go to hell," Stony sputtered good-naturedly. "And if I'm any tighter than you, Lullaby, I hope I——"

"You have been," Lullaby cut in, "tighter than me most of the time. I might say all the time."

"What in time are you talking about?" Stony demanded.

"You getting tight. It ill behooves a man who drinks as much as you do to talk about getting tight."

"Jeepers!" Stony exclaimed, starting to roll another cigarette. "You just tell me some time when I was tighter than you."

Lullaby snickered. "I can't count that high."

Stony sneered. "I didn't know you could count at all. But just name me once——"

"I could name you plenty of times——"

"I'm just asking once. Go on, be specific."

"I'd sooner be the Atlantic." Lullaby grinned.

Stony paused and eyed Lullaby with some caution. "What was that?" he asked.

"It's an ocean," Lullaby explained gravely.

Stony looked puzzled. "What's an ocean? What are you——"

Lullaby gave a whoop of delight. "Hear that, Tucson? Him

trying to needle me because he says I can't count, and he don't even know what an ocean is. What's an ocean, Poppa?"—in mimicking accents. Lullaby continued, "Son, an ocean is a large body of salt water filled with fish."

"Oh cripes!" disgustedly from Stony. "I know that, but what I was asking——"

"I suppose now you want to know what kind of fish. Well, there's mackerel and swordfish and bass and barracuda——"

"Jeepers! I know all that. I even caught some once," Stony said. "That time we went to California. Remember how sore you got when I caught a bigger weigh-fish than you did?"

Lullaby's eyes narrowed. "I can't remember that. I don't even remember anything about a weigh-fish. What's a weigh-fish?"

"One that carries scales around." Stony slapped his leg with joy.

Lullaby looked puzzled. "Don't all fish have scales——" He broke off in sudden disgust. "My Gawd! What a terrible pun. Pretty fishy, if you ask me."

"It knocked you off your perch," Stony said smugly.

Lullaby groaned and raised his eyes to heaven. "Tucson," he appealed, "don't you know some way to shut this idiot up?"

Tucson smiled and said nothing. Stony said, "Don't get Tucson to help you out. I really gave you food for thought, didn't I?" He paused suddenly and looked appalled. "Now I've done it."

"Food!" Lullaby said blissfully. "I'm hungry."

"You're always hungry," Stony said. "Look, you ate two breakfasts this morning. What's happened to the bundle of sandwiches you got at that restaurant?"

"They didn't even last until ten o'clock," Lullaby said faintly. "They were just sort of little snacks. S'help me, if I don't get some food soon, I'll be sick. I've got to keep up my strength. Tucson, when do we hit the next town?"

"Twelve or fifteen miles farther," Tucson replied. "Place called Morral City."

Lullaby shook his head. "I'm afraid I'll never make it."

"You'll make it," Stony said heartlessly. "When you pass out, we'll tie you into your saddle. Course, if the rope broke and you fell off and broke your neck, it wouldn't be my fault—just my pleasure."

Lullaby ignored this. His face looked brighter. "Say, doesn't morral, in Spanish, mean nose bag? Morral City! I think I'm going to like that town. It sounds plumb appropriate."

"Appropriate is correct," Stony sneered. "Morral also means clown, if I know my Spanish."

"What makes you think you know anything?" Lullaby asked insultingly. "If your brains were dynamite, an explosion wouldn't knock your hat off——" He paused suddenly and looked at his two companions.

As one man, the three had drawn their ponies to a sudden halt. They looked quickly at each other, all thought of joking now far from their minds. Tucson said softly, "Voices, all right."

"Sounded like somebody was mad," Lullaby observed.

"They came from just over that little rise of ground yonderly," Stony said. "Think we should investigate?" At that moment the sound of a shot was heard. Black powder smoke rose above the top of the brush a short distance away. Then more voices. Stony answered his own question: "I know damn well we should investigate."

Tucson nodded. "C'mon, pards. Move quiet."

The three slipped from saddles, dropped reins over their ponies' heads and, spreading out slightly, slipped noiselessly through the brush, heading in the direction whence the sound of the shot and voices had come. In an instant the tall brush had swallowed them up, as, moving with the stealth of three Apache Indians, they soon reached a vantage point from which they could survey the scene taking place about the body of the dead Joe Folsom. Crouching low in the thick southwest plant growth, the Mesquiteers listened silently to all that was being said.

Tucson's face grew thoughtful as, peering through the screen of leafy branches, he eyed the fat sheriff and his companions. Eventually he worked his way to Lullaby's side. "Looks to me like they're working a frame-up on that Daulton hombre," he observed softly.

Lullaby nodded, and whispered back, "I've a hunch they'll use Daulton to cover some sort of skulduggery. Think we'd better take a hand in the game?"

"I've already decided that," Tucson said. "Pass the word to Stony. You two stay back for a spell, until we see what way the wind's blowing."

"We'll be ready to back you up." Lullaby hesitated only a second before starting to work his way in Stony's direction.

Tucson remained where he was for a few minutes longer, listening to the conversation taking place in the open space about the dead man. He heard the sheriff ask if Daulton intended to "come quiet," and Daulton's reply in the affirmative with the added, "I've no intention of becoming a second victim."

"Here, Art," the sheriff continued, "put my handcuffs on the coyote——" He paused suddenly and withdrew his hand from the vicinity of his hip pocket. "Dang you, Art," he complained, "have you went and stole my handcuffs again?" Branch denied the accusation and the sheriff went on, "I must've forgot to bring 'em, then. All right, we'll just have to tie that murderin' buzzard into his saddle and——"

Sheriff Gebhardt suddenly paused. His jaw dropped in surprise as Tucson Smith rose and pushed his way through the brush and into the open, stepping widely to avoid certain prints he had noticed on the earth. Art Branch ripped out a curse. Whitlock didn't say anything, but his forehead was furrowed by a frown and his lips tightened. He wondered how long this lean redheaded stranger had been listening to the conversation. Daulton looked puzzled at the strange behavior of the sheriff and his companions, then, hearing Tucson's step, he turned his head to learn what had caused the sudden commotion.

A sudden smile parted Daulton's lips. "Welcome, mister, if you're a friend. In my situation another enemy wouldn't make much difference."

Tucson said quietly, "I'm not an enemy, anyway, Daulton."

Art Branch cursed again.

The sheriff sputtered, "Who—who the hell are you? What you want here?"

Tucson introduced himself. "Name's Smith. I've been listening to some rather interesting *habla* for quite a spell now. I can't say I cared for the sound of it. I'm not saying Daulton isn't guilty of murder, but I'd bet against it. Any takers?" He stopped a few feet from Daulton and stood eying the three men on horses. No one answered him for a moment, and he went on, "Fact is, the evidence you hombres were trying to frame against this man sounded sort of confused to me. Sheriff, you may have a suspect, but I've a hunch you're not going to hang onto him long."

"You can't stop me," Gebhardt puffed. "I'm the sheriff and ——"

Tucson laughed softly. "I'm not denying that, though it doesn't say much for the voters in your county." He cut short Gebhardt's indignant protests, and went on, "Go ahead and make your arrest. But I don't figure to see you tie your prisoner into his saddle. He's already said he'd come quietly. What more do you want—you three against one? Three to one—up to now, that is. I'd like a hand in this game."

Whitlock said coldly, "Would three against two suit you, Smith?"

"I wouldn't object," Tucson said easily. "Give Daulton his gun."

"You know damn well we won't!" Whitlock snapped. "Look here, Smith, you're butting in on something that's none of your business. Take my advice: get your horse, wherever it is, and high-tail away from here. Otherwise, you might get hurt."

Art Branch snarled, "Trax, why should we let him go? He cut into this game without no invite. He asked for trouble. Let's give it to the sidewindin' buzzard." Branch's hand dropped eagerly to gun butt.

Tucson made no attempt to draw. He eyed Branch steadily. "You'd best think twice, feller, before you pull that hawg-leg, or sure as hell you're going to get your sit-spot in a sling. Think twice!"

3. PUZZLING EVIDENCE

Branch didn't have time for any second thoughts in the matter, for at that instant Lullaby Joslin stepped into the open, his six-shooter already bearing on Branch. "Go on and jerk your iron, you bustard," Lullaby invited softly. "I'm just aching for a chance to shoot that brim the rest of the way off your Stet hat. Go ahead, draw!"

There were varied exclamations of surprise, and Branch hastily withdrew his hand from his gun. Lullaby holstered his Colt as Tucson said mockingly, "Meet my friend, Mr. Joslin"—and then to Whitlock—"Now how do you feel about that three against two proposition?"

Whitlock slowly shook his head. His face darkened. "We didn't come out here to indulge in gun fights. I don't know what you hombres are doing here, but if you interfere with the law, you'll find trouble. Why don't you two just go on about your business?"

"Maybe we're making this our business," came a fresh voice, as Stony Brooke, unable to restrain himself any longer, burst from the brush. There were more ejaculations of astonishment on the part of the sheriff and his friends, who now looked somewhat uneasy.

"And," Tucson said, smiling, "another friend of mine, Mr. Brooke."

"Sure looks like a new deal all around." Daulton grinned.

Whitlock's face had clouded up like a thunderstorm. Art Branch was uneasily craning his neck toward the brush beyond the enclosure as if expecting further opposition to pop into view. "Say—say—s-s-say," Sheriff Gebhardt stammered nervously, "how many more of you fellers is hid out in that brush?"

"We haven't had time to count 'em," Lullaby Joslin drawled.

"Anyway," Stony Brooke put in belligerently, "there's enough of us here to handle the business if you hombres are craving some *real* excitement. Just say the word!"

Tucson said quietly, "Take it easy, Stony. I don't reckon the sheriff and his friends want to make trouble for us. After all, the sheriff is just carrying out his duty."

"That's right," Gebhardt stated pompously. "There'll be no trouble of our making. All I ask is to get my prisoner to jail without a fuss."

Daulton had been looking at Tucson and his pardners. He had now lowered his arms, and was repeating half to himself, "Smith . . . Joslin . . . Brooke . . ." He suddenly addressed himself to Tucson: "Sa-a-ay, I know who you three are. You're the Three ——"

"That's possible," Tucson said quickly. "Lots of people know my pards and me." He added meaningly, "And there's some who never even heard of us. Maybe that's just as well too."

"Yeah," Daulton said slowly. "I think I see what you mean." He fell silent.

Trax Whitlock looked puzzledly at the speakers. There was something going on he didn't quite understand, some hidden meaning in the words. Just who was this tall red-haired puncher and his companions? Perhaps, Whitlock decided, it might be a good idea to go slow until he had learned more about these men. He cleared his throat and endeavored to make his tones sound friendly:

"Well, I'm glad our little misunderstanding is settled, gentlemen. For a few minutes there I was inclined to think you were going to take sides with the prisoner and kick up trouble. However, there seems little more to do, as I see it, than to load this dead man on his horse and get the prisoner to town."

"That's about correct." Tucson nodded pleasantly. "I'd like to look at this dead man first. I heard you say his name was Joe Folsom——"

"You know him? the sheriff asked.

Tucson shook his head. "Never heard of him." He approached the lifeless body and stooped down, examining the bullet holes in the man's back. Then he touched one hand to the dead Folsom's face. "Yes, I'd say Daulton was correct. This hombre's been dead around four hours—nearer five now——"

"That still doesn't prove Daulton didn't kill him," Art Branch half snarled.

"I didn't say it did," Tucson replied mildly, without looking up. He finally straightened to his feet, still eying the corpse. "Looks like," he commented, motioning toward the dead Folsom's outstretched right arm, "as if he might have been throwing something, about the time he went down. I wonder . . ."

Without finishing the sentence, he commenced to walk in the direction the outstretched arm seemed to indicate, and his steps carried him a few feet into the surrounding brush. The others saw him bend down after a few moments and pick up something from the earth. When he returned to the cleared space he carried a large metal object in his arms.

"Well, here's something," he announced, "but I'm hanged if I know what it is."

There came a half-suppressed curse from Art Branch, as he and Whitlock tumbled out of saddles and quickly crossed the hard earth to Tucson. The sheriff was slower to follow. With a good deal of grunting, he lowered his bulky figure from the saddle. Now it was plain whence came his nickname of Ducky. The sheriff not only waddled when he walked, but his feet, despite the high heels, looked extremely flat, and the toes turned out at an angle greater than average.

Whitlock scowled angrily and said something in a low voice to Branch, who was vigorously shaking his head, as the men gathered around Tucson to examine the object he had retrieved from the brush.

It was of sheet metal, cylindrical in form, and hollow, with the steel-reinforced ends equipped with a sort of axle which apparently ran completely through the cylinder. This drumlike object was about two feet long, with a diameter of approximately a foot and a half. The axle running lengthwise through the center protruded a few inches at either end and was of steel.

Whitlock broke the silence: "I'll be damned! What is it?"

"You don't know?" Tucson asked. He had been closely watching Whitlock's features.

"No, how should I? Do you?"

Tucson promptly shook his head. "I haven't the least idea. It's meant to hang between standards, I'd say, and be turned with a crank. See—one end of the axle is flattened on two sides, where a wrench, or a crank, could fit. But why?" His forehead furrowed with speculation as he turned the object in his hands.

Lullaby said, "There's a little door there—see? It's held with a kind of snap lock. Open it up."

"Don't rush me, cowboy." Tucson chuckled. "I'm as curious as you are. I can hear something knocking around inside."

He unsnapped the catch in the circular surface and opened the small door; then, stooping, he dumped the contents on the earth. The others gathered closer. There were certain exclamations as the various objects came into view: a quantity of small chunks of adobe mud and soft sandstone; two small rubber balls about an inch in diameter, such as children play with; and a packet of twenty-dollar bills, pinned together with a strip of paper. At least the outer bills were of twenty-dollar denomination. Ignoring the exclamations of the others, Tucson proceeded to count the money. There were fifty "twenties." One thousand dollars!

"Seems like a darn small amount to cause murder," Tucson commented.

"Y'know," Whitlock put in, "I don't think this money—the metal drum—any of this stuff—had anything to do with Folsom. This drum was likely dropped by somebody else—maybe a long time ago."

"Not much sign of dust on it," Tucson pointed out. "No rust."

"But what would Folsom have been doing with it—even if it was thrown into the brush by him, in the hope his killer wouldn't find it?" Whitlock persisted.

Tucson shrugged his muscular shoulders. "You tell me and I'll tell you," he answered shortly. "But if this is evidence of some sort, it's the most puzzling evidence in a murder case I've ever seen."

"Cripes A'mighty!" Whitlock swore. "That's no evidence. I don't figure it's got one damn thing to do with this murder." A sudden thought struck him. "I'll tell you what I think this drum is. Some prospector has been panning a stream somewhere. Such dirt and rocks as looks interesting he throws into this drum with some water to wash 'em when the drum is turned. Then the gold nuggets, or silver, or whatever he finds, sinks to the bottom. That makes an easy job——"

"And just where is this stream," Lullaby asked sarcastically, "where a man can turn up twenty-dollar bills, all packaged, not to mention little rubber balls for kids to play with?"

Whitlock forced a thin smile. "If I knew, I'd do some panning there myself. Say what you like, I think this metal drum is some prospector's invention. It could even be there's more to the machine, and those rubber balls are used for bearings. I'll bet that's it."

Stony snickered. "You sound like your brain runs on rubber-ball bearings, mister."

Whitlock flushed angrily, but didn't say anything. Art Branch directed a look of hate in Stony's direction, but also kept quiet. Tucson riffled through the package of bills but found nothing of import there. They looked to be ordinary bills such as are passed across hundreds of counters and tables in various transactions, running from commercial projects to poker games, every day in the year. Some of the bills appeared to be more worn than others, that was all.

"This always was my favorite picture of Andy Jackson," Tucson said dryly as he lay the packet of bills down on the earth and picked up one of the small balls.

"Who's Andy Jackson?" Sheriff Gebhardt asked dumbly.

"Former President of these United States," Lullaby said.

"What's he got to do with this business?" The sheriff frowned.

Stony sighed. "Must be you never looked at a twenty-dollar bill, Sheriff. Or don't you get many of 'em?"

"Oh, yeah—yeah." Ducky Gebhardt's fat face cleared. "I see what you mean. Mostly around these parts it's a hard-money country, though. Don't see so many bills as in some parts."

"They're coming in, though," Whitlock said. "See a lot more bills around Morral City these days than we used to." He looked angrily at Gebhardt. The sheriff swallowed hard and fell silent.

Tucson meanwhile had been exposing one of the small balls to a thorough scrutiny. It was of solid rubber and felt slightly greasy to the touch. Tucson rubbed his fingers on it, lifted it to his nose. He said to Lullaby, "What's that smell like?"

Lullaby sniffed the small black ball. "Coal oil," he said promptly.

Whitlock asked. "Does that tell you anything important, Smith?"

Tucson frowned. "I don't know as it does," he said noncommittally, "except the fact it's been soaked in coal oil, kerosene, whatever you want to call it."

Whitlock shrugged carelessly. "I don't want to call it anything. I just don't give a damn." He turned to the sheriff. "Ducky, it's about time we started back to town with your prisoner. Folsom will have to be taken to the undertaker's too. We ought to get riding."

"Yeah, we should," the sheriff agreed. He looked greedily at the packet of bills. "I think I better take charge of that money. I can give an accounting to the county——"

"Sure, you should," Tucson broke in. He dumped money, the two rubber balls, and a scraping of the mud and bits of rock back into the metal drum. "Take it along."

"I won't bother with that iron contraption," Gebhardt said, "just the money——"

"Take the whole thing, Ducky," Whitlock said quickly. "That drum and the contents will be exhibits at Daulton's trial——"

"Huh!" The sheriff looked surprised. "You already stated, Trax, that you didn't figure this stuff had anything to do with the killin'."

"Dammit!" Whitlock said impatiently, "I can't be sure. I don't know any more than you do—or Smith. Take that stuff with you."

Art Branch sneered. "Go on, pick it up, Ducky. We got to get pushin'. I'm needin' a drink. I'll tie Folsom's body onto his hawss. You keep an eye on Daulton——"

Tucson broke in. "Sheriff, you'd best take a good look at that body before you move it. You'll have to testify at a coroner's inquest, I imagine, and tell how the corpse lay and so on."

"I'm lookin' at the body, ain't I?" Gebhardt said huffily. "You don't need to tell me my business."

Tucson smiled. "Why, gosh, Sheriff, I wouldn't think of trying to do that. Maybe I talk too much. You should know your job, without any advice from me." Gebhardt softened under the flattery and Tucson added casually, "Were you and your friends riding from the west when you arrived here?"

Gebhardt shook his head. "Nope, from the east. We'd just come out from town."

"I suppose you haven't moved your horses around from the moment you stopped at the edge of this clearing?"

"Nope," Gebhardt said, "I only got out of the saddle for the fust time since you come——"

"What you driving at, Smith?" Whitlock demanded. "What difference does it make to you what we did with our broncs?"

"Not much. I just figured you had too much sense to trample

your horses over any sign that might be found near the body."

"Cripes! We're not dumb. We know that much," Whitlock stated harshly. "We pulled to a halt the minute we saw Daulton bending over the body. Ain't moved our ponies since. Besides"—glancing hurriedly about—"the earth right here is too hard to leave any sign. I already give it a look."

Tucson nodded carelessly. "Sure, it appears that way, doesn't it? I just wondered how you happened to come out here if you hadn't been riding through from the west, as we were. Did you just get an idea this was a good day to go looking for dead bodies —particularly when said body is to be found some distance off the old stage road?"

"What you hinting at, Smith?" Whitlock snapped. Branch and the sheriff had begun to look uneasy.

"Not hinting, just asking." Tucson smiled thinly. "I just got to wondering if this was a regular business of the sheriff's—you know, sort of a regular patrol he makes. Picks up a couple of pals and says, 'Boys, let's go riding and see who's been killed today.' And then he brings you right to the spot, and, by golly! there's a dead man, just as you all expected——"

"I don't like this, Smith!" Whitlock's tones quivered with anger.

Tucson eyed him steadily. "Now that you mention it, I don't like it any better than you do. You've got to admit something smells about this business—unless you've a better explanation than you've furnished so far." He swung suddenly on Gebhardt. "Sheriff, what did bring you to this exact spot?"

Some of the color drained from Gebhardt's puffy features. "Well, well, t'tell the truth, it—it was like—like this——" he began in a stammering voice, looking helplessly at Whitlock. "You see"—lamely—"we were out riding to——"

"By Gawd!" Art Branch spat hotly. "You're trying to stir up trouble, Smith. What right you got asking questions?" His eye gleamed balefully at Tucson through the torn slit in his sombrero.

"Cool down, Art," Whitlock said sharply. He turned to Tucson. "It's just as Ducky says, we were out riding, looking for Folsom—— Now, wait, don't jump to any conclusions. Folsom was a friend of ours. We'd been trying to find a job for him around town, but he was independent, wanted to find a job for himself, on some outfit. Nobody's hiring these days, but he kept trying. He'd go riding out to these different outfits. Yesterday he rode out as usual. We'd arranged to play some poker last night, but he never showed up. When this morning came and he was still missing, I got worried. Finally I asked the sheriff and Art to ride out with me and look for him. Thought maybe his horse had broke a leg in a gopher hole, or something else had set him afoot. We were following the old stage road, riding west, when we thought we heard a shot over this way. So——"

"So you thought fast and came up with an answer," Lullaby put in scornfully.

Whitlock swung savagely on Lullaby. "You calling me a liar?"

Lullaby shook his head. "No—not yet. I'll be glad to though, at some later day."

Whitlock's scowl deepened. "I don't like your attitude."

Lullaby smiled lazily. "Y'know, sometimes I get sort of tired of it myself. But what can I do? I've been wearing it all my life. Maybe it's wearing thin? What do you think? Do you crave to furnish me with another?"

Whitlock said angrily, "Oh hell," and turned away. "Come on, Ducky, I told you once we should get started. We're just wasting time here."

"Yeah, yeah, sure, Trax," the sheriff agreed. He appeared flustered. "I was just wondering if we should take Mr. Smith and his pards along as witnesses——"

"Don't worry," Tucson said. "We were heading for Morral City, anyway. We want to make sure Daulton gets there safe."

"And he'd better get there safe," Stony snapped, "or somebody will hear from me. This business of shooting a prisoner and then claiming he was killed while trying to escape is bad business."

Gebhardt turned pompously on Stony. "I resent that. As the duly elected sheriff of Carbonero County I must take exception to such insinuations. I—I——" He broke off, backing a step away from Stony. "Wha—what you looking at me like that for?" he quavered.

"I was just wondering," Stony replied in chilly accents, "how you'd taste boiled. Or maybe baked would be better. On a platter, with an apple in your mouth."

Gebhardt backed away another step, all the color leaving his face. "That's a threat——" he said weakly.

"Cripes A'mighty, Ducky," Art Branch exploded. "Don't let this hombre scare you. He's just bluffing."

Stony cast a warning eye at Branch. "You'd best keep out of this, feller, before I unscrew your head and hand it to you."

"I'd like to see you try it," Branch said belligerently.

"You mean that?" Stony snapped eagerly, a wide grin appearing on his face.

"Art!" Whitlock snarled. "Cut out that arguing and get Folsom hoisted on his horse. Smith, we don't want any trouble here. How about calling off that pard of yours?"

"I'm not his boss," Tucson said calmly, "but unless your jackal wants to see himself taken apart, he'd better do as you say."

"Get moving, Art!" Whitlock ordered.

Branch turned and hurried into the brush after the dead man's pony.

Lullaby said, "Did I hear something said about an apple a spell back? I'm hungry. Wish I had an apple."

Stony laughed. "A whole treeful wouldn't satisfy that appetite of yours."

Tucson was talking to Daulton. "And mind what I say," Tucson said seriously. "Don't give those hombres a chance to throw down on you. Not that I think they'll dare try anything now, but I don't want you to do anything to rile them, Daulton. I'll look you up when we hit town. Don't worry. I'll talk to you some more then." He was holding his voice low.

"Sure, I'll do as you say, Mr. Smith——"

"Make it just Tucson. I don't think you killed Folsom, and we'll see what can be done about getting you out of this mess."

"I don't know how to thank you for stepping in at the right time."

"Don't try it then, Jeff."

By this time the dead man had been lashed across the back of his pony, and the sheriff and his prisoner were mounted, flanked on either side by Branch and Whitlock. The sheriff carried the metal drum.

Gebhardt asked, "Smith, ain't you and your pards going to get your hawsses and start?"

Tucson nodded. "In a few minutes. We left our broncs back a spell. We'll catch up to you. If we don't catch up right away, keep going and we'll see you in town. And I want to see Daulton in town too." He added meaningly, "Alive and kicking."

"Look here, Smith," Gebhardt said indignantly, "I don't like that. As sheriff of Carbonero County——"

"Ducky," Whitlock said wrathfully, "if you start running off at the mouth again, I'm going to close it for you, so help me God. Now shut up and let's get riding."

Gebhardt shut up and the riders started off. Tucson and his two pardners stood looking after them. Lullaby said, "What a sheriff! If a crime wave ever strikes Carbonero County, I sure feel sorry for the taxpayers."

Stony nodded. "Anybody could push that blown-up windbag around—and it wouldn't surprise me none if that Whitlock hombre did more than his quota of pushing. Tucson, what you got figured out on this killing?"

"Damn little," Tucson confessed, "except that I've a hunch Daulton didn't do it."

"You think those others knew more than they let on?" Lullaby asked.

"I feel right sure of it—no, don't ask me why. I don't know. I've just got a hunch that way, that's all."

"Based on what?" Stony asked.

Tucson scowled thoughtfully. "Well, they claimed to come out here looking for their pal, Folsom, but when I was eavesdropping in the brush I didn't hear a word that led me to believe Folsom was a close friend of theirs."

"There's something in that." Lullaby nodded agreement. "What do you make of that metal drum contraption? How does that hitch in? What's it for?"

"There you've got me," Tucson admitted. "I doubt it was any device cooked up by a prospector, as that Trax hombre tried to tell it. But I've no idea what it could be used for. Course, I don't know everything. That drum likely could be employed for washing minerals."

"Do you think the sheriff and his pals knew what it was for?"

"I don't think the sheriff knew what it was. On the other hand, I think the other two recognized it. I noticed a couple of quick glances pass between them. And while that Trax hombre stated he didn't think it had anything to do with the killing, he was quick to insist that the sheriff take it along for evidence."

"Maybe," Stony suggested, "he just had his eye on that thousand-dollar package, but insisted the sheriff take the whole business so we wouldn't fall wise as to what he had in mind."

Tucson nodded. "Maybe that's it," he agreed.

Lullaby said, "If we're going to catch up to those hombres, we should get started. Want I should go get the horses?"

Tucson shook his head. "We're not going to catch up. Daulton will be all right, so long as the sheriff thinks we might be right behind him. I'm in no hurry to leave. I want to look over this ground for sign. All right, let's spread out and see what we can find. After we've given the ground a good survey, we'll check and see if our stories agree. Once that's done, if we find anything to go on, I aim to talk turkey to that fat-brained sheriff."

Lullaby groaned. "First, apples. Then, turkey. Why does somebody always have to be reminding me I'm hungry?"

"That's the first I ever heard you had to be reminded," Stony said caustically.

Before Lullaby had a chance to retort, Tucson cut in, smiling, "Now don't you two get tangled in one of your eternal arguments, or I'll have to do some reminding myself. Let's get busy and finish up here. Remember, we've got a job to do. We can't let Daulton down."

4. TUCSON RUNS A BLUFF

The setting sun had dropped behind the saw-toothed peaks of the Apparition Mountains, by the time Tucson and his companions crossed a plank bridge erected over the shallow-flowing Rio Claro —which was nearer creek than river status—and approached the main thoroughfare running through Morral City. This thoroughfare, originally named Butterfield Street, was popularly known as Main, and was crossed by four other streets, running north and south: Yuma, Kearney, Las Cruces and Dallas streets. Paralleling Main Street, to the north, was Fremont Street, given over entirely to residences. Main was paralleled on the south by the tracks of the T.N. & A.S. Railroad, and at the south end of Las Cruces Street the railroad depot was situated.

As the seat of Carbonero County, Morral City held a position of some prominence in this section of the Southwest, particularly in the fall of the year when the stockmen were shipping their cows from the whitewashed cattle pens located east of town, on a spur of the T.N. & A.S. But regardless of the time of year, there had always been a certain air of prosperity about Morral City, even after the mines in the Apparition Mountains had closed down. Most of the buildings along Main Street were of rock-and-adobe construction, though there were many of frame, with high false fronts. Several saloons were strung along this principal thoroughfare; there were two general stores, a brick-constructed bank building, a pair of hotels, restaurants, a couple of livery stables, and various other places of commercial enterprise. On either side of Main Street were plank sidewalks and an almost unbroken line of hitch racks. The street itself was unpaved and slightly curving, muddy during the wet season and dusty in summer.

As always, in a town they'd not visited before, the Mesquiteers glanced about with interest as their horses plodded along Main Street, kicking up small clouds of dust at every step. Though it wasn't yet dark, here and there lamps had already been lighted in some of the buildings. Lullaby said, "There doesn't seem to be many people in sight. Maybe they just go to bed early."

"It's suppertime, idiot," Stony replied. "Folks are shoving their hoofs under tables——" He broke off suddenly and looked uneasily at Lullaby.

"I didn't miss it," Lullaby said. "Suppertime! But I'm just too faint from undernourishment to dwell on the subject. If I can stay in the saddle long enough, I aim to 'light at the first restaurant we see——"

Stony broke in hastily, jerking one thumb to the left. "There's a hotel, Tucson. 'Cowmen's Rest Hotel,' the sign says. Want we should stop?"

Tucson eyed the dingy two-story frame building and shook his head. "That place looks to me like its beds might have contracted a mite of animal life. A town this size should have a better hotel. We'll likely find it near the center of town."

The ponies walked on. They crossed Kearney Street. Tucson caught sight of a gunsmith's shop on one corner and on another a general store. Next to the gunsmith's shop, he spied the establishment of the local undertaker. He pulled his pony to a stop and stepped down from the saddle. The others halted too and looked inquiringly at him. Tucson explained, "You hombres take my horse and look for another hotel. Get rooms for us. I'll see you later, if not at the hotel, someplace around town."

"What you aiming to do?" Lullaby asked.

"I'm going to drop into this undertaker's. Likely Folsom's body was left there. I want to see if there's anything to pick up."

They nodded, understanding. Stony took the reins of Tucson's pony, while its rider crossed to the plank sidewalk, rounded one end of a tie rail and entered the funeral establishment. "What you figure he hopes to do?" Stony said.

"Never any telling what Tucson has in mind," Lullaby answered. "All I hope is that the hotel we're looking for has good chow."

"And cold beer," Stony amended.

They continued on their way and before the end of the block was reached, had arrived at the Morral City Hotel & Bar.

It was after eight-thirty before Tucson left the undertaking establishment and again stepped to the sidewalk. There were more lights shining from windows along the street now and more people in view—cowmen and citizens, many of them Mexicans. Overhead the stars were shining in an indigo sky. The moon wasn't up yet.

Tucson found Lullaby seated in the lobby of the Morral City Hotel, reading a week-old newspaper. He got to his feet when he saw Tucson. Tucson said, "Had your supper?"

"Two suppers," Lullaby said blissfully. "I've been waiting for you. Figured I might have a little snack while you ate. Dang good chow this place puts out. I had a steak, first, so big I had to rope it down, and then——"

"I can guess what you had," Tucson said dryly. "I've seen you eat, when you really put your mind to it. I won't get a chance to feed for a spell yet. Where's Stony?"

"Swilling beer in the hotel bar. It's disgusting the way he drinks," Lullaby said smugly. "We should persuade him to sign the pledge——"

"I'll leave that to you. I'm busy right now."

"What'd you find out?"

"I'll tell it later. Did you get rooms for us?"

Lullaby nodded. "With food like they got here I even had a notion to buy the place——"

Tucson interrupted again. "Have the clerk reserve a room for Jeff Daulton. I've got a hunch he'll be out of jail before the night's over. I'm going down to visit the sheriff now." Lullaby started to say something about "nice work," but Tucson cut him short: "You and Stony meander around town and drop into a few bars. See what's to be learned about Trax Whitlock and his gang."

"We'll do that." Lullaby nodded. "See you later."

Leaving the hotel, Tucson walked west on Main Street, then at Kearney crossed diagonally over to where the sheriff's office and jail stood on the southwest corner. The building was of rock-and-adobe construction, with a narrow porch running across the front, and a wooden awning that reached to supports placed at the outer edge of the sidewalk. A swinging sign attached to one of the uprights announced that within the building could be found the office of the sheriff of Carbonero County. Tucson stepped to the porch and glanced through one of the dusty windows, placed on either side of a doorway. Sheriff Ducky Gebhardt was slumped back in a chair, feet on his desk, half asleep.

For a moment Tucson stood in the open doorway, glancing around the office. The desk was placed near a right-hand window. There were a few straight-backed chairs scattered about the room. On one wall was a rack of rifles and shotguns; a row of pegs had handcuffs hanging on them. A large topographical map of the county, considerably flyspecked, occupied a portion of another wall. Nailed up were various reward bills, yellowed with age, and a couple of calendars from meat-packing companies. The floor was thick with dust and littered with cigarette and cigar stubs. In the rear wall a closed door showed the way to the jail cells.

Tucson stepped into the office. Gebhardt roused at the sound, straightened in his chair, blinked, and then gazed with a certain nervous resentment at his visitor. "What you want, Smith?" he mumbled ungraciously.

"I want to see your prisoner—Jeff Daulton, in case you've got more than one, which same I doubt."

"Daulton's the only man I got in my cells. I run a clean town. No crime. What you want to see Daulton about?"

"That's none of your business."

"I ain't a-goin' to let you see him," Gebhardt said bluntly. "Daulton's a dangerous character. There'll be a coroner's inquest tomorrow mornin', and then——"

"Don't make things tough for yourself, Gebhardt," Tucson warned sternly. "Either I see Daulton, right now, or you'll find yourself in a mess of trouble. If I have to write to the governor, you'll lose your job——"

"Governor? What governor?" Gebhardt looked startled.

"Don't you know the governor of this territory? And you claim to be sheriff." Tucson laughed sarcastically.

"Course I know him," Gebhardt said indignantly. He now looked uneasy. "You—you a friend of his?"

"Friend of the governor's?" Tucson evaded. "Why, say, if you—— No, I won't make any boasting statements. Don't take my word for it. I tell you, you just write the governor and ask him if he knows Tucson Smith. I'll bet he'll give you the horse laugh for even asking."

"Tucson Smith." Gebhardt frowned. "I've heard your name before someplace."

"Probably," Tucson continued brazenly, "you heard the governor speak of me. But that's neither here nor there. I aim to see Daulton."

"We-ell, I don't know. Trax Whitlock said he was to be held in —in—incom——"

"Incommunicado?" Tucson furnished the word. "Who's running this county, you or Whitlock? What are you, Ducky, just a figurehead in this county? My, oh my! Wait until I tell the governor about this."

"Now, wait a minute, Mr. Smith," Gebhardt pleaded. "Don't do anything hasty. Whitlock ain't got anything to do with it, really. I'm running this county. Maybe I'll let you talk to Daulton, but I can't let you into his cell."

"I don't want to enter his cell. I just want to speak to him through the bars for a few minutes."

"We-ell, reckon I can accommodate you." Gebhardt rose reluctantly from his chair and waddled toward the entrance to the cell block, Tucson at his heels. Beyond the office doorway there was a narrow corridor, on either side of which were six cells equipped with iron-barred doors. An oil lamp, suspended from the corridor ceiling, gave a feeble light. In the first cell to Tucson's right, Jeff Daulton was seated on a cot let down from one wall on chains. He was smoking a cigarette and gazing moodily at nothing in particular. In the far wall of his cell, placed head-high, was a small iron-barred window. At sound of Tucson's step, Daulton raised his head, then approached the cell door.

Gebhardt said irritably, "Visitor to see you, Daulton."

"How you getting along, Jeff?" Tucson asked, then, to Gebhardt, "You can run along back to your office now." Daulton stated he was getting along "as well as could be expected," and Gebhardt interrupted to say he wasn't allowed to leave a prisoner alone with a visitor. "That," Tucson continued coldly, "will be just one more thing for me to take up with the governor on my next visit. He has mighty strict ideas on prisoner treatment, dictatorial law officers, lack of co-operation—and, I might add, grafting on the part of men elected to high position. Would you believe it, Sheriff, there's quite a few jail keepers steal part of the money provided for prisoners' food? Oh, by the way, Jeff, what did *you* get for supper tonight?"

"A small bowl of greasy chili, a chunk of dry bread, and a cup of hawgwash Gebhardt insists is coffee. If you don't believe me, the stuff is still here. I couldn't swallow it."

Gebhardt was nervously mopping perspiration from his face and making excuses. "I'm sorry; I should have examined that food. That dirty cook is cheating on me. By Gawd! I'll wring his neck——"

"Just forget it and get back to your office," Tucson snapped. "Somebody in Carbonero County is going to catch merry hell on this deal."

But the fat sheriff didn't even wait to hear the last of Tucson's words. He waddled sadly back toward the front of the building, and closed the door between his office and the cell block.

Daulton chuckled as he stood at the door of his cell, only the steel bars between him and Tucson. "You sure got that overstuffed hombre eating out of your hand. How do you do it?"

Tucson laughed. "He's afraid I'll take our troubles to the governor." He explained the bluff he had run on the sheriff and ended, "By the way, just who is governor in this territory now?"

"Come to think of it, I don't know either," Daulton replied.

There was some further laughter before Tucson turned serious. "Look here, Jeff, I don't think you're guilty of killing Folsom, but I'd like to hear your story. I just sort of got it in pieces today. I'd like to make sure of certain facts."

"Not much to tell," Daulton said. "I worked for various outfits, then decided to take a long vacation and see something of this country and Mexico. On the way back from Mexico, after crossing the Border, I happened to stumble on Folsom's body. Next Gebhardt and his pals arrived and got the drop on me. I admit I had my gun in my hand at the time——"

"Yeah, I know about that. Heard you tell it today. We stayed behind and read sign. Your tracks showed you as coming from the south, so that's straight. There was one sort of damp spot, and the track looked quite fresh—fresh enough to prove to me you couldn't have been there four hours earlier and killed Folsom. There were other tracks of ponies, coming from the west too. One of the ponies was lame in the off hind hoof."

Daulton nodded. "Yes, I found that when I read sign." He added. "It was the horse of a rider who followed Folsom to that spot."

"Right." Tucson nodded. "For your information, I noticed

when Art Branch left that his pony was lame in the off hind hoof. I checked the tracks later."

Daulton's eyes widened. "Cripes! I didn't notice that."

"You wouldn't. You were riding with him. What outfits did you say you'd worked for?" Daulton gave several names. Tucson nodded. "All those brands are familiar to me. But, as I get it, it's over two years since you left your last job. What you been doing since then?"

"The Ladder-B was the last outfit I punched for," Daulton said evasively. "I've just been riding around ever since."

"They must have paid well," Tucson said casually. "I never yet heard of a puncher who could save enough for a two years' vacation."

Daulton didn't speak for a moment. When he did, a certain stubbornness showed in his tones. "Maybe a wealthy grandmother died and willed me her money," he said.

"Is that so?" Tucson said dryly. "I didn't even know she'd been sick."

"Maybe we'd better not discuss it—right now," Daulton said. He changed the subject. "Say, aren't you and your pards known as the Three Mesquiteers? I thought I recognized your names."

"And I didn't even know she was sick." Tucson grinned. "All right, Jeff, don't tell your private business if you don't want to. So far, you've got a clean slate with me. I'll see you again, sooner than you think. Just take it easy."

Turning away, he headed back to the sheriff's office, this time leaving open the door between cell block and office. Gebhardt said ingratiatingly, "I hope you had a good visit with the prisoner, Mr. Smith." He pushed up laboriously from his chair. "Come around any time——"

"Sit down, Ducky, I've got a few things to say to you," Tucson said. The sheriff sank back in his chair and Tucson leaned against his desk. "In the first place, I don't figure Jeff Daulton is going to stay in that cell much longer."

"Now, now, Mr. Smith, ain't you exagerratin'? He's being held for murder——"

"Not much longer, he won't be. You just listen. I'll do the talking for a minute. Today, after you left, my pards and I read sign around that place Folsom's body was found. The time when Daulton made tracks pretty much proves he couldn't have been at that spot when Folsom was killed. Daulton's tracks were too fresh. Is that clear?"

"We ain't sure yet the exact hour Folsom was killed."

"I'll get to that. Now when you rode in there you stopped at the edge of the clearing—on the east side of the body. Is that your story?"

"That's my story," Gebhardt replied. "We didn't none of us move from that spot after we stopped, until we turned around and headed back with Daulton and the corpse."

"In that case," Tucson asked, "how do you account for hoof-prints being beyond the body—to the west side of the body?"

Gebhardt swallowed hard. "If—if that's right, there must have been somebody else there, maybe the murderer——"

"Oh, you think now that Daulton isn't guilty?"

"It—it could have been somebody else," the sheriff said weakly. "I wouldn't want to say definite, though. You see, until I——"

"It was somebody else," Tucson cut in, "and he rode a pony with a lame hoof on the hind off side."

Gebhardt's jaw dropped, then slowly closed. "Th—that's a damn good clue, Mr. Smith. Come mornin', I'll sort of look around and see can I locate such a hawss——"

"You needn't bother. When you hombres left this afternoon I noticed that Art Branch was riding a horse that had gone lame in that same foot."

The sheriff's eyes bugged out. "My G-G-Gawd!" he stammered. "You ain't sayin' Art killed Folsom?"

"I didn't say that. What I do maintain is that he's a liar if he claims he never went there until he rode with you and Whitlock."

"B-b-but——"

"But me no buts. I'm still talking. When I hit town this evening I dropped into your local undertaker's to see if Folsom's body had been delivered and to check into a couple of other things. The body was there, and the undertaker informed me a doctor was shortly coming to examine the body. While I was waiting for the doctor, I slipped out and visited your town blacksmith. He was in a very angry frame of mind against one Art Branch, who had brought a horse in to be shod. It seems that rather than pay the blacksmith's fee, Branch had done the shoeing himself the last time it was done, and he'd done such a lousy piece of work the pony's hoof may be ruined forever. What do you think of that? Think that blacksmith might make a good witness against Branch?"

Gebhardt swallowed hard. "Art always was a tightwad," he said weakly. "I hired him to shoe a hawss for me once, and——"

"Save it for another time, Ducky. By the time I got back to the undertaker's, Dr. Graham had arrived and was probing out the bullets from Folsom's back. Oh, by the way, Sheriff, what did you do with Daulton's rifle when you arrested him?"

"Rifle?" Gebhardt frowned. "Daulton didn't have no rifle—just a six-shooter. Are you claiming I took a rifle from him? I tell you, Mr. Smith, he didn't carry a rifle. I'll swear to that."

Tucson smiled. "That's the way to talk up, Ducky—just what I wanted you to say, because I'll bet you're going to be surprised when I tell you it was two .30-30 Winchester slugs that Doc Graham took from Folsom's body. I sort of had an idea those wounds looked like they'd been made with rifle slugs, and Graham proved I was right. And just to top things off, Ducky, both Doc Graham and that blacksmith tell me Art Branch has quite a rep as a rifle shot in these parts. Now, do you still feel like holding Jeff Daulton?"

Gebhardt's face was wet with nervous perspiration. "G-g-gosh A'mighty!" he stuttered. "I—I—I don't know what to say. There must be some m-m-mix-up some place——"

"Mostly in your head," Tucson snapped. "And here's something else: Dr. Graham agrees with Daulton on the time that Folsom died, and Daulton was a long way from that spot at the time the murder was committed——"

"You telling me I should arrest Art Branch?" Gebhardt said faintly.

"I'm not trying to tell you your duty. That, you should know. But I am insisting that you release Jeff Daulton. At once!"

All the color was drained from the sheriff's porcine features. He raised one protesting, trembling hand. "I—I don't know what to say, Mr. Smith. I'll go see Trax and ask——"

Tucson swore impatiently. "Does Trax Whitlock have any legal standing in this community as a law enforcer?"

Gebhardt gulped and shook his head. "Not—er—exactly. But he's an important man round Morral City. His word carries weight."

"His word doesn't carry a lousy two-bit ounce for me," Tucson snapped, "nor for anyone else with a backbone. Either you're sheriff of this county, or you aren't. What's the answer?"

"Well, I'm sheriff, all right, but——" Gebhardt mumbled.

Tucson didn't wait for him to finish. One muscular right hand swept out and caught Gebhardt by the collar, jerked the bulky figure bodily from the chair. "I'm sick of this palavering, you cheap, no-account, tin-horn excuse for a sheriff," Tucson said wrathfully. "Now you get Daulton's things together, find his six-shooter, and unlock his cell. If he isn't out here within two minutes, there's going to be hell to pay and no pitch hot. Now, damn your fat carcass, get a move on!"

"Y-Y-Ye-e-s-sir-r, Mr. S-S-Smith." Gebhardt's teeth chattered as Tucson released him. His features were the color of water-soaked liver; his knees knocked together. "I'll do j-j-just as you s-say, but T-T-Trax ain't goin' to like it."

"And I'll like it still less if you mention Whitlock's name once more. Now jump to it!"

5. ROUGH OPPOSITION

On the shadowed porch of the Brown Bottle Bar, Trax Whitlock sat talking to Art Branch. They were seated on a pair of upturned empty beer bottle cases, placed against the front wall of the saloon. Through a dust-grimed window could be seen the bar's interior, where a few customers stood drinking. There was considerable raucous laughter, buzz of conversation, and the clinking of bottles and glasses. But the place where Whitlock and Branch sat was in deep shadow.

"I'm damned if I understand what that Smith hombre is doing in Ducky's office so long," Whitlock growled.

Branch glanced diagonally across the street to a corner building where a light could be seen shining from the sheriff's window. "Why don't you saunter over, drop in casual-like, and see what's up?"

Whitlock shook his head. "I wouldn't give Smith the satisfaction of thinking I was bothered. Just our luck to have him and his nosy pals bust in on us that way. Otherwise we could have laid the whole business at Daulton's door——"

"I still think you should go over there and see what's doing."

"Don't worry. Ducky will come to report as soon as Smith leaves." A note of anger crept into Whitlock's voice. "You telling me what you think? Cripes A'mighty! You don't even think——"

"Now look, Trax, let's not start all that again. If you've bawled me out once, you've bawled me out a dozen times. How was I to know Folsom thrun that metal drum into the brush? He was dead by the time I got there, and there was no sign of the drum. I figured he must have thrun it away someplace while I was chasin' him——"

Whitlock cursed a lurid stream. "Got eyes, haven't you?"

"Now, Trax, be reasonable. He was ridin' quite a way ahead. Ridin' through those low hills, he was bound to be out of sight from time to time. All's I know he had that drum when I saw him, just before I fired my first shot. Then he dropped behind a rise. When I next saw him I let him have it again, but he kept ridin', hangin' on like a stubborn mule. Then he dropped into that hollow. Like I say, when I got there, he was deader'n a butchered beef and no sign of the drum. Then, I prompt lit out for town to tell you——"

"Goddammit! I know all that. We've been through it a dozen times——"

"Just what I was sayin'," Branch cut in earnestly. "No use cryin' over spilt milk, Trax."

"One more mistake like this," Whitlock said savagely, "and you'll be crying over spilt blood. Your dumb trick has put us all in a bad fix."

"Mebbe so, mebbe so, but I ought to get some credit for downin' the nosy bustard."

Whitlock brushed aside the remark. "With the inquest tomorrow, and all, we're in a tight if we don't think fast. That drum will be on exhibit. Maybe somebody will know, or guess, what it can be used for. Then where'll we be?"

"We haven't faced anything we couldn't lick yet, have we? Look, Trax"—eagerly—"I've got an idea about that drum. Ducky don't know what it's for and you can imagine what a mess he'd make describing it—particular with a few hints from us. Now, here's what we could do . . ." His voice dropped to a lower tone and he talked steadily for several minutes. When he had finished:

"That might be a good idea, Art. Think you could handle it?"

"You should know better than to even ask," Branch bragged. "It'll be a cinch."

Somewhat mollified, Whitlock said, "I think maybe we've got a good idea there, Art." Branch noticed, but didn't mention, that no part of the proposed scheme had been Whitlock's, except consent to carry it through. "Art, I think we should have a drink on this. Go inside and get a bottle and a couple of glasses from the barkeep—no, wait, get three glasses. Here comes Lee. He'll want a drink."

An undersized individual—Lee Cantrell, by name—had just drawn his pony to a stop before the Brown Bottle tie rail and slipped down from the animal's back. He wore faded corduroys, a slouch-brim sombrero; his spurs jangled as he crossed the sidewalk and stepped to the porch of the saloon.

Whitlock spoke from his seat in the gloom. "Got here at last, eh, Lee? Where you been all day?"

Cantrell squinted against the darkness. "You, Trax?" He ignored Branch as the man made his way inside the saloon.

"It's me. Come and sit down. Art's getting a bottle."

Cantrell dropped to the top of a beer case, rolled a cigarette and lighted it. He didn't say anything. Whitlock waited a minute and then said impatiently, "I asked where you'd been all day."

"Out to the ranch." Cantrell's voice was flat, cold.

"When I left, you told me you'd be in later."

"Well, here I am."

"Goddammit, Lee!" Whitlock said testily. "You know what I mean. I expected you in by noon, anyway."

"Maybe I didn't want to come in. Maybe I'm sick of this whole section, seeing the same faces in town. No action. Same thing, day after day."

"I pay you well," Whitlock said defensively.

Cantrell said, "Oh hell," in a disgusted tone. Whitlock fell silent. Branch returned with an opened bottle and three glasses. He poured the whisky and then found a seat on the porch railing. The men downed their drinks.

Whitlock went on, "Lee, if you'd been with me today you might have had a chance for some action."

"I doubt it," Cantrell said in an emotionless voice. "What happened?"

Whitlock related the day's activities. Cantrell heard him through in silence. ". . . so you see," Whitlock concluded, "only for this Smith hombre and his two pals butting in, we'd have had Daulton charged with murder. Now, maybe, we're going to have some trouble making our story stick. It occurs to me it's about time for you to earn some of that money I'm paying you. How'd you like to carve another notch on your gun—maybe three of 'em—for Smith and his pals? You could catch 'em off guard——"

"Damn you, Trax," Cantrell said fiercely. "I don't have to catch nobody off guard. I'm fast enough without using your measly scheming tricks."

"All right, all right," Whitlock said placatingly. "Don't get mad, Lee. Do it your own way. These hombres should be easy——"

Cantrell swore. "Since when have I asked for easy marks? I

didn't make my rep that way, as you damn well know. I'm no Art Branch, shooting a man in the back."

Branch started a protest, thought better of it and fell silent. Men on the Hatchet outfit knew better than to argue with Lee Cantrell. Instead, Branch poured another round of drinks.

Cantrell said after a time, "Where's this Smith hombre now? From what you say, he sounds like he might have guts. Maybe he's got ability too. I'll look him over. Where is he?"

"Like I've been telling you, he's over in Ducky's office. Been in there for some time. I hope he hasn't talked that dumb bustard into anything——" Whitlock broke off suddenly and cursed with some feeling. "By God, there he is now! And Daulton's with him!"

Tucson and Daulton had just emerged from the sheriff's office. They stood a moment in the light shining from the windows, then started along the sidewalk in the direction of the Morral City Hotel.

"Ducky's released Daulton!" Whitlock said angrily. "Now——"

"I kept telling you to go over and see what was doing," Branch reminded his boss. "You'd best get over there pronto, and——"

"*You* kept telling me?" Whitlock sneered. "Art, you talk too much and do nothing right."

"All right, if you feel like that," Branch said sullenly, "but just the same you'd best see Ducky——"

"Ducky will come to me," Whitlock said confidently. "What do you think I pay money for? But damn his hide—— See, here he comes now."

The sheriff had emerged from his office and started across the street, his pointed-out toes coming down flatly at each step, his body waddling at every stride. Whitlock raised his voice: "Damn you, Ducky, hurry it up! What's been going on in your office?"

The sheriff came panting up on the porch, words tumbling from his lips. "I done my best, Trax, but he knows the governor——"

"Who knows the governor, and what about it?" Whitlock snapped.

"This Smith—Tucson Smith. Not only that, but he's put the bee on Art. Art had better slope outten town . . ." The story gradually came out, with many promptings and interruptions from Whitlock. "And—and that's all, Trax. I don't know what else we could have done."

"We!" Whitlock snarled. "Why, you stupid, fat-headed no-good son-of-a——" Words failed him, and rising to his feet, he lifted one hand and brought it sharply down across Gebhardt's puffy features. "You dumb bustard!"

Gebhardt cowered back, wiping at his face. "Now I don't take that kindly, Trax. You got no call to treat me like——"

"Shut your mouth!"

Cantrell interposed, "Better cool down, Trax. Sure, this Smith hombre"—he paused momentarily—"sort of rode roughshod over Ducky, but I'm damned if I know what else Ducky could have done. It looks to me like all the evidence points at Art. And if Art is smart, he'll high-tail it out of town as fast as his bronc will carry him."

"By Gawd, that's right." Branch sounded frightened. "My bronc's at the blacksmith shop. Can I use your horse, Trax?"

Whitlock said, "Sure you can use my horse, but don't be in a hurry. Remember, you promised to do a job yet tonight."

"But, Trax"—Branch's voice was almost a wail—"I can't stay. I'd better slope——"

"Don't lose your nerve, dammit!" Whitlock said irritably. "Who's going to arrest you, even on suspicion? Not Ducky. You stick around town until after midnight. Keep out of sight. Get that job done and then high-tail it for the ranch. You can lie low out there. I'll swear you stole my horse for your getaway. Later on, when things quiet down and Smith and his pals have been disposed of, you can put in an appearance again. Just don't lose your nerve. You're not going to be hurt. Lee's going to take care of Smith, aren't you, Lee?"

There was no answer for a moment, then Cantrell replied in flat tones, "Mebbe I am." He turned to the sheriff. "Did you say this Smith hombre called himself Tucson? Is he a tall redheaded jasper?"

Gebhardt nodded. "Yes—to both your questions."

"And what was the names of his pals?"

Whitlock cut in, "Brooke and Gosling—no, Joslin was the name. Stocky blond feller and a lean black-haired cuss. Why, Lee? Do you know 'em?"

A harsh, grating laugh was the response. "I'll say one thing for you, Trax, when you take on some opposition, you get the best. No, I don't know those three, but I've always had a cravin' to meet 'em—but in this case just one at a time. They play rough!"

"Dammit, Lee, who are they?"

"Ever hear of the Three Mesquiteers, Trax? Mebbe you don't know it, but you've taken on a job."

Whitlock was silent for a minute, then in a shaken voice he said, "Jesus!" And added, "I wonder who sent for 'em to come here."

Again Cantrell's harsh, short laugh. "Don't let it worry you, Trax. I think I've found some meat worthy of my chopper at last."

6. HAUNTED MOUNTAINS

Tucson and Jeff Daulton, after a brief stop at the hotel, eventually located Stony and Lullaby in a saloon known as the Goldfinch, which was situated on the north side of Main, just east of Las Cruces Street, and owned by a genial red-haired individual named Pat Finch. The bar was placed to the right of the swinging-doored entrance, the remainder of the room being given over to a scattering of round wooden tables and straight-backed chairs. On the walls were pictures of burlesque actresses, prize fighters and race horses. Oil lamps, suspended above the bar, were reflected in the mirror of the back bar, which was spotless, and which also reflected shining pyramids of polished glasses and rows of bottles.

At present there were only a few men at the long bar. Stony and Lullaby stood alone at the far end. As Tucson and Daulton pushed through the batwing doors, Lullaby caught sight of them in the bar mirror and spoke to Stony. Both swung around from the bar. "Damned if he didn't do it!" Stony exclaimed.

Lullaby's mouth was too full of food for speech at the moment. He swallowed hard, reached into a bowl of pretzels before him and asked, "How'd you work it, Tucson?"

Stony said, "Glad to see you out, Jeff."

"No more so than I." Daulton laughed. "Say, those pretzels look good." He dipped into Lullaby's bowl. "Couldn't eat that jail food they gave me."

"Ah, a man after my own heart." Lullaby chuckled. "I always like to see a feller who enjoys food—not that swills beer, like some folks I could name."

"Cripes," Stony sneered. "Always food. Pretzels! Crackers with the cramps, I call 'em. Tucson, just try some of this beer. It's plumb elegant."

Pat Finch worked his portly frame down the bar. "What'll it be, gentlemen?"

"Pat," Stony said, "meet my friend, Tucson Smith. Tucson, this is the best bar in town. Believe it or not, the beer is iced. Pat gets it shipped in by freight once a week. Only other place gets ice is the hotel."

Finch and Tucson shook hands. Daulton was introduced. Finch touched his flaming thatch, then pointed to Tucson's red hair. "Brother!" he said, grinning.

"Cousins, leastwise." Tucson chuckled. He gave his order for a bottle of beer. Daulton asked for "a touch." Beer, glasses, and a bottle of whisky were placed on the bar, and Finch moved down to the far end of the long counter where another patron was requesting service.

"How'd you get Jeff out of Ducky Gebhardt's clutches?" Stony asked.

Tucson glanced along the bar. "I'll tell it later, when there's not so many folks to listen." He lowered his voice. "We're all due to testify at the coroner's inquest tomorrow. I'll say this much, but don't spread it. Evidence sort of points to Art Branch as being the killer."

"I can't say that surprises me too much," Lullaby said through a mouthful of pretzel crumbs. He washed them down with a swallow of beer. "I figured him or Whitlock had a hand in it—particularly after we read those lame pony tracks. Didn't figure the sheriff as having guts enough for the job."

Stony asked, "Is Gebhardt arresting Branch?"

"I don't know what he intends," Tucson said. "I've got a hunch he'll have to see first what Whitlock wants—he seems to take orders from him. Personally, I don't care whether he arrests him or not. There's something damnably queer going on around here, and if Branch is given enough rope he'll hang himself—and some other people besides."

"Look here," Daulton put in, "you three are the Mesquiteers, aren't you?"

Tucson smiled. "Have I got to start talking about your grandmother's health again, Jeff? Oh shucks! Forget I inquired as to your personal affairs. Yes, we've been called the Three Mesquiteers—and a lot of other names, some of them not so complimentary." He turned back to Stony and Lullaby. "What have you picked up in your roaming around town, anything important?"

"One or two things," Stony replied. "This Trax Whitlock is

the owner of the Hatchet brand, for one thing. The ranch lies about twenty-two miles north of here, and he's supposed to have a sort of rough outfit. Also, Whitlock owns the Brown Bottle Bar and the Cowmen's Rest Hotel, not to mention various other pieces of town property here and there."

"His Hatchet spread must be pretty prosperous," Tucson observed.

"Just so-so," Lullaby put in, "as far as we can learn. Not as big an outfit as the Bar-BH, which lies west of the Hatchet. Incidentally, the Bar-BH is run by a girl. Seems her father was killed awhile back, though we didn't get details. Lying east of the Hatchet, twenty miles northeast of here, is the Rocking-T, owned by a man named Talbert, and next to that, some fifteen miles northeast of town, is Royce's Bench-R. These last two spreads are smaller than the Hatchet. Then there are three or four smaller ranches scattered here and there."

"Also," Stony took up the story again, "Trax Whitlock apparently gives orders to Sheriff Gebhardt."

"As we already know." Tucson nodded. "Looks to me like Whitlock has sort of set himself up as a boss hereabouts."

Lullaby looked disappointedly at the empty pretzel bowl before him, then nodded. "So far as we could learn," he said, "that Folsom who was killed today wasn't any particular friend of Whitlock's. No one seemed to know much about Folsom. He just dropped in here, hung around town, took rides—nobody knows where—and didn't mix with anybody in particular. Maybe he had a date to play poker with Whitlock last night, but if so no one else has heard about it."

"Does Art Branch work for the Hatchet outfit?" Tucson asked.

"I don't know how much work he does," Stony answered, "but he draws his pay from Whitlock. He seems to have quite a rep as a rifle shot." Tucson said he had heard that, and Stony went on, "In addition to Branch, Whitlock seems to have another jackal in his pay—some gunman named Lee Cantrell. As I get the story, there was some sort of crooked deal pulled on the original owner when Whitlock bought the Cowmen's Rest Hotel. The original owner claimed he never got all the money that was due him. Knowing he couldn't match Whitlock's speed, he imported a gunman. Whitlock imported Cantrell. The two gunmen met, and Cantrell stayed aboveground. Whitlock didn't even have to get into a fight, and the former owner of the hotel left town in disgust. We were given to understand that this Cantrell is hell on wheels with a six-shooter."

Tucson frowned. "Hmm. Cantrell? Lee Cantrell? Yes, I think I've heard of him—and his reputation's not good. He was operating up in Virginia City a few years back, I heard someplace."

"I guess Whitlock keeps him as a sort of bodyguard, or something," Stony said. "Here's something else too. Whitlock has a brother here, too—Stowell Whitlock by name. Stowell owns the Morral City bank."

Tucson smiled. "Looks like old man Whitlock's boys just about have this town in a sack."

"Not together, anyway," Lullaby said. "Stowell Whitlock, the banker, is a different sort. The two brothers hate each other's guts. Stow claims that Trax cheated him out of his share in the Hatchet Ranch, and he bucks Trax at every turn. Last election he put up a candidate against Gebhardt, but Trax got Gebhardt reelected. He's bucked Trax in other ways too, and has talked right freely against him in this town. We talked to one or two hombres that thought Trax might bump his brother off someday—or have it done."

Tucson looked thoughtful. "And then Trax could inherit the bank, eh? Well, that would be one way of controlling a heap of financial arrangements around here."

By this time the other patrons of the Goldfinch Bar had taken their departure. The proprietor walked down to ask if further drinks were desired. Daulton asked, "Closing-up time, Pat?"

Pat Finch shook his head. "Lord, no! It's never closing time so long as someone stands beyond that side of the bar and drinks and talks." Orders were given and served, and Finch settled down opposite Tucson and his friends, after placing a fresh bowl of pretzels before Lullaby.

Tucson said, "We're just trying to get a line on the doings hereabouts, Pat. I suppose you've heard about Folsom being killed. Jeff, here, was a prime candidate for suspect, but Sheriff Gebhardt learned a few details that made him change his mind——"

"Faugh! That Ducky Gebhardt," Finch said disgustedly. "A windbag if there ever was one."

"I can't understand the people of the county standing for him," Tucson commented.

"Voters will stand for anything so long as there's no trouble," Finch said. "Until recently there's been none, and the county has been prosperous. Then, last month, Ben Hampton was found dead, out on the range. He'd been shot. Hampton owned the Bar-BH, and a better man you'd never meet. Not an enemy, so far as anybody knew. His daughter, Laure, is running the outfit now. A fine girl."

"Hampton's killer was never found?" Tucson asked.

Finch shook his head. "Ducky Gebhardt issued the usual statements about having clues and being ready to make an arrest, but nothing ever came of it, of course. And now today this Folsom feller is killed. If ever we needed a good law officer, it is now."

"Nobody even makes a guess as to who killed Hampton, eh?" Lullaby said.

Finch shrugged his shoulders. "Sensible people admit they don't know. The dumb ones blame it on the ghosts."

"Ghosts?" Tucson frowned.

"Hampton's body was found in the foothills of the Apparition Mountains. Some folks say the Apparitions are haunted by the ghosts of people who were killed by the Indians a long time ago."

"Do you believe that?" Tucson asked.

Finch snorted. "Do I look like a damn fool?" He hesitated, then, "There's folks claim they've seen ghosts over that way—one ghost anyway, galloping on a white horse."

"Have you ever seen any ghosts in the Apparitions?" Tucson asked.

Finch shook his head. "Not me. I'm not enough interested to make that long ride to see a ghost. Ghosts do not exist, so how could I see one, even if I went to look?"

"And I suppose it was a ghost bullet that killed Hampton?" Daulton said.

"It was not," Finch replied promptly. "It was a good solid chunk of forty-five lead that took Hampton in the mid section." He swabbed the bar with a damp towel for a few moments. "But you know how it is. These legends about ghosts get started and some folks are dumb enough to believe in 'em. And then there's some people, like some of these Mexes, say, they've never had a chance to learn things. They're a superstitious lot. For that sort, ghosts are pretty real occasionally. I've heard more than one Mexican say he's seen a ghost riding through those foothills. Take over in Coyotero Tanks, for instance, which is ninety-nine per cent Mex populated. They believe the Apparitions are haunted. There's even a tale told of four Mexicans who disappeared in the mountains, about four years back. You can't tell the people in Coyotero Tanks ghosts ain't responsible."

"Coyotero Tanks." Tucson frowned thoughtfully, then, "Oh sure, I know where it is." He spoke to Lullaby and Stony, "Remember we stopped there on our way through this morning, right after we'd come through that pass in the Apparitions."

"Sure," Lullaby remembered, "that was the place where I got that good chili and beans, and the *tortillas* just about melted in your mouth——"

"*Your* mouth," Stony put in. "I didn't have any——"

"I said 'your' mouth," Lullaby snapped. "What you correcting me for? You wouldn't remember, anyway. You were too busy swilling *aguardiente*."

Tucson chuckled. "Anyway, it wasn't a large enough town to argue over."

"Just a handful of houses, couple of cantinas, and a general store." Finch nodded. "I guess it wouldn't be there if the trains didn't have to stop to take on water before climbing over the pass. Otherwise it's mostly goats, chickens, and Mexicans. I sort of envy 'em, at that. They live peaceful lives and raise their own fodder. A few of 'em work on the railroad. At least they don't have a Whitlock to put up with."

"Trax or Stowell?" Tucson asked.

"I was referring to Trax," Finch said. "Stow's all right. And there aren't too many bankers I feel that way about, either. But you'll like Stow. He and Trax have been feuding a long time now, ever since Trax done him out of his half of the Hatchet Ranch."

"How'd Trax work that?" Tucson asked.

Finch explained. "The two brothers owned the ranch together, though I can't say Stow ever cared for stock raising. The bank here was put up for sale and Stow wanted to buy it, so he sold his half of the ranch to Trax. Trax gave him some cash and a note, as I get the story. Then somebody stole the note from Stow, and Trax never paid another cent. It put Stow in a bad fix, as he needed the money to pay for the bank. But he's a hustler. He scrambled around and raised money someplace out of town, and now the bank is on a firm footing, but I reckon Stow nigh killed himself putting it there."

"I suppose," Stony put in, "Stow suspects Trax of stealing that note."

"He sure does," Finch said. "He accuses Trax to his face, but Trax just laughs at him. Says he'll pay off someday, but without the note Stow can't force payments. I'd hate to tangle with that Trax man, but I'm afraid I'll have to one of these days." He went on to explain. "I take part of the carload of ice that comes through every week, the hotel takes the rest. Trax wants ice for his Brown Bottle, but the railroad won't carry less than a carload, which same Trax doesn't want so much. So he's been trying to make things tough for me, hopin' to scare me into selling my ice to him. But I won't."

"How's he been making things tough?" Tucson asked.

"Sends his crew in here and they start roughhousing. I threw a scatter-gun on 'em one day last week and ordered 'em out. Later I told Trax I didn't want the Hatchet's trade. He laughed and said I'd not be bothered again, but I know he'll cook up something as soon as he gets around to it."

"Maybe," Stony said, "he'll put that Lee Cantrell on your trail."

Finch shook his head. "Branch, or some of the other Hatchet hands maybe, but not Cantrell. Cantrell wouldn't ever bother with me. Shooting me wouldn't increase his reputation. He just wants to cross guns with hombres who have a big rep as gun fighters, then he not only takes credit for downing them, but all the fellers they've downed as well. I tell you, gents, that Cantrell is a cold-blooded proposition if I ever saw one. It makes me shiver just to look at him. I always feel like I'd come on a sidewinder unexpected."

The men talked a short time longer, then prepared to seek their beds. On the street, headed for the hotel, Tucson laughed softly. "Crooked hotel deals, crooked ranch deals, two murders—not to mention the four Mexicans some time back—ghosts and a cold-blooded killer. Pards, I've got a hunch they all tie in. This may prove to be an interesting place after all."

"Maybe we'll find some *real* excitement," Stony said.

Daulton put in suddenly, "Cripes! I forgot about my horse. You said, Tucson, the sheriff took it to the Wilkins Livery?"

Tucson nodded. "I dropped in there to make sure, before I saw the sheriff. I told the liveryman to give it a rubdown and feed, so you don't have to worry about the bronc." He added slyly, "Anyway, with all that money your grandmother willed you, you don't have to worry about a misplaced pony. You could always buy another horse."

Daulton smiled thinly. "Yeah, I could, couldn't I?" He didn't say any more, beyond, "Thanks for taking care of the horse, Tucson."

Tucson said politely, "Don't mention it, Jeff."

Stony and Lullaby glanced curiously at Daulton, but the man's face was set in hard lines of thought. A few minutes later the four entered the Morral City Hotel and climbed the stairs to their rooms.

7. ROBBERY

Tucson and his friends slept late the following morning. It was after eight o'clock when a knock on Tucson's door first roused him. Tucson asked what was wanted, and the hotel clerk informed him that Dr. Graham was in the lobby and wanted to know if Tucson could see him for a few minutes. Tucson said he'd be down as soon as he could get into his clothing.

Dr. Matt Graham was a tall, spare, middle-aged man with graying hair and alert eyes, dressed in a sort of indiscriminate gray suit and a weathered Stetson hat. Tucson found him impatiently pacing the lobby. "Sorry to wake you up, Mr. Smith," Graham said as the two shook hands.

"I should have been awake a couple of hours ago, but we had a sort of full testing day, yesterday. And you can forget the 'mister.' What's up? Were you afraid I wouldn't get to your coroner's inquest on time? It was set for eleven o'clock, wasn't it?—or have you changed that?"

"No, eleven is right. My jury is ready. They're down at the undertaker's now, viewing Folsom's body. That's more or less of a formality, of course, but the law calls for it——"

"Jeff Daulton and my pards and I will be on time to give our testimony," Tucson said. "Is anything else worrying you?"

Matt Graham scowled. "That damnable Ducky Gebhardt!" he exclaimed wrathfully.

"What's the sheriff done now?"

"It's what he hasn't done," the doctor said angrily. "Tucson, you mentioned last night that you found certain objects near Folsom's body. I didn't pay particular attention, as I figured Gebhardt would have them at the inquest this morning. The sheriff will describe them, of course, but I'd like to get your description, so I'll know——"

"Why not wait until the inquest and see the things with your own eyes?" Tucson asked.

Graham snapped out an oath. "For the simple reason they

won't be there," he explained. "Somebody broke the lock on the sheriff's door during the night and stole them while Gebhardt was asleep at his boarding house."

Tucson frowned. "Don't they keep a jailer or anybody at the sheriff's office?"

"When there are prisoners in the cells, Gebhardt sleeps on a folding cot he keeps at his office. There were no prisoners, so——"

"It looks to me," Tucson said slowly, "as though somebody doesn't want those objects to appear at your inquest. And it couldn't be done just for the money, else why take the drum too?"

"How much money was there?"

"A packet of bills containing a thousand dollars. Then there was this metal drum"—Tucson broke off to give a detailed description of the drum—"and inside the drum there were two small rubber balls that looked like they'd been soaked in coal oil—smelled that way too—and some chunks of small rocks and adobe mud. Gebhardt hasn't said who he suspects of the robbery?"

"You should know better than to ask," Graham snorted. "He says he hasn't the least idea. He's more interested in spreading it all over town that Art Branch killed Folsom——"

"Branch!" Tucson exclaimed. "That's been my idea right along, but I can't understand Gebhardt agreeing. Has he arrested Branch?"

The doctor shook his head. "Claims he tried to, but can't find him. I'm just hoping my jury won't hear of it, but they probably will. I don't like to have opinions formed before an inquest. Something else—Trax Whitlock's horse was stolen last night. He claims he gave it to Branch to take to the livery, but this morning he found it never got there. So there's a horse-stealing charge against Art Branch as well."

The doctor stuffed tobacco into a smelly brier, scratched a match and puffed furiously for a few minutes. The door of the hotel lobby opened and a rather gaunt man of forty-five or fifty entered. He was dressed in gray trousers and a rusty-black long-tailed coat. A black, stiff-brimmed soft hat set squarely on his head. His features had a drawn look and his eyes appeared tired. He said, "Howdy, Doc."

Graham said, "Howdy, Stow," then, "Stow, I'd like to have you shake hands with Tucson Smith. Tucson, this is our banker. Incidentally, he's also Trax Whitlock's brother."

"Which is nothing to my credit, I'm afraid," Stow Whitlock stated. He shook hands with Tucson. "If you've not already heard, Mr. Smith, you likely will before the day has passed, that my brother and I don't get along."

"That's something that happens in many families," Tucson said quietly.

Stow Whitlock nodded. "I guess so. But it's a shame when a man can't trust his own flesh and blood. But then, Trax always did have a wild streak in him. Now that he's gone money-mad, there's no telling where it will end. I was talking to Ducky Gebhardt a few minutes ago"—he forced a wan smile—"and that's nothing to boast of either, and Ducky claims that Folsom fellow had a thousand dollars with him when he was killed. I haven't the proof, but I'd be willing to wager that Trax had something to do with that money disappearing."

"You haven't any evidence in that direction, have you, Stow?" Graham asked quickly. "I'll have you at the inquest, if——"

"No, worse luck, I haven't. Wish I did," the banker said vindictively. "I'd testify like a flash. No, sorry I can't help you, Matt. . . . I was just on my way to the dining room to get breakfast. Have you gentlemen eaten?"

"I'll go along with you," the doctor said. He nodded to Tucson. "Thanks for your information. I'll see you at the inquest—unless you're coming to the dining room."

"I'll wait until I've cleaned up a mite more," Tucson said. He nodded to Graham and the banker and turned toward the stairway leading to the second floor.

At that moment Stony, Lullaby, and Jeff Daulton were descending. All three had donned clean shirts and were freshly shaven.

Stony said, "Lullaby, look at Tucson. He hasn't even redded up yet. Look at that face—reminds me of a worn footmat."

"If he had a face like yours, he wouldn't even need to shave," Lullaby said sarcastically. "All you have to do is cover your mug with cream and get some cat to lick the whiskers off—if you can call that blond fuzz whiskers. Reminds me of something might've grown on a peach—— Peach! Something to eat! Let's get to that dining room!"

"Yeah," Stony said, "if there's any licking of cream to be done, no cat will ever get near it—not with you around."

Daulton asked Tucson, "Do these two always go on like this?"

Tucson nodded. "Yeah, only sometimes it's worse." He delayed the men only long enough to pass on the information he'd received from Dr. Graham, then left them to proceed to the dining room while he hastened up to his room to get into fresh clothing. As he left the three he noticed a whisky flask protruding from Stony's hip pocket, but thought nothing of it at the time except to gain a vague impression that the contents of the bottle, somehow, didn't look like whisky.

When Tucson joined the three in the dining room, some thirty minutes later, Daulton and Stony were laughing uproariously, and a waitress was just setting a fresh platter of pancakes and ham and a pitcher of syrup before Lullaby, who was looking extremely embarrassed. Tucson drew his chair up to the table and gave the waitress his order, then, "What's so dang funny?"

Daulton grinned. Stony let out a howl of laughter, and pointed to Lullaby. "Get him to tell it, Tucson. All's I was trying to do was break him from eating so much."

Tucson glanced questioningly at Lullaby. Lullaby looked sheepish. "S'help me, I'll even up for that one, if it's the last thing I do," he threatened. He turned to Tucson. "Of all the dirty underhanded tricks!" He pointed an accusing finger at Stony. "After that keg-shaped no-account pard of ours had finished pecking at his birdlike breakfast, I ordered some more flapjacks, like any real man wants for his breakfast, and when I wasn't looking, he poured some harness oil or something into my syrup pitcher."

Tucson grinned. "I wondered, Stony, what you carried in that bottle I saw sticking out of your pocket. I suppose you picked that up when you were booming around town last evening."

Stony went off into another paroxysm of laughter. "So he doesn't like the taste of harness oil! I had a mite of axle grease and some windmill oil mixed in too——"

"Practical jokers!" Lullaby said disgustedly. "Don't you know, you wind-broken, gall-sored ranny, that practical jokers are always hombres of immature mental development. Never mind, I'll even out with you yet."

There was some further laughter. Breakfast was eventually finished and the four men set off in the direction of the courthouse, where the inquest was to be held. A number of people were already entering the two-story brick building, which stood on Main Street, just west of Kearney, and Tucson and his companions joined the throng.

The inquest was of relatively short duration. It was shortly after twelve, noon, that the coroner's jury rendered its verdict to the effect that Joe Folsom had met his death at the hands of a person, or persons, unknown, though suspicion and evidence strongly pointed toward Branch, and Sheriff Gebhardt was directed to at once take steps to apprehend the person of Arthur Branch and hold him for trial. Thereupon, the sheriff as well as the jury retired to the nearest saloon to talk over the inquest and speculate as to who had actually killed Folsom. Much of the audience took a similar action.

Tucson and his friends stood on the plank walk before the courthouse, watching the men who were leaving. Within a short time Dr. Graham joined them. "Well, nothing startling came of it," the doctor observed.

"Just about what we already knew," Tucson replied. "Of course, there were those two witnesses who testified they saw Branch come thundering into town, carrying his rifle, and a short time later, after Branch's stop at the sheriff's office, the sheriff, Branch, and Trax Whitlock rode out of town."

"Yeah," Stony said skeptically, "the story Gebhardt and his pals told yesterday, about being worried about Folsom and starting out to look for him, sort of got knocked in the head when Gebhardt testified that Branch had come riding in to say he'd found Folsom's body. And then admitting that Folsom's rifle was in his office——"

Daulton put in, "Gebhardt and Whitlock were under oath this morning. Yesterday they didn't need to care what they told us."

"They had to talk pretty straight in the face of our evidence," Stony said.

"Funny thing," Lullaby put in, "no one on the jury, so far as I could tell, was particularly interested in that metal drum and the money."

Tucson smiled. "They weren't just sure who to believe. We're strangers here, and Gebhardt was so mixed up in his story that you couldn't make much sense of it. Imagine him saying that drum was 'sort of shaped like a cartridge box, only larger,' as he remembered it."

"And he couldn't," Graham said, "remember whether there was a hundred or a thousand in that packet of bills."

"I'm dam'd if I understand, Doc, why you put up with such a sheriff in your county," Tucson said.

Graham's features clouded. "We've just been too easygoing, I reckon, but people are commencing to wake up. I doubt he'll be elected another term, and I don't care if Trax Whitlock's money is behind him. Once the voters are aroused to crookedness, they always do throw crooks out of office, but sometimes it takes awhile for 'em to realize what's going on. Well, thanks for helping out, gentlemen. I've some patients to call on and must be on my way."

They glanced after the doctor as he hurried along the street. By this time most of the audience had left the courthouse. Tucson heard a step in back of him and turned to find Trax Whitlock speaking to him. "First," Whitlock was saying, "I want to apologize to Jeff Daulton for sort of going off half cocked and accusing him of murder. Can you forget it, Daulton?"

"It's already forgotten," Jeff said quietly. "Not necessary to say anything more." He started to turn away.

Whitlock forced a nervous laugh and fingered his blond mustache. Tucson was thinking that here was a very different type from his brother Stowell, the banker. Whitlock continued, "I probably owe an apology all around"—looking at Tucson—"for that misunderstanding we had. There were some hard words passed, and I don't like that. But I admit it was my fault as much as the sheriff's. Had I known who you and your pardners were, Smith, I'd have thought twice."

"And just who are we?" Tucson smiled thinly.

Whitlock chuckled. "Well, the news seems to have pretty much spread through Morral City that the Three Mesquiteers are spending some time here. Y'know, when I first heard your names, it didn't occur to me, and then—well, shucks, a reputation like yours can't be kept hidden. Morral City is proud to have you staying here."

"The way you and the sheriff were talking yesterday," Tucson pointed out, smiling, "I'd an idea you were ready to run us out of town—if possible."

Whitlock sighed. "I'm sorry about the whole business. I was at fault, no doubt of it. I'd like to make partial amends by asking you to have a drink with me. I don't want hard feelings. My

Brown Bottle Saloon is handy—right next to the courthouse. I can't promise you iced drinks, but I do think my place carries a little higher grade of liquor than any other place in town. Will you join me?"

Tucson glanced at his companions, then nodded. "I don't see why not," he replied. He wondered just what Trax Whitlock had in mind.

8. KILLER CANTRELL

There was a vast difference between the Goldfinch Saloon and the Brown Bottle Bar; a certain cleanliness made the Goldfinch stand out. The Brown Bottle's glasses were streaked and greasy looking; the bar mirror, fly-specked. The man behind the bar, a beetle-browed surly-looking individual named Kosky, wore a soiled and spotted apron. As Tucson and his companions followed Trax Whitlock through the swinging doors of the entrance, Tucson spotted Ducky Gebhardt standing at the bar with a bottle and glass before him.

Whitlock swore with some irritation. "You, Ducky," he said sharply, "it's time you hauled out of here and got on Art Branch's trail."

"But I don't know where to look, Trax," Gebhardt whined, glancing nervously at Tucson and the others.

"Well, anyway, get out and try, will you?" The sheriff put down his unfinished drink and waddled out to the street without another word. Whitlock said disgustedly to Tucson, "I have to start a fire under that lazy bustard every so often."

"Well," Tucson said, "I don't suppose he does know where to start looking for Branch, does he?"

Whitlock called to the barkeep to "set out the best," and turned back to Tucson. "I wish *I* knew. That Branch coyote stole the best horse I ever forked."

"Take your saddle too?" Tucson asked.

"And my saddle." Whitlock nodded gloomily. The men drank from their glasses and found the whisky not so bad as might have been expected. Tucson threw a couple of dollars on the bar and called for another round. Whitlock said casually, "You hombres expecting to stay around for a spell?"

"We might and we might not," Tucson said. "I don't know what Jeff plans."

Daulton said, "So long as I was suspected of murder, I'd sort of like to stay around and see if they actually catch the real criminal."

"You and your pards just happen to be passing through?" Whitlock asked Tucson. Stony and Lullaby exchanged glances and in a low voice said something about Whitlock's curiosity.

"Just passing through." Tucson nodded. "We've been up in Utah looking at a strain of horse flesh a dealer there has been working on. Sort of thought we might pick up a few studs and introduce it on our 3-Bar-O spread."

Despite himself a look of relief passed across Whitlock's features. He'd been wondering if somebody had sent for the Mesquiteers to come to Morral City. He continued, "I suppose you've been hearing things since you've been in town—that I don't get along with my brother, and so on." Tucson admitted the truth of this. Trax continued, "Nobody else could get along with him either, if they knew him as well as I do. He's always claiming I cheated him out of his half of the Hatchet, but if you knew all the details, you'd see——"

"Frankly," Tucson cut in, "I'm not interested in your feud. I'm more interested in other things—ghosts, disappearing Mexicans, a man by the name of Hampton murdered——"

"Somebody filling you up with that guff about ghosts, eh?" Whitlock laughed. "Take my word for it, there's nothing to it. I've scoured the Apparition Mountains many a time, and I've never seen hide nor hair of any ghost. Probably these superstitious greasers keep the tales alive. As to Ben Hampton"—he sobered—"that was too damn bad. Fine fellow, Ben. If we had a sheriff worth anything, he'd have run down Ben's murderer——"

"I understand," Tucson cut in, "that you backed Gebhardt at the last election."

"I did," Whitlock admitted. "Never regretted anything so much in my life. I had an idea I could do something with Ducky, but I was wrong. We all make mistakes. That was one of my worst. Come next election, he's due to go out on his rear, and we'll put in a good man. Anyway, Smith, if you're staying around here to look into any ghost story, you're just wasting your time."

"That could be," Tucson said noncommittally.

There were a few other customers at the other end of the bar. About the time they finished drinking, the swinging doors banged back and Lee Cantrell entered. Trax Whitlock lifted his voice, "Hey, Lee, come here and meet some friends of mine. You've heard of the Three Mesquiteers. Smith, Joslin, Brooke—oh yes, and Daulton—shake hands with one of my punchers, Lee Cantrell."

No one offered a hand to shake. Cantrell looked over the four men with a sort of sneer twitching at his lips. He was undersized, wiry, probably weighing in the vicinity of a hundred and thirty pounds. His cheekbones were high, his mouth wide, with thin lips. It was Cantrell's eyes that Tucson noticed most. There was a sort of flat, opaque look to them that prevented a man's reading anything that might be taking place in his mind. His voice was cold, emotionless as he said, "Yeah, I've heard of the Mesquiteers, Trax. What do you expect me to do, give three cheers?"

"Now, Lee, don't be grouchy," Whitlock commenced.

Tucson said quietly, "No, Cantrell, we wouldn't expect anything from you that had to do with 'cheer.' "

"Very funny—very funny indeed," Cantrell said. He stepped to the bar a few feet from Tucson and ordered a drink, then his eyes slid sidewise toward Tucson. "Let me see," he mused, half aloud, "where was it I saw the Mesquiteers before? Oh yes, at a court trial in El Paso. You hombres were acting as witnesses against a bunch of train thieves who'd been stupid enough to be caught by you."

"That," Tucson said quietly, "is over five years back. You've got a good memory, Cantrell. I wonder why we didn't catch you with that gang."

Cantrell's laugh was harsh, grating. "Not me, Smith. Oh sure, I knew that crowd. I warned 'em they was monkeying with dynamite, but I wasn't in on their game."

"Too smart for 'em, eh?" Tucson said.

Cantrell nodded. "And I wouldn't have to be very smart for that, either," he said contemptuously. He reached for his drink, bumped it with his hand, and knocked over the glass. "Goddammit!" he snarled, calling to the bartender, "what do you do, put rockers on these tumblers?" Without reply, the barkeep set out the bottle again, and Cantrell filled his glass, spilling some over the side.

"Dam'd if you don't have a habit of knocking over glasses, Lee." Whitlock chuckled.

The flat colorless eyes moved venomously toward Whitlock. "Sometimes you talk too much, Trax," he said coldly.

"You know, Cantrell," Tucson said quietly, "I had an idea you might still be in Nevada—Virginia City, wasn't it?"

"And what if it was?" Cantrell demanded.

"They called you Killer Cantrell up there, didn't they?" Tucson asked.

Cantrell's lips tightened, then he relaxed. "Yeah, they did—until I taught a few fellers different. Killer. I always resented that name, like it was somebody that went around knocking over men promiscuous-like just to get a rep as a gun fighter. That's not me. No man can say I never gave the other feller an even chance with his draw, and I don't bother with amateurs, either."

"I've heard that too," Tucson admitted. "I understand you just like to draw against a man who already has a pretty good rep."

"Put it that way if you like," Cantrell said, his tones emotionless. Tucson wondered what was going on behind those flat opaque eyes. He learned in a minute, when Cantrell continued, "Say like you, Smith. You have a rep for being fast with your hawg-leg."

"I've been fast enough when it was necessary, Cantrell," Tucson said quietly. A certain tension was building up in the barroom. "You talk like you had something in mind." The words were a direct challenge.

Cantrell considered. His eyes slipped toward Lullaby, Stony, and Daulton, then back to Tucson. "Maybe I have, Smith, but not today. You got too many pals with you."

"Don't let that stop you," Tucson said easily.

"All right," Cantrell said, "let's put it another way. This just isn't my day for arguments."

The tension in the room eased. Cantrell drew out his sack of Durham. His cigarette papers slipped from his fingers to the floor, and he stooped, fumbling there a moment before retrieving them. He straightened up, swaying a trifle at the bar, and called for another drink. Whitlock said, "Lee, don't you think you've had enough to drink for today?"

"If I thought that," Cantrell said coldly, "I'd not be ordering another shot. And I don't remember asking you for advice, Trax."

Whitlock fell silent and turned away. Cantrell laughed harshly and swung back toward Tucson. "Y'know, Smith, that's one trouble with this world. Somebody's always butting in on somebody else's business." He shoved his sombrero to the back of his head and now Tucson saw the ugly livid scar that paralleled the man's eyebrows and traced its fiery line above one temple to disappear in the hair. "And I don't like folks that can't mind their own business. Maybe if you were smart, Smith, you'd get along home. There's nothing here to interest your law-enforcement instincts. So you might as well ride."

"And suppose we don't feel that way?" Tucson asked coldly.

"Didn't think you would. Hoped you wouldn't. One of these days, Smith, you and me will have to get together."

"Any time you say, Cantrell. Just name the day."

Cantrell said coldly, "Oh, to hell with you," downed his drink, swung savagely away from the bar, and barged out to the street.

Whitlock drew a long breath. "Lee's having one of his bad days, I reckon."

"Bad days?" Tucson asked.

"Headaches," Whitlock replied. "He gets a terrific headache every so often. It makes him mean. Actually, he's a fine hombre."

"I've seen fine wildcats too," Stony put in, "but I never wanted to associate with 'em."

Whitlock said, "I'm afraid Lee's taken a dislike to you, Smith. Unless you have something important to keep you here, you could avoid some trouble by leaving."

Tucson laughed softly. "I'm afraid I have something important to keep me here, Whitlock."

"The same being?"

"When I find out I'll let you know. Meanwhile, we're staying."

Whitlock shrugged. "On your own head be it."

"Or on Cantrell's. After all, Whitlock, he works for you. Can't you control him? You're the one who wants to see trouble avoided."

"I don't figure there's any man on earth can control Lee, once he makes up his mind to take the warpath."

"That," Tucson said quietly, "remains to be seen."

The conversation switched to other, general topics, and within a few minutes Tucson and his companions started for the street. Whitlock followed them outside. As they stepped to the sidewalk, they saw Cantrell standing at the hitch rail, gazing east along Main Street.

Cantrell, hearing voices, glanced around, then spoke to Whitlock. "Trax," he said, "there goes Ducky, crossing toward the Warbonnet Saloon. That fat slob is going to be liquored up before night's here, if you don't stop him." His tones took on a sort of mocking touch. "He never will catch Art Branch and your horse if you don't keep him sober."

Whitlock squinted along the thoroughfare. "By cripes," he said, "there's nothing wrong with your eyesight, Lee. Damned if I see Ducky, though."

"Cantrell's right," Tucson said. He could make out the sheriff's bulky form just stepping to the sidewalk, some three blocks distant. "That's Gebhardt all right."

"Anybody ask for your opinion, Smith?" Cantrell snarled.

"No," Tucson snapped, "but somebody sure as hell is going to get it, whether they want it or not."

Cantrell's laugh grated harshly. "We'll get together on something yet, Smith. You see if we don't."

"Any time you like, Cantrell," Tucson said. He nodded shortly to Whitlock and started along the street, accompanied by Lullaby, Stony, and Jeff Daulton. They were half a block away before anyone spoke. Then Stony said:

"That Cantrell hombre is sure flirting with a bruise."

"If not worse"—from Lullaby. "Did you ever see a meaner little cuss? He acts like he hates the world. I thought for a minute, back there in the Brown Bottle, that he and Tucson would tangle."

"Tucson made him back down," Daulton said. "That's the reason they didn't."

Tucson frowned. "I'm not sure I did," he said. "I think all that business was more in the nature of a warning than anything else. Whitlock wanted to fish around, find out why we were here, if we were staying, and so on, and then they tried to scare us out. So far as I'm concerned, it didn't work."

"What's the next move?" Stony asked.

"Dinner," Lullaby said.

"Dinner," Tucson agreed. "Then I think I'll take a ride out to the Bar-BH, get acquainted with the Hampton girl who runs it, and see what we can learn about the death of her father."

"Mind if I tag along?" Daulton asked.

"We'll be glad to have you," Tucson said. "There doesn't seem to be anything more to learn in town right now. We'll see if the Bar-BH has anything to offer. Somehow I just don't like it when people—Whitlock in particular—try to scare me out of town. I'm aiming to stay until a few mysteries are cleared up."

9. LAURE HAMPTON

It was shortly after two o'clock when Tucson and his companions got their horses from the livery stable and rode west along Main Street toward the end of town. Crossing the plank bridge over the Rio Claro, they found the hoof-chopped and wheel-rutted trail that ran northwest in the direction of the Bar-BH Ranch. The country was rolling, dotted with mesquite, greasewood, cacti, and yucca; there seemed to be plenty of grazing land, and from time to time the riders passed small bunches of white-faced Hereford cows, branded on the left flank with the Bar-BH iron. Off to their right a short distance they could see the long line of cottonwood trees and willows which flanked along either bank the shallow Claro River—if river it could be called. At the end of an hour's loping, the men swung their ponies toward the stream and watered them. Then, after the ponies had quenched their thirsts, they turned back toward the trail once more.

The riders were walking their ponies now to give them a slight rest. They rode four abreast along the trail. On Tucson's right was Jeff Daulton; on his left was Stony, and Lullaby rode at Stony's side. Stony sifted grains of tobacco from his Durham sack into a brown paper and began to roll a cigarette. He shoved the sack back into the breast pocket of his shirt, ran his tongue along one edge of the paper, and started to reach for a match. At that moment Tucson reached across and plucked the cigarette from Stony's fingers.

"And once more I'm much obliged, pard." Tucson grinned, sticking the cylinder of tobacco between his lips and striking a light.

Stony looked his exasperation. "Blast your hide, Tucson. You've gone and caught me off guard again. If you'd only try that *every* time I roll a smoke I'd be ready for you, but it just seems to happen when I'm thinking of something else——"

"Or," Tucson said, chuckling, "you might just say it happens when I'm needing a smoke. What are you kicking about? You should be flattered that I appreciate such rolling of smokes. You're really good at it."

"I can't believe that," Lullaby protested, shaking his head. "Not with those fumble fingers of his. I never could understand how his cigarettes stuck together——"

"There's a hell of a lot you don't understand," Stony snapped. "To have understanding a man has to have brains, and so——" He broke off, then, "But it's just like Tucson says, my cigarettes have a certain extra quality in the rolling. They're packed nice and tight, and yet they draw easy. No wonder he likes 'em."

"Yaah!" Lullaby said scoffingly. "He's just too lazy to roll his own."

Stony smirked. "You're just jealous of my smoke-rolling ability. Well, you know what they say about mousetraps and builders."

Lullaby eyed him suspiciously. "Why should anybody talk about mousetraps? What do you mean?"

"It's a saying," Stony explained loftily, "as only people with education understand. I'll bet you don't know what happens when a man builds a better mousetrap."

"He catches rats instead of mice, I suppose," Lullaby said hopefully.

Stony looked disgusted. "No, stupid. The saying goes like this, 'If a man builds a better mousetrap, the world will beat a path to his door.' "

Lullaby shook his head. "Sounds dumb to me. If this hombre's mousetraps are so much better, he wouldn't have to sell 'em at home. Any hardware dealer on any Main Street would be glad to handle the business. And why wouldn't the feller already have a path to his door, anyway, if not a sidewalk? You trying to tell me some hombre is going to go out on the range by himself, just to build mousetraps? Gopher traps, maybe, or coyote traps, to save the stock. But mousetraps, no!"

"You're hopeless," Stony said wearily. "Trying to educate you is just a waste of time." He started to reach for his tobacco again, then seeing that Lullaby had started to roll a cigarette he paused, a sudden gleam coming into his eye.

"Educate, hell!" Lullaby said, sifting grains of tobacco into his paper. "I'm just trying to make some sense out of your dumb remarks. You say 'the world will beat a path to his door.' The *world,* mind you! That means from all over, across oceans and everything.

Now whoever heard of anybody making a path on water? Even if it could be done, would anybody go to all that work just to get a mousetrap, I ask you?"

He curled the cylinder of tobacco deftly between his fingers. Stony was watching him closely. "It's like this, pard," Stony said, pretending to be patient. "Maybe I should have made myself a mite clearer. Let me explain——"

"A *mite* clearer!" Lullaby paused, the cigarette halfway to his lips. "One hell of a lot clearer." He completed the operation and ran his tongue along the edge of the cigarette paper.

And at that moment Stony reached over and quickly took the cigarette from Lullaby's fingers and placed it in his own mouth. A guffaw left his lips as he reached for a match.

"Dang your thieving soul, Stony," Lullaby said irritably. "Of all the underhanded tricks!" He glared resentfully at his pardner.

"Underhanded nothing." Stony grinned. "I'm just smart. Look how quick I picked up Tucson's trick——"

"Quick?" Lullaby snorted. "After he's been doing that to you for years, you just get around to trying it today."

Stony chuckled. "That's a heap faster'n you, anyway, pard. But don't let it fret you. Someday, with good luck, you might catch up to my intelligence."

"Your intelligence. Bah!" Lullaby growled.

Grinning widely, Stony struck a match and touched it to the end of the stolen cigarette between his lips. He had started to draw in the smoke when an abrupt *puff!* occurred. The cigarette burst into flame, making a sort of miniature explosion that went out instantly, leaving a shred of powder-blackened paper dangling from his smudged lips and chin.

"Wha-wha-what the hell!" Stony gasped, his jaw dropping. He plucked the scrap of paper from his mouth, stared at it a moment, then glanced with sudden suspicion at Lullaby.

Lullaby asked politely, "Was something said about traps, Stony?" Suddenly he was rocking with laughter. "Traps! You sure walked into that one with your eyes open, feller. And just to save you beating a path to my door for more of that excellent smoking mixture I concocted, here, I'll give you the sack." He reached over and thrust the partially filled Durham sack into Stony's shirt pocket.

Stony drew away resentfully and began to wipe at his blackened mouth with his bandanna. He was swearing under his breath. Tucson and Jeff Daulton were shaking with laughter.

"Cripes!" Lullaby said, in a sudden burst of generosity, "I'll even reveal the secret formula of my prime smoking mixture. It's plumb simple to concoct. First, you take a .45 ca'tridge and pry the lead slug out of the shell. Then you take some of the black powder and mix it into a sack of Durham. The important part, of course, is to wait for the proper sucker to think he's put it over on you with his thieving propensities——"

"Aw, you go to hell," Stony growled, though a hidden gleam of reluctant admiration for Lullaby's well-laid plan had commenced to appear in his eyes. "A fine trick to play on a trusting pard!"

"I'll admit that," Lullaby said complacently. "It was a very low sort of stunt—almost as low as the joker who put harness oil in my flapjack syrup——"

"Jeepers!" Stony exclaimed. "You sure hold a grudge——"

"Not any longer I don't, sweetheart," Lullaby said smugly. "We're even now."

"T'hell we're even." Stony grinned suddenly. "But from now on I roll my own smokes."

"And leave my syrup alone?" Lullaby persisted.

"Hah!" Stony exclaimed. "I wouldn't be so simple as to promise that."

Tucson broke in, "C'mon, you hombres, let's prod our broncs. It'll be suppertime before we reach the Bar-BH, if we don't hurry."

"And what's wrong with that?" Lullaby wanted to know, drawing a fresh sack of tobacco from his pocket and rolling another cigarette. When it was finished he offered it to Stony. Stony drew back, shaking his head.

"I don't trust you," Stony said. "Like Tucson pointed out, we'd better hurry a mite."

The horses were urged to a swifter gait; miles unrolled before their flying hoofs. It was nearly four-thirty by the time the buildings of the Hampton Ranch were sighted. The ranch house proper was surrounded by tall cottonwood trees, and was constructed of adobe reinforced with chunks of rock. A short distance to its rear were the combination bunk- and mess house with its adjoining kitchen, from the chimney of which blue smoke was rising toward the sky. There was a large barn, blacksmith shop, corrals, and a couple of miscellaneous buildings. As the four riders drew near they could hear a faint squeaking from the windmill, its vanes turning lazily in the soft breeze that lifted across the range. The hot sun made the dark shadows among the trees look doubly welcome, and before long the horses had loped past the ranch house and were heading in the direction of the bunkhouse.

As they drew near the bunkhouse and pulled to a halt, a lean grizzled man in cow togs stepped from the doorway and raised one gnarled hand in greeting. "Welcome to the Bar-BH," he said. "I'm Jed Carrick, rod of this spread—though what good I do nowdays, I'm not sure. Miss Laure runs things and runs 'em well."

Tucson started to introduce himself and his companions, but the foreman cut him short. "I know you all by name," he said, shaking hands. "Heard you testifyin' at the inquest this mornin'. Somehow I got an idea you'd upset the applecart for Whitlock and that fat-headed sheriff. And I've heard of you Mesquiteers before, of course."

Tucson frowned. "I don't remember you testifying at the inquest."

"Didn't," Carrick replied. "Just went in to sort of take in the show. Been interested in what's going on around here ever sence Ben was killed. Ben Hampton, I mean. He owned this spread. His daughter Laure took over after he was killed. She was at the inquest too, but stayed in town to visit friends a spell. She should be getting in most any time now—but turn your ponies into the corral and rest your saddles." He turned his head toward the kitchen and called, "Hey, Java, you'd best put a few more spuds in the pot. We'll have company for supper."

A bald-headed individual with a long red nose appeared in the kitchen doorway, wiping his hands on an old flour sack he wore about his waist in lieu of an apron. "You don't need to tell me," he said sourly, in the manner of all ranch cooks. "I heerd 'em ride in. My Gawd! More hungry mouths to feed. Seems like the range is overrun with saddle tramps, nowadays."

"These are no saddle tramps," Carrick denied. He performed introductions, concluding ". . . and if they can stand the cooking of one Java Jenkins, they'll have proved their stomachs are made of cast-iron and rawhide."

"I don't think it will be that bad." Tucson laughed.

The cook unbent a trifle. "I'll leave it to you gents to decide.

Trouble is, this Bar-BH outfit don't appreciate good cookin'."

Lullaby said suddenly. "You're not *the* Java Jenkins? Cripes! The fame of your cooking has reached clear back home to Texas."

Jenkins eyed him somewhat suspiciously. "What do you mean, *fame?*"

"Don't you make a sort of special dried-apple pie?" Lullaby asked.

"I certain do," the cook said promptly.

Lullaby turned to his companions. "Pards, we're in luck! This is the one and genuine Java Jenkins. Now I know we'll really feed tonight. Isn't that so, cookie?"

Java Jenkins was grinning broadly now. "Appreciation at last." He beamed. "A by Gawd Daniel come to judgment! Well, I'll see you at supper, gents." He withdrew into his kitchen.

The horses were started toward the corral. Jed Carrick said to Lullaby, "What's all this bosh about Java's fame reaching Texas—and his dried-apple pies?"

Lullaby chuckled. "Did you ever know a ranch cook who didn't try to turn out something special in that kind of pie? I was just trying to put him in a good humor. Aces to tens he'll outdo himself tonight."

"He'll have to," Stony said darkly, "once he sees you eat."

Carrick laughed and the men and horses continued on toward the corral.

When the men returned to the bunkhouse, they lounged and smoked on benches placed against the front wall of the building. The sun dropped lower in the west, touching the peaks of the Apparitions now and forming deep purple shadows in the draws and ravines of the mountains.

Carrick said at last to Tucson, "You hombres aiming to stick around a spell?"

Tucson nodded. "We're sort of interested to see what will follow Folsom's death. Besides, an attempt was made to scare us out today, and we just don't like to be pushed around." He told Carrick of his conversation with Trax Whitlock and Cantrell.

Carrick shook his head. "A bad pair," he said seriously. "Particularly that Cantrell—a killer if I ever saw one. There's some damn bad things happening on this range, and I'd like to know what's behind it."

"That's the way we feel," Tucson replied. "Put us down as just plain curious, if you like—but, as I say, we don't like to be pushed around. That's why we rode out to see you today. We heard about Ben Hampton being killed, and we thought maybe you could give us some information about that. There's a chance there may be some link between his death and Joe Folsom's."

Carrick didn't reply at once. Three cowhands came riding in from the range and put their ponies in the corral. On the way back, they stopped and were introduced to Tucson and the others, then continued on into the bunkhouse. Carrick had been stuffing tobacco into his pipe. He drew meditatively on it for a few minutes then said to Tucson, "T'tell the truth, I've sort of had a hunch that way myself. No, don't ask me why. It's just a hunch, and no reason behind it I can put a finger on."

"Did Ben Hampton and Joe Folsom have anything in common?"

"Both cowmen. That's all so far as I know. I don't think Ben ever spoke to Folsom more'n once or twice when Folsom happened to stop by here for a short time. Folsom claimed to be looking for a job, punching. I think Ben might have made a place for him on the outfit, though we won't be needin' any extra help until beef roundup comes along. At the same time, Folsom didn't appear too anxious to go to work. But he did do a lot of riding over the range. Every so often one of our hands would cut his trail. Dam'd if I know what his business was, if he wa'n't lookin' for a job."

Two more Bar-BH cowboys rode past. Tucson said, "And you haven't any idea why Ben Hampton was killed?"

"Not the slightest." The foreman frowned. "So far as I know, Ben didn't have an enemy in the world. There'd been no trouble between the Bar-BH and the other outfits." He paused as the two cowhands returned from the corral and he introduced them to Tucson and the others. When they had entered the bunkhouse, Carrick said, "Them's the two who found Ben's body. He'd been dead some hours when they saw him layin' out on the range. Ben's hawss had come home, which was how we happened to start searchin'. Like I say, them two found him, and he'd been plugged plumb center with a forty-five slug."

"Do you know where he was going at the time he was killed?" Tucson asked.

Carrick nodded. "He owned an old cabin over in the Apparitions that he rents to a lunger—feller out here for his health—and he'd gone to collect the rent." Carrick paused at a question from Stony, then went on, "Yeah, he'd been there and got the money all right, so he must have been on his way home."

"Robbery?" Lullaby asked.

Carrick shook his head. "The amount wasn't enough to cause murder. Anyway, he had the money on him—so he wasn't killed for that."

Hoofbeats sounded along the road leading to the ranch and a rider turned in. Tucson saw it was a girl. Carrick said, looking somewhat relieved, "Here comes Laure now. It was certain a hard blow when Ben was killed, but Laure has snapped out of her grief in fine shape. Took over and runs this outfit like she'd been doing it all her life."

"With considerable help from her rod, I imagine," Tucson commented.

"Not so much's you'd think," Carrick replied.

The girl pulled her pony to a halt and dismounted. She was tall and boyishly built, with dark hair, a clear olive complexion, and long eyelashes. She wore a green corduroy divided riding skirt, mannish flannel shirt, and riding boots. A flat-topped sombrero covered her head, and a beaded quirt dangled from her left wrist.

"Wondered if you was goin' to get in by suppertime, Laure," Carrick said in a grumbling tone. "Feel easier now that you're here."

"Shucks, Jed." The girl laughed, her voice low and throaty. "Nothing's going to happen to me." She stripped off her buckskin gloves and approached Tucson, right hand outstretched. "Heard you testify this morning, Mr. Smith, so I feel as though I already know you—and you others as well." She shook hands with each man in turn, her eyes seeming to dwell longest on Jeff Daulton. Jeff seemed reluctant to relinquish her hand and when he finally did so his face looked somewhat redder than usual.

"Golly, I'm starved," Laure Hampton said. "Jed, will you take my pony to the corral? I'll drop into the kitchen and get Java to fix a couple of plates for me. Then you bring Mr. Smith and his friends up to the house later and we'll talk."

"I'll take care of your pony, Miss Hampton," Daulton said quickly.

The two exchanged glances and it was the girl's turn to color.

Then she said, "Thanks," gave a quick nod to the others, and entered the cookhouse, where she could be heard in conversation with Java Jenkins. Daulton took the horse's reins and led it away. Within a short time Laure reappeared, carrying a covered platter of food and a tin pail of coffee. "I'll see you all later," she said as she passed. A moment later she entered the rear door of the ranch house.

Carrick's eyes followed the girl's form until she had disappeared, then he glanced down toward the corral, where Daulton was just closing the gate. He said dryly, "It looks as if our friend Jeff was sort of impressed with Laure. Well, I ain't surprised. Most of the young bucks in this neck of the range have tried sparkin' Laure at one time or another. And I can't say's I blame 'em. She's a right pretty girl."

"She is that," Tucson agreed. "Does Miss Laure live all alone in that house since her father was killed?"

Carrick shook his head. "She has an Injun woman stayin' with her, to redd up the house and help with cookin' and so on when Laure gets her own meals——"

A loud pounding on a dishpan interrupted the words. "Come and get it or I'll thro-o-ow-w-w it away!" Java Jenkins bawled loudly.

"Let's eat," Carrick said, and the men entered the mess house.

10. DUBIOUS PROOF

It had grown dark while the men were at supper. A few faint stars showed overhead, though as yet there was no sign of a moon, when Tucson and his friends, led by Jed Carrick, left the mess house. "That," Lullaby commented, "was a right good meal."

"I'm surprised you didn't just call it a light snack," Stony said sarcastically. "I'll bet Java thinks one of the starving Armenians descended on him."

Lights shone from the ranch house. Laure met them at the door and ushered the men into the main room, a long chamber that stretched the width of the ranch house. There was a big rock fireplace, now dark, in one wall. The furniture looked comfortable. Animal skins and Indian rugs were spread on the pine floor. An oil lamp, covered with a glass shade, burned on a round oak table in the center of the room. By this time the girl had changed her riding outfit for a high-bodiced dress of some soft blue material, with lace at the throat and wrists. Her dark hair was gathered into a bun at her nape.

Carrick looked at her in surprise. "Sort've got dressed up, didn't you, Laure?"

The girl flushed and glanced quickly at Jeff Daulton. "Good grief, Jed! You wouldn't expect me to stay in those hot riding clothes?" She quickly changed the subject. "How did you work it, Jed?" She gestured to the others to be seated.

"I didn't," the foreman replied. "They came out here on their own account."

Tucson looked questioningly at the girl and she explained, "When we heard you testify at the inquiry this morning and learned who you were," Laure said, "I suggested to Jed that it would be a good idea if he could persuade you and your friends to stay on for a time and learn, if possible, just who killed Dad, and why."

Carrick took up the story. "When it come time to find you, you weren't to be seen anyplace. That must have been about the time you were in Whitlock's Brown Bottle. Never dreamed of you going there. I'd figured to ride in tomorrow and see you at your hotel——"

At that moment a door into the living room opened and a comely Indian woman entered, bearing a tray of glasses. Laure said, "Mr. Smith, I hope you like mint."

"Mint?" Tucson asked.

The girl nodded, smiling. "I grow a patch at the side of the house. Dad used to like it. I sort of fix it up with some bourbon and sugar and cold water."

Tucson laughed. "I gather your meaning, Miss Hampton."

"I'll drop the 'misters' if you men will forget the 'miss'," the girl suggested. Drinks were passed and the Indian woman withdrew. Laure placed a box of cigars on the table and opened it, then seated herself. Conversation was general for a few minutes. Laure asked if Jeff Daulton intended to stay with the Mesquiteers right along.

Jeff shook his head. "I'm just a cowpunch taking a vacation at present."

"Perhaps the Bar-BH could use you later on," Laure said. Jeff said that would be fine, and the girl again turned to Tucson. "Am I to understand, then, that you do intend to stay and look into things that are going on here?"

Tucson nodded. "We were talking to Cantrell and Trax Whitlock today after the inquest and they appeared so anxious to have us leave that we thought it might be interesting to find out why." He asked a few questions about her father but she could tell him little more of the murder than Jed Carrick had. Tucson said next, "I understand the Bar-BH is the biggest of the outfits hereabouts. Have you had any trouble with the other stock raisers?"

"Not a bit." Laure shook her head. "We get along with all of them. In fact, Webb Talbert, who owns the Rocking-T, and Scott Royce, who runs the Bench-R iron, were close friends of Dad's."

"I notice you don't say the same for Trax Whitlock," Tucson pointed out.

"Dad didn't like him, but there was no cause for enmity between them. They'd never had any trouble—we-ell, maybe there was a little. You see, from time to time Trax Whitlock has tried to buy the Bar-BH. Dad wouldn't sell."

"Why?" Tucson asked.

"Two reasons," the girl said. "Dad was satisfied here. He liked to raise beef. That's one. The other is that Whitlock never offered near what the outfit is worth. Since Dad was—since he died, Whitlock has raised the offer, but I said no."

"He still doesn't offer enough?"

"That's it. Eventually if he'll meet my figure I may sell out. Trax Whitlock is too ambitious. I think he'd like to own this whole range. Folks are getting tired of his highhanded methods. That's going to mean trouble, maybe a range war. I don't want to get mixed in anything of that sort. I don't like killing."

Jeff Daulton put in, "I understand Whitlock's Hatchet outfit is a right sizable spread. Have you had any trouble with rustlers?"

Laure shook her head. "This range has been pretty free of rustlers for some years now. Oh, there's a little goes on, right along, as you'll find on any range, but it's nothing to concern anybody." She added further details: nearly all the ranchers were fairly prosperous, they worked well together on the roundups; there was no mortgage nor were there any notes due on the Bar-BH. She sighed deeply. "So you see I can't think of one reason why anybody should want to kill Dad. The only way I see it, he must have been mistaken for somebody else."

"That seems hard to believe too," Tucson put in. "I hate to dwell on a painful subject, but the fact remains that he was shot from the front and that he was killed during the day, if the doctor was right in designating the time of death. So it wasn't a case of wrong recognition, as I see it. . . . What about Stow Whitlock and his feud with Trax?"

Laure told him what she knew, and nothing was added to Tucson's information in that direction. "You'll find Stow Whitlock a far different proposition from his brother," the girl said. "He's respected in Morral City. Just recently he promised to donate quite a chunk of money to a church-building fund."

Lullaby changed the subject. "What's this we've heard about the Apparition Mountains being haunted, Laure?"

"Just a lot of foolish talk, I reckon, based on rumor and old Indian legends. You see, the occupants of a wagon train were massacred as it was passing through the Apparitions one time when the Apaches were on the warpath. Then, in reprisal, a lot of Indians were killed in the mountains. People began to say that ghosts were seen. You know how that sort of a story grows.

There's an old house over there in the foothills—it's on Bar-BH holdings, by the way—where a prospector once lived with his wife and daughter. The Indians dropped down on them and killed them. They say the daughter got a horse and almost made an escape, but the Indians followed and killed her." The girl laughed shortly. "There are people who claim to have seen the ghost of that girl and her horse galloping through the foothills. That's ridiculous, of course, but a great many people believe it——"

"More than you'd think." Jed Carrick nodded. He puffed hard on his cigar.

Laure said, "When I was in town today, Jed, I dropped around to see Teresita for a few minutes." She broke off to tell Tucson and the others, "Teresita is a Mexican woman who worked for us some years ago, before she got married and moved to Morral City. Anyway, one of Teresita's relatives from Coyotero Tanks was there, and he had heard from another relative that the ghost galloped last night."

Carrick said "Bosh!" in a disgusted voice.

"Laure," Stony asked, "have you ever actually talked to anyone who claimed to have seen that ghost?—anyone you'd put faith in?"

Much to his surprise, Laure replied in the affirmative. "Yes. One of our hands, Johnny Merker. He swears he saw it, and we can't shake him out of the idea." She turned to the foreman. "Jed, why not get Johnny up here and let Tucson hear his story?"

"That's a right suggestion." Carrick nodded. He got to his feet and left the house.

Tucson asked, "You mentioned an old house over in the foothills, Laure. Is that the house you rent to some lunger, where your father collected the rent the day he was killed?"

"That's the house," the girl replied. "It's not much of a house, really, just one room. It was there when Dad bought the Bar-BH. I don't know who originally built it, unless it was the prospector who was killed by the Indians. You see, there was quite a bit of silver mining in the Apparitions at one time. Then the vein petered out, and mining was done for. So far as rent for the place was concerned, Marden could have had it for nothing, but he insisted on paying something——"

"Is Marden the lunger?"

The girl nodded. "Gridley Marden. He'd had lung trouble and

couldn't live anyplace else except out here. Dad let him have the place. Occasionally he'd ride over to visit and get the rent, but the rent was the last thing he thought of."

"Does this Gridley Marden live there alone?" Lullaby asked.

"No—he has a sort of man-of-all-work named Riley Comstock. Riley's quite a character in these parts. One of those who prospected in the old days. He still prospects—unsuccessfully—whenever Marden hasn't enough to keep him busy."

"Has either of them ever seen the ghost?" Jeff Daulton asked.

"They not only state emphatically they haven't seen it, but they say anybody is cracked who claims it exists," Laure answered.

Footsteps were heard at the door and Carrick entered with Johnny Merker, a slim-hipped, angular-jawed young puncher with leathery features. Laure offered him a seat and went to get him a drink. Tucson came to the point after a few minutes. "Look here, Johnny," he asked, "do you still think you saw a ghost such as Laure and Jed have been telling about?"

"If it wasn't a ghost," Merker said doggedly, "it's the nearest thing to a ghost I ever heard of." He looked uneasily at the others as though expecting to be laughed at for his gullibility.

"You make it sound right certain," Tucson said seriously. "Do you mind telling us about it?"

Merker smiled a trifle sheepishly. "No, I don't mind tellin' about it. I already been hoorawed so many times by the boys in the bunkhouse, once more shouldn't make any difference, I reckon. First, let's get something straight. I wasn't drunk that night, as a heap of folks seem to think. Hadn't had a drink since the previous day."

Tucson chuckled. "All right, we'll take it for granted your eyesight was all right, as well as your mind."

"Second," Merker went on, "I've never believed in ghosts. I don't believe in 'em now. Howsomever, I do know what I saw." Again that dogged tone in his voice.

Tucson nodded. "We're waiting to hear."

"It was one night," Merker commenced, then, "No, I'd best tell it from the start. It was like this. I'd ordered a new mail-order saddle and had gone to town to see if it had come in yet. It hadn't, but while I was at the railroad depot the man at Coyotero Tanks telegraphed that a saddle for me had been put off the train at that point by mistake. It made me mad as—as the deuce, but I figured I might as well make the ride to Coyotero Tanks as wait for the saddle to be sent back to Morral City and then have to ride in for it another day. And so I started for Coyotero Tanks."

Merker paused to take a swallow from his glass. "I didn't push my pony too hard—didn't want to wear him out on the ride. I got my saddle at Coyotero Tanks, then started across country for the Bar-BH. By that time it was dark. There wasn't much moon to speak of, even when it did show above the horizon. Anyway, there I was, just moving along easy, ridin' parallel to the Apparition Mountains, when all of a sudden I see something moving——"

"How far were you from Coyotero Tanks when this happened?" Stony asked.

Merker frowned. "I don't know exactly. At a guess I'd say between ten and fifteen miles, and probably a mile or so from where the high mountains really start to lift toward the sky. I was just traveling through the lower foothills. Like I say, I saw something moving, but at that moment I was just dipping down a slope and my view was cut off. By the time I reached the crest, it was all dark like before, so I thought I must be mistaken. I went on about half a mile, still sort of thinking about that white thing I thought I'd seen, and I gave another look toward the mountains just as I'd reached a stretch of high level ground. Well, damned —beg your pardon, Miss Laure—darned if I didn't see it again."

"And it looked like a galloping horse and rider?" Daulton asked.

Merker shook his head. "Not at first. When I first saw it it was just a sort of movin' white blur. And then gradual it commenced to take shape. Dog my hide! I just couldn't believe my eyes. But there it was. A girl and a horse—sort of a shivery white like—and the horse movin' fast, with the girl's hair streamin' out behind. Her feet was movin' fast like she was spurrin' that ghost horse in the ribs. I didn't know what to think. And then, while I watched, that danged apparition started to fade away. First the horse's head and front legs sort of dissolved to nothing, then the girl's body. The horse's tail was last to go and it just seemed to kind of melt into thin air. Just like that, the whole danged ghost vanished." Merker heaved a sigh, shook his head perplexedly and swallowed another drink.

"And that's all there was to it?" Lullaby wanted to know.

"Cripes! Ain't that enough?" Merker retorted. "It gave me cold chills down my back. I'd heard about those mountains being haunted, but had laughed at the idea. Now I don't know what to think."

"Did you see the ghost again that night?" Tucson asked.

Merker shook his head. "I waited around nigh an hour too. I don't mind admittin' I felt plumb spooky. I was all over in a cold sweat. I waited a long spell, but the ghost didn't show up again, so I lined out for here. When I got in I woke the boys up and told 'em, but they just laughed at me."

"It's all bosh," Jed Carrick growled. "Probably Johnny just saw moonlight shining on a rock, or somethin', and as he moved he thought it was a ghost movin'. What do they call it—the power of suggestion? Johnny had heard there was ghosts in the mountains, so when he saw white moonlight, his mind tricked him, and——"

"That's not so, Jed," Merker said earnestly. "There wasn't much of a moon—not enough to—aw, cripes——" He broke off. "It's no use. We've augered all this before. No use startin' again."

"I'll tell a man there ain't." Carrick snorted. "You and Steve Plummer went out the next night lookin' for that ghost, hung around until dawn, and you both admit you didn't see a thing."

"Maybe the ghost doesn't ride every night." Laure smiled. "Or perhaps Johnny and Steve couldn't find the right spot to view it."

"That could be possible," Tucson said. "Anyway, Johnny has given us a certain proof of the ghost's existence."

"If a ghost can exist," Lullaby said. "And sort of a doubtful proof."

"You don't believe me?" Merker bristled, looking at Lullaby.

"Sure I believe you." Lullaby laughed. "Don't get proddy, Johnny. Only I feel dubious about what you saw. I believe you saw something—what it was, I can't say—but I don't believe it was a ghost. And you've said yourself you don't believe in ghosts. You can't expect me to accept what you don't believe yourself."

"That's right," Johnny conceded. "But what did I see?"

Lullaby shook his head. "I haven't the least idea."

Tucson asked, "Does anybody know anything about four Mexicans disappearing in the Apparitions a few years back? Have their ghosts been seen?"

"I've never heard of anyone having seen their ghosts," Laure said, "but I can tell you a little about them. Those four were hired by Gridley Marden when he rented that house of ours in the foothills."

"Hired? What for?" Tucson asked.

"The house was in pretty bad shape. It needed repairs and Marden wanted cleaning up done around the place—brush taken out and so on. The four Mexicans were from Coyotero Tanks. When they'd finished their job, he paid them off, but they never got back to their homes, though they had started for Coyotero Tanks that same day."

"Weren't their bodies ever found?" Stony asked.

"Not that I know of," Laure replied. "I never heard they were."

Tucson questioned Merker further, but could get no more information regarding the ghost than Merker had already given. Merker again pointed out that there hadn't been much of a moon that night, so that seemed to dispose of Carrick's idea that Merker had been looking at moonlight shining on rocks. Merker finally arose and started for the bunkhouse. Tucson mentioned that he and his friends should be starting back to town too. Carrick suggested they stay the night.

"We've got plenty of bunks and blankets," the foreman said.

"I think that's a good idea," Laure seconded the invitation.

"Matter of fact," Tucson confessed; "I'd like to stay. I sort of figured on taking a ride over to Coyotero Tanks in the morning and perhaps stopping off to see this Marden man on the way. I know my pards will be willing. How about you, Jeff?"

"I really should push back to Morral City," Daulton said. "There's a telegram I want to send. Should have sent it today, but it slipped my mind."

"To your grandfather, I suppose." Tucson chuckled.

"Grandfather?" Daulton frowned.

"You already told me your grandmother was dead," Tucson pointed out.

Daulton's face cleared. He laughed. "No, not my grandfather. Let's say my uncle."

The others looked at Daulton and Tucson, realizing there was some hidden meaning in the words, but no one spoke for a few minutes. Finally, Laure said, "Look here, Jeff, if your telegram could wait until morning, we could make the ride to town together. I've got to get some thread to match a piece of material——"

Daulton cut in promptly, "In that case I'll be glad to stay over. My—my uncle can wait a spell longer for his telegram."

The men left for the bunkhouse a few minutes later. When they arrived, only a single lamp, turned low, was burning. The Bar-BH hands were already snoring in bunks. Tucson and his friends undressed quietly and crawled between blankets. Carrick extinguished the light and followed suit. A variety of snores filled the bunkhouse. Tucson distinguished Lullaby's and Stony's from the others, as he lay there pondering the ghost story Merker had related. There was a slight noise in the next bunk. Tucson asked softly, "What's the matter, Jeff, can't you get to sleep?"

Daulton whispered back, "I'm wide awake as a hoot owl."

Tucson smiled in the darkness. "What you thinking about?"

Daulton didn't answer at once. Finally he said, "Same thing as you are—ghosts."

Tucson said dryly, "Oh." After a minute he asked, "Say, Jeff, that uncle of yours—his name wouldn't be Sam, would it?"

Again a long silence. Finally Jeff said, "That could be possible, Tucson."

Neither spoke again and within a short time the sound of their heavy breathing mingled with that of the others.

11. TROUBLE BREWING

By making an early departure from the Bar-BH the following morning, Tucson, Lullaby, and Stony managed to reach Gridley Marden's place around ten o'clock. They had loped the horses steadily, stopping now and then to breathe the animals, and then pushing on again. The sun overhead was bright; a few scattered clouds drifted lazily in the turquoise sky. The foothills grew higher as the riders approached the mountains, and by the time Marden's house was sighted, the jagged peaks of the Apparitions seemed to tower almost overhead, their saw-toothed crags tipped with golden morning light.

As they drew near the men saw that the house was situated at the mouth of a wide box canyon, and faced the east. Back of it rose the precipitous heights of the Apparitions; ahead lay rolling foothills. Scattered about the canyon were gigantic stratified rocks which had tumbled from the peaks in past ages; some of these rocks were as large as the house itself and a few had stunted bits of plant life growing from cracks. The house had at one time been surrounded by tall brush—catclaw, mesquite, greasewood, and prickly pear—but this had been cleared away from the front of the building so the view across the foothills might not be obstructed.

Countless centuries of rain had washed down from the farther recesses of the mountains a wide band of deep sand, which passed across what might be considered the front yard of the house; across this stretch of sand the riders traveled, their ponies sinking to fetlocks at every step, until firmer terrain was reached. Now they were near enough for Tucson to see that the building was constructed of random rock, bound together with a sort of adobe mortar. A small bed of red geraniums stood at either side of the closed door, and the earth in the vicinity appeared to be neatly swept. Farther up the canyon the men could see a small shed and a corral, in which were three horses, one a dirty white, the other two chestnuts.

There weren't any humans to be seen about the place, but as the riders dismounted the door of the house opened and a scrawny, bewhiskered individual with lined features and watery blue eyes put in an appearance. A small opening, intended for a smile, parted his chest-length beard. "Thought I heerd saddle leather squeakin' out here," he stated. "Thet sand wash yonderly plumb muffles hoof trompin'. Was the Injuns still on the war-path, we could be snuk up on and massacreed afore we could say Jack Robinson." He turned his head back toward the interior of the house. "Grid! We got company."

"Well, not company exactly." Tucson smiled. "My pardners and I are on our way to Coyotero Tanks and we stopped off to see if it would be possible to get a drink of water for our ponies—that is, if water isn't scarce."

" 'T'ain't scurce a-tall." The whiskered man spoke. "We got a plumb dandy well out back—ain't never run dry——"

He broke off and stepped to one side as a thin, cleanly shaven man of about forty-five appeared. "Welcome, gentlemen. Of course we've plenty of water. I'm Gridley Marden."

Tucson introduced himself and his companions. Marden was dressed in a white collarless shirt, dark trousers, and city shoes. His skin had the reddish look of the easterner not used to the burning southwest sun, the sort of skin that never darkens. "But come in, gentlemen." He turned to his companion. "This is Riley Comstock. I'd die of loneliness if it weren't for Riley. He cooks and cleans up for me. . . . Riley, why don't you water these horses while Mr. Smith and his friends enjoy such hospitality as we can offer." He smiled at Tucson. "You'll have some coffee, of course."

"I'll take keer of the broncs, Grid." Comstock hitched up his overalls, one scuffed boot kicked a small pebble out of his way, and he seized the reins of the three ponies to lead them around to the rear of the house, whistling tunelessly as he went.

The interior of the house was neatly, if sparsely, furnished. A pair of bunks with folded blankets stood against one wall. At another wall, near a window, was a cookstove, above it shelves holding canned goods and other supplies. A door at the rear was closed. A shelf of books stood in one corner, and there were several straight-backed chairs, in addition to two armchairs. An oil lamp with shade was suspended from the beamed ceiling. The floor was of bare pine boards, and there were a couple of Navajo rugs. On an oilcloth-covered table stood a coffeepot and some dishes of food.

Marden said, "We were just at breakfast. Can I offer you a bite?" Tucson and Stony refused anything but coffee; Lullaby accepted a plate of fried potatoes and bacon. "It's good to see new faces," Marden went on. "Riley rather gets on my nerves at times, as I suppose I get on his. But he can get away occasionally and do what he calls his 'prospectin.' So far he's had no success finding any precious metals. About all I can do is putter about my geraniums out in front. I've even got a vegetable garden in the back, but"—he smiled ruefully—"it's not too much of a success. It requires continual weeding, and Riley doesn't always happen to be in the mood for weeding. I can't do too much myself. I'm a semi-invalid, you know. Lungs. Doctors tell me this is the only place I can remain alive. Now and then I ride a little, but too much sun isn't good for me either, the doctors tell me. So most of my time is spent in reading or thinking, and to tell the truth I'm getting a bit tired of both——" He broke off, laughing. "I seem to be monopolizing the conversation. That's what it is to be a hermit. When you do see a new face, you promptly proceed to talk an ear off its owner."

"We'd heard you weren't well," Tucson replied. "We stayed at the Bar-BH last night——"

"How is Laure Hampton? She's a very nice girl. I suppose you know all about her father being killed?"

"We know very little about it, as a matter of fact," Tucson said. "Though I'll admit we're interested. We thought you might be able to tell us something about it. You see, we've become interested——"

"I'm not surprised," Marden answered, "considering who you are."

"Are we somebody special?" Stony chuckled.

Marden laughed. "We're not quite so isolated here as you might think. Quite frequently I have a visitor. Yesterday afternoon a rider passing through dropped in for a few minutes. He'd been at that Folsom inquest, so of course he told me all about you gentlemen—— Oh, Mr. Joslin, can I give you some more food? It won't take more than a minute to fry up another pan of potatoes."

Lullaby said no, that he was satisfied for the time being.

Stony said sarcastically, "I can't believe it."

"Company manners," Lullaby said with a smirk.

Riley Comstock entered the back door, the loosely holstered gun at his belt banging against his right leg. He looked at the table, then the empty pans on the stove. "Looks like somebody was hungry," he growled.

"It was me," Lullaby said meekly. "Hope I didn't eat your breakfast."

"Oh, that's all right," Comstock said. "Kind of late for breakfast, anyway. I'll cook up extra for dinner."

"Matter of fact," Marden put in, "we've fallen into the habit of sleeping late. Consequently, our meals are always behind time." He turned back to Tucson. "No, I can't throw any light on Ben Hampton's murder. Can't imagine who'd do such a thing. He was a good friend, and I miss him."

"Did you know Joe Folsom too?" Stony asked.

"We-ell," Marden answered, "I can't say I knew him. He was here, one day. Dropped in like you men to water his horse. We really didn't talk much." He paused, then, "Do you suppose the same man was responsible for both killings?"

Tucson shrugged. "Could be, I suppose. I'd like to know." He changed the subject slightly. "Can you throw any light on the disappearance of those four Mexicans a few years back?"

Marden's face darkened and he shook his head. "I only wish I could. In a way, I feel a certain responsibility there. Those men had been working for me, and after they left here they were never seen again——"

"Thet ain't no fret of yourn, Grid," Riley Comstock said. "Ask me and I'll tell you thet them four greasers lit out for other parts. Mebbe they was sick of their wives in Coyotero Tanks. Mebbe they jist hankered after a change of scenery—landscape and fimmle." He guffawed. "You take four of them Mexes with two hundred dollars atween 'em and they ain't goin' home to no same woman."

"Two hundred dollars?" Tucson said.

Marden explained. "Their pay for a month—fifty dollars each."

"And the way them Mexes worked, considerin' we fed 'em, you was robbed, Grid," Comstock put in.

"Oh, I don't think so, Riley." Marden shook his head.

Tucson asked, "What sort of work were they doing?"

"I wanted a lot of the brush cleared off and burned," Marden explained. "And there were some repairs to the house. Odds and ends to be done. When I first came here you could scarcely see this place for the high brush. Ben Hampton would have done anything I wanted done, of course, but I preferred to do it myself. He didn't even want to take rent from me, but so long as I have the means——" He shrugged his shoulders and reached for a box of cigars which he tendered his guests. All three refused and got to their feet.

"We've got to be on our way," Tucson said.

Marden looked disappointed. "I was hoping you'd stay longer. It's so seldom we have guests."

"Come back some time and help me prospect," Comstock invited. "I know three-four likely spots. Aimin' to hit 'er any day now. Better throw in with me, and we'll git ter be millyunaires. When I make my pile, ye can bet I'm a-goin' to light a shuck outten here. Goin' East, I am. Clear far as Denver, mebbe, where I can see some laig-shows and drink fancy at the bars. I heer'n tell 'bout a dandy drink named pussy's-cafe. Allers aimed to try 'er, should I ever get a chance. And I'll do it yit, by grab!"

"Anything we can do for you at Coyotero Tanks?" Tucson asked. "Do you need any supplies or anything sent out?"

Marden shook his head, but Riley Comstock said, "Tell Andy King should he know of a rider comin' this way, to bring me a box of .45 ca'tridges. Forgot 'em the last time, and I'm nigh fresh out."

"Cripes!" Lullaby said. "I can fix that. I've got a box of .45 slugs on my saddle you can have. It'll pay for my breakfast—or I guess it was your breakfast I ate."

"Yo're welcome to it, son," Comstock said through his whiskers. "Now I can boast I once fed the Three Mesquiteers." He cackled. "And 'member whut I said about prospectin' with me. We'll all git wealthy and hit the high spots. Wine, women, and song! Thet's for me!"

Five minutes later Tucson and his pardners were again in the saddle, crossing the stretch of deep sand. Now they could look ahead on a steadily dropping vista of rolling hill lands. They had been riding not more than five minutes and had just passed beyond view of the house when Tucson suddenly reined his pony to a halt. He climbed down from the saddle, and stooping low to the ground, picked up something from the earth. Then, after scanning his surroundings a few moments, he remounted. Lullaby and Stony had reined their ponies in to wait for him. Simultaneously, they asked him what he had found.

"This," Tucson said, holding out a small round rubber ball.

Stony said, "I'll be damned!"

"Oil-soaked?" from Lullaby.

Tucson nodded. "Just like the pair we found in that metal drum. It could be this is one of that pair."

"But how did it get here?" Stony asked.

"You got me"—from Tucson. "I just spied it by chance. Happened to glance down at the ground and there it was. Lucky it hadn't rolled into some grass or brush."

Stony and Lullaby examined the rubber ball and handed it back, their features scowling. "I don't know what to think," Stony said at last. "Finding it so close to Marden's place——"

Lullaby said, "You think Marden and Comstock have anything to do with this, Tucson? After all, that drum was stolen from Ducky Gebhardt's office. It might have been brought back here and maybe the ball fell out—maybe both balls fell out. Did you see any tracks?"

"Couple of hoof prints. Not too fresh."

"Lame in the off hind hoof?" Stony asked quickly.

"These were both made by near hoofs," Tucson said. "There might have been more prints, but I didn't want to waste time looking for 'em. Both prints were headed toward town——"

"Meaning that the ball was dropped when the drum was taken east of here by Folsom?" Lullaby said.

"That's possible." Tucson nodded. "I just don't know, though."

"Maybe," Stony proposed, "we'd better go back and talk to Marden and Comstock some more."

Tucson shook his head. "We've got to have more than this to go on. If they knew anything, they'd just deny it, and what could we do? Did you notice anything suspicious about that pair?"

Both Stony and Lullaby said they hadn't. Stony added, "Did you, pard?"

"Maybe. I noticed Marden cough a couple of times. I've heard lungers cough. Marden's cough didn't sound the same. It seemed sort of forced. Maybe he was trying to convince me of something. I don't know. I just feel there's trouble brewing for somebody, before long."

"What did you think of that pair, anyway, Tucson?" Lullaby asked.

"I don't know what to think—now," Tucson replied soberly.

The men kicked their ponies in the ribs and loped on.

12. CONFUSING ADDRESSES

The sun was well past meridian by the time Tucson and his companions first sighted Coyotero Tanks. It wasn't, actually, much of a town, just a huddle of adobe buildings and two or three frame shacks, of various sizes, clustered about the twin rails where the T.N. & A.S. trains started through the pass in the Apparition Mountains. On either side of the town rose a rough escarpment of yellowish granite, on the sides of which an occasional yucca or stunted manzanita had gained a roothold in a bit of shallow soil.

Near the center of the town, placed alongside the rails, stood a paint-blistered water tank on a wooden trestle. Water leaked from various points in the big container and furnished some life for the straggly plants and withered sage growing in the gravelly earth below. A short distance away was a wooden building painted railroad red, with a narrow-roofed porch stretching across its width. There was a tie rail at one end of the building, and here the riders dismounted, then came around to the front. A couple of Mexicans lounging on the porch nodded and smiled. More Mexicans could be seen moving among the scattering of adobe shacks. A couple of chickens pecked desultorily between the rails, and on the far side of the rail bed a small Mexican child was playing with a mongrel puppy.

The door of the building stood open and the men entered. The place appeared to be a sort of combination general store and railroad depot. A long counter ran across the back, behind which were shelves of canned goods. There were a couple of round-topped tables not far from the door. Deep-ledged windows were covered with dust, and several calendars hung on the walls. At one end of the counter a middle-aged man with a sagging middle, dressed in faded overalls, was lazily plying a broom, though it looked to be a hopeless task, considering the litter of paper, cigarette and cigar stubs and other forms of trash covering the rough pine boards. A casual observer might gain the impression that the room was never swept clean, but that the litter was just moved from one end to the other on alternate days.

The instant the man with the broom spied Tucson and his pardners, he ceased sweeping, reached behind the counter and donned a train conductor's faded cap. "Railroad business?" he queried.

Tucson shook his head. Instantly the cap was removed. Tucson said, "We just dropped in to see what you had to eat."

The man looked dubious. "You might do better to look out one of the Mex joints and eat chili. All's I got is canned goods." Tucson said canned goods would do. The man looked disappointed, then said, "I'm Andy King."

Tucson gravely acknowledged the introduction and furnished his name and that of his pardners, then said, "Can you sell us what we want, or do you just act as an executive for the railroad?"

"Oh, shucks, I can sell you what you want. Far's the railroad's concerned, I just 'tend the water tank and handle a mite of freight now and then. Never figured you'd want to eat here. I got some beer too, but it ain't cold."

Tucson said that beer, warm or cold, was still beer. Lullaby meanwhile had been wandering along the counter, scrutinizing the goods on the shelves. Finally he said, "We'll need about three cans of sardines, some tomatoes, couple of cans of peaches—— What's that, corned beef in cans? Couple of those too. And a bottle of pickles. Better get a couple of pounds of soda crackers out of your barrel too——"

Stony chimed in with his choice. Andy King's jaw dropped. "Land's sakes! You fellers outfittin' for a trip?"

Stony jerked a thumb toward Lullaby. "Him—he's always outfitting. And it doesn't have to be for a trip, neither."

Food and bottled beer were placed on one of the tables. King furnished some forks and a can opener. The men produced Barlow knives, and drew up chairs. Andy King hovered attentively nearby. "Seems like," King commented, "I saw you gents in town two days back, didn't I?"

"You might've at that," Tucson replied, then went on before King could pursue the subject further. "Andy, I understand these Apparition Mountains are haunted. What do you know about it?"

King made a derisive sound. "All poppycock, if you ask me. I ain't never seen no ghosts around here. I'll tell you what, though. There ain't a Mex in Coyotero Tanks that won't swear there's ghosts in these mountains. Some of 'em even swear they've seen the ghost of a gal, ridin' through the foothills. Seems like this gal was supposed to have been overtook by Apaches and killed, sometime or other. Crazy idea, a course. But things like that skeers hell outten the Mexes. Bein' mighty religious, they believe in spirits and such." He paused, then, "Now you take sensible men like you gents, you wouldn't put no stock in any such cockin' bull stories, would you?"

Tucson looked doubtful. "I don't know. You never know what to believe. For instance, somebody was telling me that four Mexicans disappeared from this town and never have been found. What became of them?"

"That's right," King admitted. "And I can't say where they disappeared to. Their wives sure as hell think ghosts grabbed 'em. I got a hunch, though, they just lit out for parts unknown when they found themselves with some money in their pockets. They might even show up here again someday——" He broke off and snickered. "If'n they do, three of 'em's got surprises comin'?"

"How's that?" Lullaby asked through a mouthful of food.

"Three of their wives done got hitched again. The fourth remained faithful though. Josefa says she'll wait for her man, in case he does come back, but I guess she give up hope long ago."

"Is that Josefa Pico?" Tucson asked.

King shook his head. "Nope, her name's Rayón—Josefa Rayón. Right enterprisin' Mexican woman, Josefa. There was two kids to feed, so she opened up a little restaurant, with chili and such. She's makin' her way, 'thout dependin' on no charity."

Tucson rose after a few minutes and donned his sombrero. He rolled a cigarette and lighted it, then said, "You hombres take your time with your food. I'm going to take a *pasear* around town and see what it looks like."

" 'Tain't worth your time," Andy King stated. "Nothin' to see in this burg. You'd be better off to stay and drink my beer."

"Maybe it's *tequila* I want now." Tucson smiled. He nodded to the others and sauntered out.

Stony and Lullaby continued eating. Lullaby asked, "Do you get much freight to handle here?"

King shook his head. "Mostly the freight I get is for this store. Ain't much else comes."

"I thought maybe," Stony said idly, "there'd be freight for the ranches hereabouts, or perhaps that hombre who lives with Riley Comstock might get packages from time to time."

"Nothing to speak of." King shook his head. "Riley rides here two or three times a month for supplies. Ain't nothin' much come for Marden in a long spell. The ranches take their deliveries at Morral City."

"Do you operate a post office here too?" Lullaby asked.

King snickered. "Now who in this town would be writin' letters—or who would be gettin' them? Oh, occasional, a letter is addressed for somebody by way of Morral City, and the train drops it off when it stops for water. Or, say, if somebody does want to mail somethin', I give it to the conductor, with enough money for postage. Like that Mister Marden, say. 'Bout once a month he gives Riley a couple of packages to mail. Riley gives me the money for stamps, and the train conductor mails the packages. Marden always has Riley add enough money so's to buy the conductor a drink."

Stony yawned widely. "I suppose Marden sends his laundry someplace to be washed. Probably he's particular who does his shirts."

King shook his head. "Naw! The packages ain't big enough to hold laundry. I'd say mebbe they was the size of a couple of books. . . . What? No, I don't know what he sends off, but it wouldn't be laundry. He could get some Mex woman here in town to do his laundry if he wanted to——"

"Funny thing about mailing letters for fellers," Stony said casually. "A man can give you a letter to mail for him, and even if you look at the address, you've forgotten it a minute later."

"No siree!" Andy King said triumphantly. "I've got a good memory, I have. Course, in the case of them packages Comstock mails, they always go to the same addresses, so that makes it easier."

"And then a town like El Paso is easy to remember," Lullaby prompted.

"El Paso?" King looked bothered. "Did I say them packages went to El Paso? I must be dreamin'. They go to Denver and San Francisco."

"Sure, Lullaby," Stony said, "that's what Andy told us—Denver and San Francisco. John Smith of Denver and——"

"If I said John Smith," King interrupted, "you must have heard me wrong, or my tongue slipped. It was Denver of San Francisco and Francisco of Denver."

"Huh?" Lullaby looked a trifle startled. Stony observed that he'd better wash his ears better hereafter.

King giggled. "Kind of confusin', ain't it? Mebbe that's why I remember those names so well. It's what you might call a quincedince, sort of. But them's the names—Harry Denver, of San Francisco, and Pablo Francisco, of Denver."

Lullaby laughed. "Sounds like you got your geography tangled."

A little more conversation, apparently casual, extracted from King the post-office-box addresses of Denver and Francisco. More beer was opened and after a time the conversation lagged. Lullaby and Stony shoved back the empty cans and rolled cigarettes. Money was placed on the table and King informed he could keep the change, then the two men wandered out to the porch to await Tucson's return.

Nearly two hours passed before he put in an appearance. Lullaby and Stony were about to go looking for him when he strolled up to the porch, carrying under one arm a large newspaper-wrapped parcel. "Where in time you been?" Stony asked.

"I'll tell later," Tucson replied. "As soon as we fill our canteens, we can get started again. No need to rush, though. We don't want to kill our ponies before we get to Morral City."

13. THE GHOST RIDES

The three men were riding north through the Apparition foothills before Stony spoke again. "This isn't the way to Morral City, Tucson."

Tucson smiled slightly. "There's no hurry. I thought we'd head this way first. Did you two learn anything from Andy King?"

"Denver of San Francisco, and Francisco of Denver," Lullaby replied.

"Sounds like a train schedule." Tucson chuckled. "You don't make sense, Lullaby."

"Can you name me a time when he ever did?" Stony grinned. The men were riding abreast, the ponies traveling at a walk.

Lullaby said, "They're addresses, Tucson. Harry Denver, of San Francisco, and Pablo Francisco, of Denver." He added the post-office-box numbers where these names could be reached. Tucson frowned and asked for further information.

"Gridley Marden sends packages to those addresses every month," Stony answered. "And it isn't his laundry he sends, because the packages are about the size of two books—maybe smaller."

"I noticed some books at his house," Tucson said.

"You wouldn't have noticed any, if he sent a couple away every month," Lullaby pointed out.

"Maybe he receives new books every month," Tucson suggested.

"Andy King didn't say so," Stony said.

The horses plodded on. Lullaby asked, "What have you got wrapped in that newspaper, Tucson?"

"Beans and chili, rolled in *tortillas,*" came the reply.

Lullaby brightened. "By cripes! A man after my own heart."

"You're getting as bad as Lullaby," Stony said disgustedly.

"I hope not," Tucson said dryly. "Seeing as we won't be getting back to town for a spell, I figured we'd need some supper."

"You get that chow from Josefa Rayón?" Lullaby asked.

Tucson nodded. "Along with some conversation. It took a time to gain her confidence, but when she finally realized I was trying to learn what happened to those four Mexicans who disappeared, she opened up some. Sent a kid to find the former wives of the other three Mexicans too. I talked to them. Josefa is a pretty sensible woman. She doesn't put much faith in this ghost talk. All she knows is that her husband went to work for Marden and never returned. The other three women got tired of waiting and married again. Josefa feels that her man is dead—she said he was a good man, a hard worker, and not the kind to run away from her. Besides, they had two children and he was nuts about the kids."

"Did he tell her what sort of work he was doing for Marden?" Stony queried.

"As much as he knew, I guess," Tucson answered. "The four Mexes worked two weeks for Marden, clearing out brush and making some repairs to the roof and so on. At the end of each week they returned home with their salary. On Monday they'd return to Marden's place. Finally Marden told them the trip home and back again was just a waste of time. He told the Mexicans if they'd stay right through until the job was finished, he'd raise their pay. He had about a month's straight work for them and he told them to bring picks and shovels from Coyotero Tanks when they came back next time. He also warned them he didn't want their wives to come visiting while they were there. The Mexes agreed. After all, fifty dollars for the month, and their board, was right good pay. So the last time Josefa ever saw her husband he was leaving with a pick and shovel over his shoulder, with the intention of being away a month. The burros the Mexes rode off on wandered home two months later."

"What did Josefa's husband have to say about Marden?" Lullaby asked. "Did he ever tell her?"

"He liked Marden all right, I guess," Tucson said. "Nothing to the contrary was said."

"Picks and shovels," Lullaby mused, half aloud. "Sounds like digging."

Tucson said, "According to what I heard, Marden wanted a garden plot laid out."

Stony swore. "Four Mexicans to work one month digging a

garden plot. Marden must have been figuring to go into the vegetable business. Sounds like a lot of squirrel fodder to me."

Lullaby scowled. "Y'know, I heard one time about a mine down in South America where they kept the miners captive so the outside world would never learn how rich the mine was."

"Maybe there is something in that prospecting talk of Riley Comstock's," Stony said.

"If those Mexicans are kept captive to mine ore," Tucson said, "what becomes of the ore?"

"Sent to Denver of San Francisco, and Francisco of Denver," Stony said promptly.

"In packages the size of two books, I suppose." Tucson smiled skeptically.

"All right, say it isn't ore," Stony said doggedly. "Maybe Marden and Comstock have opened up a diamond pit in the mountains. Even industrial diamonds could run into money——"

"Or it could be turquoise or rubies, or some other jewel stones," Lullaby agreed.

Tucson shrugged his shoulders. "Damned if I know what to think."

"Could diamonds, maybe, be smuggled someplace in rubber balls?" Stony wondered.

"Don't be so dumb," Lullaby said. "Nobody'd want to smuggle diamonds out of this country. It's coming in they'd be smuggled."

"How do you know?" Stony snapped.

"Well, I don't know——"

"Why try to talk about it, then?" Stony demanded. "And you call me dumb! If there's anything inside a rubber ball, it could be your brain, giving you such a stretch of imagination. Get it, Lullaby? Rubber—stretch!"

"Ver-r-ry funny." Lullaby sneered. "Like all your puns, that one doesn't have any bounce."

"It snapped you right where it hurt, though." Stony snickered.

And so they wrangled while the ponies plodded on, with Tucson deep in thought. The sun was dropping below the peaks of the mountains now, and reflecting redly on the undersides of clouds drifting lazily across the sky. After a time Tucson called a halt in a small hollow surrounded by brush. Saddle girths were loosened when the men dismounted, then bits of dry wood and brush were gathered—the sort that would make a minimum of smoke when a fire was lighted. The three men sat about the glowing embers, warming the rolled *tortillas* on slender sticks or knife points. Draughts of lukewarm water from their canteens and cigarettes completed the meal.

By this time it had grown dark. An occasional star showed through the drifting clouds. A faint line of light spread slowly along the horizon, but it would be some time yet before the moon rose. There was a chill touch to the breeze ruffling the tips of the brush and the men huddled closer to the fire and from time to time tossed additional fuel on the low flames. The wind grew stronger after an hour. Stony asked suddenly, "How much longer we going to stay here, Tucson? And if you're ready to talk, I'd like to know why we stopped when we did."

The fire glowed red on Tucson's smiling features. "I wondered how long it would take to get your curiosity aroused. Look here, if there's a ghost that makes nightly rides, I aim to see it. We all know that ghosts do not exist. At the same time there's *something* in these parts that people have seen. Right?"

"Right," Stony said. Lullaby agreed.

"We know of no one except Marden and Comstock living in these parts," Tucson continued, "so there's a chance they may be behind this ghost stunt that's being pulled. I plan for us to hide out in the vicinity of Marden's place, lay low and see if there's anything to be seen. If that's agreeable to you hombres, we'll get mounted again."

The wind died after a time, but the clouds it had carried across the sky remained. Now and then the moon, still not high, peered through the drifting masses, but for the most part the range was submerged in gloom. "Just our luck," Tucson said testily. "If there's a ghost to be seen, I wanted plenty of moonlight to see it by."

The horses were again moving through the foothills. Off to their left the peaks of the Apparitions made a faint silhouette against the sable sky beyond. "Maybe the ghost will show up better against the dark," Stony offered.

"It's not that so much that bothers me," Tucson admitted. "I was planning to hide out somewhere in the vicinity of Marden's place, but now it's so dark I can only guess at the location, against those black mountain sides. I should have memorized a landmark this morning when we visited him."

"Cripes!" Lullaby offered in Tucson's defense. "Things always look different at night, anyhow. This morning you didn't know anything about Marden's mailing off those monthly packages, and you hadn't talked to those Mex women, to arouse our suspicions. Between the three of us we should manage to get somewhere near Marden's place."

"I didn't want to be 'somewhere near,'" Tucson said. "I wanted to be damn close. Now we don't dare try to get too close for fear of stumbling on Marden's place too soon and being heard. So we'll have to stay well away."

The horses pushed on for another three quarters of an hour, then Tucson called for a halt as they were dropping down a long hilly decline. The men dismounted and dropped reins over the ponies' heads. "I figure," Tucson said, "we should be fairly opposite Marden's place, about now. Let's see if there's anything to be seen."

They left the ponies behind and made their way on foot up a long slope covered with brush. At the top they dropped to their stomachs and peered across the undulating hills toward the mountains. The precipitous peaks could be seen as before, rising against the darkened sky, but down below there was nothing but dense gloom. The moon was casting very little light. Tucson said, "You hombres see anything that looks like lights in a house?"

Neither Lullaby nor Stony could answer in the affirmative.

Tucson went on, "I still think we're not more than three or four hundred yards from Marden's place. Well, let's wait here awhile and see if anything happens."

Cigarettes were rolled and the flame shielded from view while they were lighted. The men smoked in silence. Somewhere in the far reaches of the mountains a coyote's mournful howling took on a spectral quality. The wind moaned eerily among the mountain crags, died away, rose again to mingle with the echoing yip-yipping of coyotes.

Stony stirred uneasily. "You know, there is something sort of spooky about this setup."

Lullaby laughed. "Is that your teeth I hear chattering?"

"Cripes!" Stony protested. "That's a chilly wind. I'm getting cold sprawled out here. And my teeth weren't chattering, as you damn well know——"

"T'hell they wasn't," Lullaby scoffed. "Sounded to me like your jaws were performing a clog dance."

Involuntarily, the men had been keeping their voices low. "All's I started to say," Stony began aggrievedly, "is that I don't wonder some folks believe in ghosts. Take a setup like this, and if a feller was alone, he wouldn't want to linger around if he knew those mountains were haunted—even if he didn't believe in ghosts. And how do we know they don't exist? Some pretty big men claim to have seen ghosts. I've heard some right plausible stories, too, with a lot of proof behind 'em——"

"Shut it!" Tucson whispered suddenly. "I think I saw something."

The other two fell silent, straining their eyes toward the lower slopes of the mountains. Then something like a gasp left Stony's lips and his voice wasn't quite steady. "By God, there is something moving off there—looks sort of white—and with a kind of glowing to it, like it was on fire, or fire was showing through——"

"But not red and yellow like a fire," Lullaby cut in. "Sort of pale greenish white."

Tucson spoke again and talk died away. At first there was just a vague shapeless mass moving against the darkness. Then, gradually, it took on form, and the three men saw the horse's head and running forequarters. Next, the spectral figure on its back came into view, and then the rest of the horse. It was moving fast across their line of vision, though there wasn't a sound to be heard. No pounding of galloping hoofs reached their ears. It was this last that gave an unearthly quality to the proceeding.

The apparition was too far off for the men to distinguish features, but they could make out the form of a girl in a long flowing dress and the loose hair flying about the girl's head as she bent forward over the horse's neck as though urging it to a faster gait.

Then, slowly, the uncanny vision faded from view. Finally, only the horse's rear quarters were to be seen and its flowing tail, then those dissolved into darkness and the black night was as impenetrable as before. There remained now only the eerie soughing of the wind through the mountain draws and the continual echoed howling of coyotes. And then these sounds too faded to sudden silence.

Tucson drew a long breath. He said, "Well, there you are. We've seen it too."

"What's the next move, pard?" Lullaby asked.

"Let's stay here a spell and see if it appears again," Tucson said. "I'd like to have another look. When it first showed up, I think we were all too surprised to do anything but let our jaws drop. Say what you like, a man doesn't see something like that without getting a sort of shock, and that kind of throws his thinking out of whack for a few moments."

"Dammit!" Stony exclaimed, puzzled. "That horse wasn't making the slightest sound. It was just as though that ghost was sort of floating over the ground."

"There's got to be an explanation for that too," Tucson said calmly. "Anyway, now that we know where the ghost appeared, we can head over that way and get a closer look later on. Right now, we wait and see if it appears again."

Five minutes, then ten minutes passed and drifted into a quarter of an hour. "One performance nightly, I reckon——" Lullaby commenced, then suddenly stopped.

"There it is again," Stony interrupted.

The three men lay there on their stomachs, peering through a screen of brush, once more seeing the weird specter gradually take form and move across their astonished line of vision. There appeared to be no change in the apparition; it was the same as before—the noiseless galloping hoofs, the flying mane and tail of the ghost horse, the flowing skirt of the girl, her long hair floating in the wind behind her as she rode.

There was even something uncanny in the dead silence. The coyotes had ceased their howling, and for the minute not a breath of air was stirring. All the world seemed hushed during that eerie ride. . . .

Stony swore suddenly, reached for his six-shooter. Orange fire and powder smoke erupted from the muzzle of his gun. The echoes of the shot went crashing against the peaks and canyon walls.

Tucson said, "Darn you, Stony, now you've——"

"Look at that ghost ride!" Lullaby interrupted. "Spurring like all the devils of hell, instead of Apaches, were on its trail!"

It was true. The "ghost" was frantically kicking the horse in the ribs, urging it to greater efforts, and bent lower still over the animal's outstretched neck. And this time there was no slow dissolving of the ghostly horse and rider; moving swiftly, it seemed to disappear with an almost unseemly speed.

But an instant later, to the listeners' ears came the faint clattering of shod hoofs on rock and baked earth, and then these sounds too faded away.

Tucson said, "Well," and again, "Well!"

"I'm sorry, pards," Stony said contritely. "I shouldn't have fired that shot." He was plugging out the empty shell and inserting a new load in his cylinder. Then he replaced the gun in holster.

"Anyway," Lullaby said, "that target was sort of far off for accurate shooting with a six-shooter."

"Wasn't trying to hit it," Stony said. "After all, I wouldn't want to hurt a girl. Just wanted to throw a scare into her. If I'd only used my head a minute, I wouldn't have done even that. But I was so danged mad at myself. Y'know, the first time I saw that blasted ghost I was almost convinced it was real—or rather that it wasn't real. And then I got to thinking what a damn fool I was, believing in ghosts, so next time it come past I just jerked and fired without thinking. Tucson, I reckon I've spoiled something."

Tucson laughed. "Forget it. I just sort of had an idea we might get that ghost's course fixed in our mind, and then tomorrow night hide out there and capture it. But it's sure a slick piece of work to fool folks. I wonder how they do it?"

"Do you reckon it would do any good to go back for our broncs and get on that ghost's trail?" Lullaby suggested.

Tucson shook his head. "The ghost has too much start on us now, and could probably be hid out in one of those draws or ravines in the mountains. Unless we had a heap of luck, we never would find it. But it might be a good idea to pay a visit to Marden and see how we find him."

They hurried back down the slope and got into saddles, then started toward the mountains. The moon broke through drifting clouds and shed more light now. Lullaby said, "Who do you reckon that girl is, Tucson?"

"You got me," Tucson replied.

Stony speculated, "Could one of those Mex women be mixed up in this—you know, one of the wives of the missing Mexes?"

Tucson shrugged. "Could be—but I doubt it. I just don't know what to think."

They pushed the ponies a little harder now, but slowed down as they neared Marden's house. There were no lights showing from the building. As the ponies passed over the broad wash of deep sand that ran past the house, they sank to fetlocks and the men drew their mounts to a walk. Stony said, "I figure it was just about here that ghost was traveling. You note, pard, that our horses move plumb quiet in this deep sand." He held his voice low while he talked.

Tucson said, "I was just thinking of that. Maybe that explains the ghost moving so silent."

They left the sand and reached firmer ground. There was still no sign of life about the house. As they dismounted, Lullaby said, "I seem to remember that Marden said this morning that they always went to bed late."

"Maybe this night is an exception," Tucson said as he knocked on the door. There was no answer to the knock. Tucson tried again without success. He raised his voice. "Hey, Marden, wake up!"

Still no reply. Stony said, "Maybe he went off prospecting with Riley Comstock."

"I doubt that," Tucson said and again knocked. Then he tried the door. It was unlocked. The knob turned easily under his hand and he pushed open the door. All was dark within. He called again, "Marden, are you there?"

A lighted match a few moments later showed that Marden was there—at least all that was left of Gridley Marden. The man was lying face down on the floor, only partially dressed. His nightshirt had been tucked into his trousers and his feet were bare. From his back protruded the bone handle of a heavy butcher knife, and blood was slowly congealing as it dripped to the floor.

14. WARNING?

At the coroner's inquest, held two days later, nothing of import was brought out to show who had been responsible for the death of Gridley Marden. The Mesquiteers testified to finding the body when they had halted that night "to get water for their horses." They hadn't mentioned seeing the ghost. In their opinion Marden had been stabbed to death shortly before their arrival. No, Riley Comstock hadn't been there and Riley's white horse was missing from the corral. No one else had been found in the vicinity, and they had headed straight for Morral City to inform the sheriff of their discovery.

Ducky Gebhardt testified he had sent men with a wagon when daylight came, and had himself accompanied them. The wagon drivers testified, with Ducky, that Riley Comstock had put in an appearance as they were leaving with the body, and was extremely shocked at the death of his friend. He had accompanied the wagon back to town.

When it came his turn to speak, Comstock told how he had left the afternoon of the day—or night, rather—upon which Marden was killed, to go prospecting in the mountains, and had only returned when Marden's corpse was being removed. He testified that the butcher knife, the murder weapon, had been around the house a long time. No, he didn't remember when it had been purchased. Comstock swore that he and Marden were good friends and had never had any differences. He had liked working for Marden. Of Marden's life before they met he knew nothing. Occasionally, while giving evidence, Comstock gulped and dabbed at his eyes with a soiled bandanna, and Dr. Graham didn't keep the oldster on the stand any longer than was necessary.

Laure Hampton had been called to tell what she knew of Marden. There was little Laure could tell beyond relating how Marden had arrived in this country a few years before, stating he was a semi-invalid and desired to rent the old house which stood on Bar-BH holdings. Her father had let Marden have the house.

No, Marden and the Bar-BH had never had any trouble of any sort. Nor did Laure know anything of his former life or who his friends were, if he had any aside from Riley Comstock. So far as she knew, he had no enemies.

When the evidence was all in, and the testimony of a few other witnesses had been heard, the coroner's jury had nothing definite to go on so far as concerned clues to the murderer. Gridley Marden, it appeared, was a near recluse about whom no one knew a great deal, nor was anyone found who could state where the man had originally come from. The upshot of the inquest was that the jury rendered a verdict to the effect that Gridley Marden had met his death as the result of a knife wound, the murder weapon having been held in the hand of some person unknown, and Sheriff Duckworth Gebhardt was directed to take all steps necessary to effect the apprehension of the murderer.

At the close of the inquest, Lullaby and Stony left Tucson to go to the Goldfinch Bar for a drink, while Tucson turned his steps in the direction of Morley & Wade's general store to buy a box of cartridges for his six-shooter. As he stepped from the store he almost collided with Jeff Daulton, who was hurrying along the plank sidewalk. Tucson said, "Where you heading in such a rush, Jeff?"

Daulton jerked one thumb in the direction of Wilkins Livery Stable, which stood across the street on the opposite corner. "Oh, hello, Tucson—I wanted to see you. I was just heading for the livery to get my horse and Laure's. I'm going to ride back to the Bar-BH with her."

"Oh, so it's Laure already, is it?" Tucson said dryly. "Only three nights ago I heard you calling her Miss Hampton."

Jeff colored. "Maybe you'll remember she asked us to call her by her first name?"

Tucson nodded. "Comes easy too, doesn't it?"

"Sure does." Jeff's color deepened. He laughed a trifle sheepishly. "Laure's a dang nice girl and I'm aiming to see as much of her as possible."

"Like that, eh?"

"Just like that, Tucson. Once I get a few things settled——" He broke off, his smile widening. "In case you're interested, I was out to the Bar-BH visiting two nights ago—the night you found Marden's body."

"That so?" Tucson looked thoughtful. "I remember now you weren't in your room at the hotel when we arrived. I happened to wake up a spell later and heard you going in your room."

"It was late when I left the Bar-BH. You see, Laure wasn't there when I arrived. She hadn't been expecting me. You remember that morning I rode to town with her, when she came in to buy some dress goods or something. When she left town, she headed out to the Rocking-T to visit with Webb Talbert's wife. She stayed there for supper and then headed home. I was just about to pull out when she rode in. Then she insisted that I stay a spell and have some coffee and a piece of cake she'd baked, and—well, time just slipped by."

Tucson chuckled. "Too bad there wasn't a full moon that night. You'd really have had an excuse for staying late." Jeff laughed and said he didn't need an excuse. Tucson went on, "I can believe that." He grinned. "It looks to me as though you're getting pretty deeply involved. You'd best be careful."

"Cripes! Who wants to be careful?" Jeff laughed happily, then suddenly sobered. "Oh yes, I nearly forgot I wanted to see you." Tucson asked the reason. Jeff continued, "When you and your pards were testifying at the inquest, I noticed you just answered questions. None of you three furnished anything extra——"

"Meaning what?" Tucson asked.

"Meaning," Jeff replied, "that I don't think you told everything that happened that night. I sort of had a feeling you were holding out. Did you learn anything I should know?"

"Maybe." Tucson glanced along the street. A few men passed here and there along the sidewalks. The early afternoon sun was making deep shadows between buildings. Men lounged on porches. Wagons and ponies waited at hitch racks along the thoroughfare, the horses switching their tails at the flies. There was no one in the immediate vicinity of the two men, though. Tucson said, "We saw the ghost that night. But keep that information under your hat——"

"T'hell you did!" Jeff looked startled. "What did it look like?"

Tucson told briefly what had happened that day and night. A brief smile flitted across Jeff's face when Tucson spoke of Stony's shooting at the galloping ghost, but was quickly erased. "I'll be damned!" he said seriously. "Well, that sort of proves the ghost is human. And you say it was a girl?" His frown deepened.

"Looked that way." Tucson nodded. "You see, we were some distance away and couldn't see features, but we could see the long skirt and the hair flying out behind."

Jeff was silent for a moment. "And you really couldn't find any sign of Marden's killer near the house?" he asked next.

"We didn't figure it was worth while looking too long. Of course, we did cast around outside to see if there were any prints or important sign, but we found nothing, and that murderer might have been hid anyplace around that canyon. It was quite dark too and we didn't want to act as sitting ducks for lead slugs."

"And no sign of Riley Comstock?"

"Have you forgotten he was away prospecting? One horse was missing from the corral. Only those two chestnuts were there. The white was missing——"

"I haven't forgotten he said he was away prospecting," Jeff cut in, "but he could have perjured himself."

"Do you figure he did?"

Jeff swore. "Damned if I know what to believe."

"I'll tell you one thing," Tucson continued. "When we went in that night there was only one man there—Marden. And he wasn't what you'd call a man by that time. But there were two hats hanging on pegs. One I figured as Marden's. The other was battered and dirty. It must have been Comstock's. But Comstock was away prospecting."

Jeff's eyes narrowed. "It could be Comstock owns two hats." Tucson agreed, and Jeff went on, "Did you notice anything else?"

Tucson scowled. "Yes and no. But from the time we were there in the morning, until we returned, some change had taken place in that house—there was a difference in the appearance, somehow, but I'm blasted if I can say what it was. Things just looked different. There's some sort of idea nudging at my brain, but I can't seem to dovetail it."

"Maybe you'll figure it out later."

"That's possible." Tucson considered a moment. "Jeff, I don't want to appear too inquisitive, but I don't think you've ever mentioned the address of that uncle you spoke of."

Daulton's features tightened to a blank mask. "What about it?"

"Could his address be in Washington?"

For nearly a minute the two men stared steadily at one another. Finally Jeff said quietly, "I think you've made a good stab at it, Tucson. So what if it is?"

"Here's a couple more addresses that might interest you. Harry Denver of San Francisco, and Pablo Francisco, of Denver."

Jeff frowned. "You joshing me? It sounds sort of crazy."

"I'm not joshing you, Jeff." Tucson added the post-office-box numbers of the two names. "Does it mean anything to you?"

Jeff shook his head. "Not yet it doesn't. Tell me some more."

Tucson related what they had learned in Coyotero Tanks. "Every month, regular, Gridley Marden used to send packages to those addresses—packages about the size of two books wrapped up. Now does it mean anything to you?"

Jeff's face had lighted up. "By the Almighty!" he exclaimed. "I think my uncle is going to be interested in those addresses. I've got to send a telegram." He swung away, then turned back. "Tucson, do me a favor. Get my pony and Laure's from the livery and bring them down to the hotel. Tell Laure—she's waiting for me there—that I've been detained a few minutes, but that I'll be right along." Tucson nodded and Daulton hurried off.

Tucson was getting the horses at the livery stable when he noticed a saddle leaning against one end of a stall, and asked the attendant, "Whose saddle is that?"

"Trax Whitlock's," the livery man replied. "Left his horse here for a feed and a rubdown when he come in for the inquest today. Hasn't come back for it yet."

"What's Whitlock riding these days?" Tucson asked casually.

"That pinto hawss in the stall there."

Tucson nodded carelessly, took the reins of Jeff's and Laure's ponies, and, mounting Jeff's horse, started off in the direction of the Morral City Hotel. Arriving there, he left the ponies at the hitch rack and started up the steps leading to the hotel porch, where a number of chairs were ranged along the porch railing. Tucson was about to enter the lobby when he heard his name called, and, turning, he saw Laure Hampton talking to Stowell Whitlock at the far end of the porch.

The banker looked nervous, and was mopping perspiration from his lined features. He acknowledged Tucson's greeting, then sank limply into one of the chairs at the railing. Tucson looked at Laure, saying, "Jeff asked me to bring your horses up here. He's delayed, but will be along within a few minutes." Again he glanced at the banker. "Is anything wrong?"

The girl looked a trifle pale, but now color was returning to her face. "Not wrong, exactly—not now. Though there might've been." Tucson asked for information and Laure explained, "Lee Cantrell just left before you got here——"

"What about Cantrell?" Tucson asked quickly.

"I was waiting here for Jeff," the girl went on. "Mr. Whitlock had just come out of the hotel and we were standing here talking. Cantrell was crossing the street from across the way, heading in this direction. As he stepped to the sidewalk out there he stubbed his toe and went sprawling." A smile curved the girl's lips. "It was really very funny the way he went down. I know I laughed, as did several people passing along the street. Mr. Whitlock started to laugh and couldn't stop——"

"If I'd had any sense"—Whitlock smiled wryly—"I'd have stuffed my handkerchief into my mouth. I might have known that Cantrell wouldn't take to ridicule."

"Cantrell snarled something," the girl went on. "I didn't get the words, but everybody stopped laughing except Mr. Whitlock. The next thing I knew Cantrell was up here on the porch with his gun out, threatening to shoot Mr. Whitlock if he didn't keep still. His face was like a maniac's. He was furious!"

"I thought my end had come," Whitlock said, nodding.

Laure continued, "I asked Cantrell if he couldn't take a joke, and that seemed to cool him down some, though for a moment I thought he'd turn his rage on me. He just looked at me for a minute, with that hard flat look of his—you know how he is, like a snake getting ready to strike—then he relaxed. He even removed his sombrero and made a sort of mocking bow, saying something about not wanting to make trouble in a lady's presence——"

"He also added," Whitlock cut in, "that I owed Laure a lot, because her being here had saved my life."

"He stumbled again going down the steps from the porch," Laure said. "He didn't fall again, though—and nobody laughed again."

"Well, all's well that ends well." Tucson smiled. "Was Cantrell drunk?"

Both Laure and Stow Whitlock answered in the negative.

Whitlock added, "Cantrell doesn't have to be drunk to act that way. It's just his nature to be ornery." The banker was recovering his self-possession again. "I've heard he's that way on my brother's ranch. He refuses to mix with the hands, and they've learned to leave him alone. Nobody but Trax would hire a man of that breed. If we only had a law-enforcement officer worth his salt, he'd do something about Cantrell." He added darkly, "And my brother as well."

Jeff Daulton put in an appearance and they told him what had happened. Jeff looked serious. "If I were you, Mr. Whitlock," he said, "I'd carry a gun."

Stow Whitlock shook his head. "I don't think it would be very fitting for Morral City's banker to go around toting a six-shooter. Even supposing I did, what good would it do me? I'm not much of a hand with firearms, and if I carried a dozen guns I'd still have no chance against a man like Lee Cantrell."

"I reckon you're right at that," Daulton agreed. He turned to the girl. "We can get started for the Bar-BH now if you're ready, Laure. Sorry I had to hold things up."

The girl said that didn't matter, and they descended the porch steps and got into saddles. Tucson stood talking to Stow Whitlock for a time. The banker said, "You seem to be running true to form, Mr. Smith."

"How's that?"

"I've heard you have a reputation for stepping into stormy situations—you and your pards—wherever you go. Morral City doesn't seem to be any exception. First Folsom was killed and then this man, Gridley Marden."

"And Ben Hampton and the disappearance of four Mexicans before that," Tucson said.

"Do you think all the deaths and the disappearance of the Mexicans are related in any way?" Whitlock said.

Tucson shrugged. "Frankly, I don't know what to think, Mr. Whitlock."

Whitlock smiled. "You don't believe, then, that the ghost had anything to do with Marden's death?"

"That's ridiculous." Tucson laughed. "Do you?"

"Certainly not," the banker said promptly, "but there are a lot of people around town who do. There's plenty of talk along those lines. I don't suppose you saw anything that resembled a ghost the night you found Marden's body."

Tucson grinned. "There was certainly no ghost in the house to be seen that night."

They conversed a few minutes longer, then Tucson left to seek his pardners. He went first to the Goldfinch Saloon. Just as he was about to enter he spied Trax Whitlock and four of his punchers approaching along the sidewalk. The punchers, Bert Yost, Gus Wolf, Luke Steed, and Hump Pelton, were a hard-bitten lot, rangy men with unshaven muscular jaws.

Trax Whitlock nodded and started to pass, then paused when Tucson said, "Did you get the horse back too, Whitlock?"

Whitlock frowned. "What horse you talking about, Smith?"

"Your horse that Art Branch stole. Or maybe I'm not covering enough territory. Maybe you—or the sheriff—caught Branch too."

The lines on Whitlock's face deepened. The other punchers gathered around, staring hard-faced at Tucson. "Certainly Branch ain't been caught," Whitlock growled. "It's all that fool sheriff can do to catch his breath. But where did you get an idea I got my horse?"

"Noticed your saddle down at Wilkins Livery a spell back," Tucson explained.

"Hell! That's a pinto I'm riding——" Whitlock commenced.

"I'm not talking about horses now," Tucson cut in. "Just noticed you had the same saddle you had the day we found Folsom's body. Thought maybe you got the horse back too."

"What in hell gives you the idea that's the same saddle?" Whitlock scowled. "That's a different——"

"Oh, isn't that the same saddle?" Tucson asked innocently. "I just noticed a scratch on one stirrup fender that was there the day I first saw you."

Whitlock didn't speak for a moment. Then he gave a short laugh. "Dam'd if you ain't got sharp eyes, Smith. But you're mistaken. I know the scratch you mean. That's on all my saddles—I own three, you know."

"No, I didn't know. Must be I'm mistaken." Tucson smiled thinly.

"You sure are, Smith. Yeah, I always manage to scratch up my fenders that way. Reckon I rasp my rowels across 'em when I'm mounting."

"Could be, could be," Tucson said carelessly. "There's never any telling what position a feller will sling his foot when he piles on." He nodded and started to pass.

Whitlock caught his arm. "Look here, Smith, did you think I had my horse and saddle back? Were you hinting that I knew Art Branch's whereabouts?"

Tucson glanced at the hand grasping his arm. After a moment Whitlock released his grip. Tucson said, "No—I wasn't *hinting.*"

"By God, Smith! I don't like the way you say that."

Tucson said coldly, "I don't give a damn whether you like it or not. You got anything more to say?"

Whitlock glared at him a moment, then relaxed. "Oh hell," he snarled. "I've no more time to argue with you." He turned to his men. "C'mon, fellers, there's a drink waiting for us at the Brown Bottle."

The men started on. One of them, Luke Steed, paused to sneer at Tucson. "I got a hunch I know a hombre what's flirtin' with a chunk of forty-five lead," he said in nasty tones.

Tucson swung back to face Steed. "That so?" he said easily. "I don't see your cards."

"Cards?" Steed's jaw dropped. "What cards you talkin' about?"

Tucson laughed. "Weren't you telling your own fortune?"

He didn't wait for Steed to reply, but again turned and entered the Goldfinch.

The interior of the saloon was cool and dim after the glare of the street. There was but one customer, standing at the far end of the bar. When his eyes became accustomed to the light, Tucson recognized Lee Cantrell standing in moody silence over a glass of whisky. Pat Finch rose from a seat at the opposite end of the counter. "H'are you, Tucson?"

"How's it going, Pat? You seen Stony and Lullaby?"

"They dragged out of here about a half hour since. What you drinking?"

Tucson said, "Beer," and moved on down the bar. "Hello, Cantrell."

Cantrell lifted his head, stared in Tucson's direction a moment, then grunted something that might have been a greeting or an invitation to go to hell. Tucson moved up closer and Pat brought a bottle of beer down the bar. Tucson said to Cantrell, "I just ran across your boss and some of his jackals on the way to the Brown Bottle. I'm surprised you're not doing your drinking there."

Cantrell's flat, obsidian-like eyes rested on Tucson a moment. "There's a hell of a lot that might surprise you, if you knew it," he snapped. "In the first place, Trax Whitlock ain't my boss, even if I do draw wages from him. In the second place, I don't like to drink with them damn cow nurses. Now you satisfied?"

"Oh, cripes." Tucson laughed. "I was satisfied before. Just making conversation."

Cantrell didn't reply. He downed his drink and asked for another. Pat Finch served it, gave Tucson another bottle of beer, then retired to the other end of the bar. Cantrell downed the whisky and started to roll a cigarette, spilling a good deal of tobacco on the floor in the process. When it was finished, Tucson struck a match and held the light for Cantrell. The man swayed a trifle as he drew on the tobacco, and one hand grasped the bar for support.

Again he turned his hard opaque eyes on Tucson. "I didn't ask for that light," he said belligerently, and before Tucson had a chance to reply called to Pat to bring the bottle and leave it on the bar. Pat complied, casting a worried look at Tucson as he did so.

Tucson said, "How about letting me buy that drink for you, Cantrell?"

Cantrell shook his head. "Not a chance." He spilled some bills out on the bar.

Tucson asked, "Any particular reason?"

"I never drink on a man I'm intending to kill," Cantrell said, cold-voiced.

"Well, that's a fair warning, anyway," Tucson said quietly. "Just when is this going to happen, Cantrell?" He wasn't unduly alarmed; Cantrell's hand was nowhere near his gun.

"A hell of a lot sooner than you'll like," Cantrell stated. "I——" He broke off, cursing. "Why in hell should I stand here talking to you?" he rasped. Swinging away from the bar, he started toward the doorway.

Pat Finch called to him, "Hey, Lee, you got some change coming."

Cantrell paused at the entrance. "Keep it to buy flowers for Smith." He hesitated a moment longer. "Oh, yeah, Smith, there's something else. Was I you, I wouldn't go nowhere near the sheriff's office today."

"Why not?"

"I'm just telling you, that's all. Take my advice."

And without another word the man turned and rocked through the swinging doors to the street.

"Now what in the devil," Finch exclaimed, "do you figure he's talking about?"

"You got me." Tucson looked puzzled. "If Cantrell hadn't already declared himself an enemy, I'd say that sounded like a warning of some sort. But why should *he* warn me?"

15. POWDERSMOKE!

Ten minutes after Cantrell had departed, Stony and Lullaby entered the Goldfinch Bar. "Danged if we haven't been looking all over for you, pard," Stony said.

"That's why you didn't find me." Tucson smiled.

"What do you mean?" Lullaby asked.

"I haven't been all over," Tucson explained. "Just been here, at the hotel and—oh yes—at the livery."

The pair joined Tucson at the bar. "We passed Cantrell down the street a spell," Stony said. "He looked ornery mean."

Tucson said, "He was in here a few minutes ago. I offered to buy him a drink but he said he never drank with anybody he was intending to kill—words to that effect."

"T'hell he did!" Stony exclaimed.

Lullaby said seriously, "You're due to have trouble with that hombre yet, pard."

"If it comes, it comes," Tucson said quietly. "Maybe he's all talk——"

"You know better than that," Lullaby snapped. "Killer Cantrell's rep wasn't made on talk."

"I don't know as I ever saw so much poison wrapped in an undersized frame," Stony said. "Reminds me of a sidewinder—undersize, but plumb vicious. Mean all the time, like a rattler too."

Pat Finch put in, "I reckon he's having another of his bad days. I understand he's plagued with some terrific headaches, on and off."

"Likely due to that scar across his forehead," Tucson commented, "or what lies behind it. Maybe some pressure there, affecting Cantrell's brain."

"Could be," Pat Finch agreed. "Trax Whitlock was telling me, one time, how Cantrell come by that scar. Happened in a corral with a killer horse. The horse used its hoofs plenty. Trax didn't know all the details, but for once, I guess, Cantrell met his match.

They had to take him to the hospital. Didn't expect him to live, but he pulled through. Probably been a good thing had the horse finished him——"

"When was this?" Tucson asked.

Pat Finch shrugged and scratched his red head. "You got me. Back about ten years ago, I think. Cantrell was just a kid——"

"Sure," Tucson said, "that's it."

"What's it?" Lullaby asked.

"I remember now," Tucson said slowly, "reading a piece in a newspaper about that. Sure, Cantrell—Lee Cantrell was the name. They shot the horse later—too dangerous to keep. Might be that old injury that makes him so mean. Probably he drinks a lot to kill the pain."

"I can't say I ever saw him downright drunk, though," Pat Finch said. "He just sort of keeps his skin soaked in whisky all the time. I reckon he's built up one of these here immunities to alcohol."

Lullaby asked, "Stony, don't you wish you could do that?"

"Do what?" Stony queried cautiously.

"Build up a community to alcohol."

"Pat didn't say community," Stony pointed out. "It was an amenity to alcohol, he was talking about——"

"You mean equanimity," Lullaby cut in.

"No," Stony said, "what you've got in mind is unanimity."

"Wait a minute, wait a minute," Finch said earnestly. "You're both wrong. I was talking about a commodity—alcohol—and an immunity to same."

Stony and Lullaby swung around and stared at the barkeeper, their eyes narrowing in thought.

"An immunity to a commodity," Stony repeated slowly, as though striving to understand. "An immunity—to—a commodity." He brightened. "But wouldn't that bring about an impecuniosity?"

"Pat probably means," Lullaby said, "a conformity to inebrity."

Stony shook his head. "I don't think so. He wouldn't sanction a compatibility to impropriety."

"Perhaps you're right," Lullaby agreed gravely. "That would denote a complicity in importunity, wouldn't it?"

The barkeep stared at the two in growing bewilderment. His jaw sagged and he passed one hand wearily over his face. Finally he found his voice. "Look," he said hoarsely, almost pleadingly, "all I'm talking about is a commodity—something I can sell at a fair profit—wares, goods, alcohol."

"Alcohol always wears good with me," Stony said promptly. "What are you arguing about, Pat?"

"What am *I* arguing about!" The barkeep's voice was shrill with indignation. Noticing the smiles on the men's faces, he slumped suddenly, then turned away, shaking his head. "All right, I've been took in," he conceded glumly, and placed fresh bottles of beer on the bar. "The drinks are on me. Tucson, are these two pards of yours always this crazy?"

Tucson chuckled. "It comes natural to 'em, I reckon—though I guess part of it can be blamed on that Encyclopaedia Britannica we keep back home on the ranch——"

"Encyc—Encyc——" Finch broke off, something appealing in his tones. "Now don't you start using them off-trail words too."

A small Mexican boy pushed hesitatingly through the swinging doors at the entrance and lifted his voice to ask for Señor Tucson Smith. Tucson said, "Here I am, son. What do you want?"

"Ees *nota* for you," the boy said, "send by the señor sheriff." He handed a folded sheet of paper to Tucson.

Tucson tossed the boy a quarter, then unfolded the sheet while the boy was returning to the street. Lullaby said, "What's up, pard?"

Tucson glanced through the note, then passed it over for Lullaby's and Stony's perusal. The note read:

Mister Tucson Smith—Dear Sir—If you can come to my office as soon as possible I have something important to see you about.

Yrs. truly,
Duckworth Gebhardt
Sheriff of Carbonero County

Lullaby glanced up. "What do you suppose that windbag wants?"

Tucson shrugged. "I've nothing better to do so I guess I'll drift down to his office and see."

"Want us to go along?" Stony asked.

Tucson shook his head. "I don't figure Ducky Gebhardt has anything important to offer. You two stay here. I'll be back before long. *Adiós, compañeros!*"

Tucson pushed his way through the batwing doors and stepped out to the sidewalk, then started west at an easy gait, staying on the shady side of the street. At the corner of Las Cruces Street, he crossed diagonally to the opposite side and continued his progress. He was halfway to the next corner, where Kearney Street met Main, on the southwest corner of which stood the sheriff's office, when he paused suddenly, remembering the warning Lee Cantrell had given him in the Goldfinch Bar. What was it Cantrell had said? Oh yes . . . *Was I you, I wouldn't go nowhere near the sheriff's office today.* Tucson frowned. Now what in the devil had Cantrell meant by that?

"It could be," Tucson muttered, slowing his steps, "that Cantrell knows of some scheme Trax Whitlock cooked up. But I still don't know why Cantrell should warn me. Maybe it will pay to go slow, though."

He glanced around and found that he was standing in front of the Morral City Post Office. The sun beat down on the wooden awning stretching above the post-office doorway. A few people passed both ways along the sidewalk. Tucson glanced up toward the corner of Kearney and Main, but could see no one near the sheriff's office at the moment. Just the same, it might pay to approach with caution. In his mind Tucson considered the layout of the sheriff's building: in the front was the office, and from the office a doorway led into the block of twelve cells, with a corridor, or passageway, running between them. Tucson pondered. It seemed likely there would be a door at the rear of the jail building.

"I'd like to bet," Tucson speculated, "that with those cells hardly ever holding anybody, and in view of Ducky Gebhardt's slovenly, careless ways, that door would be left unlocked. It's worth trying, anyway."

Adjoining the post office, in front of which Tucson was standing, stood a hay and feed store. A narrow passageway ran between the two buildings. Tucson turned and made his way through this passageway, emerging at the rear of the structures ranging along Main, behind each of which stood a trash pile. Seventy-five feet away stretched the twin tracks of the T.N. & A.S. Railroad. Beyond the rails it was all open country, except for a scattering of adobe huts that were almost submerged in the sea of mesquite and greasewood. At the moment there was no one in sight. Tucson hesitated but a moment longer, then started walking toward the jail building.

A moment later he had crossed the end of Kearney Street and found himself standing near the bars of a corral, constructed at the back of the jail. At the present moment, in addition to the sheriff's mount, a second horse stood within the enclosure. Tucson scrutinized the animal. It looked as though it had been ridden hard, though not recently. Its hide was streaked with dried sweat and dust. The animal had not had the care a good mount deserved. Tucson studied the horse. He frowned. "I wouldn't say for sure, but that sure looks like the bronc Art Branch ran off—Trax Whitlock's pony. Now I wonder if Branch has returned."

He didn't hesitate longer, but quickly slipped through the bars of the corral and approached the rear door of the jail, which was closed and situated at a corner of the building. Tucson tried the doorknob. It turned easily under his hand. Opening the door a slim crack, he stood listening. Voices came to him from somewhere in the front of the building, but he couldn't distinguish the words. Moving noiselessly, he opened the door, slipped within, and closed it again. Now he stood listening in a half gloom, waiting for his vision to adjust itself to the change of light.

He found himself standing in a narrow corridor at one end of a cell block. Across the way, on the opposite side of the building, was the other cell block. A passageway led between them to the front of the jail and thence to the sheriff's office. Moving with extreme caution, Tucson peered around the corner of the nearest cell and glanced along the passageway. From this vantage point he could see straight through to Main Street, though his view was partly obstructed by two silhouetted figures, one crouched near the open doorway that led from the jail into the sheriff's office, and the other blocking the front entrance from the street.

Tucson waited, then he heard the man nearest him growl, "For geez' sakes, Ducky, is he comin', or ain't he?"

Ducky Gebhardt turned half back from his doorway. "I tell you, I saw him startin' down this way——"

"Dammit! That was ten minutes ago. What's he doin', crawlin' on his hands and knees?" The voice sounded familiar, but Tucson couldn't place it for a minute.

Then the sheriff spoke again. "It looked to me like he stepped into the post office. Probably stopped to write a letter on his way. Don't be so impatient, Art. He swallowed our bait."

Art? It must be Art Branch. A feeling of exultation ran through Tucson. If he could capture Art Branch, make him talk, a number of mysteries might be cleared up. *If* he could capture him. Damn it, Tucson told himself, I've simply got to take that hombre alive.

Branch was talking again, snarling something unintelligible at Gebhardt. Tucson stepped into the passageway, where he could get a better view. Though the man's back was to him, Tucson could recognize Branch now—the man's slovenly make-up, the torn hat brim, hanging lower in front than in the rear, the loosely dangling six-shooter holster. Branch had already drawn his gun, and held it in readiness.

Tucson spoke quietly from his end of the passageway. "Weren't waiting for me, were you, Branch?"

Branch cursed and whirled around. "Who's back there?" he demanded. He'd been peering toward the sun-bright street for so long that for a moment or so he couldn't make out Tucson's features.

Then, Ducky Gebhardt's tones, "D-D-Did somebody come in that rear door, Art?"

Tucson still hadn't drawn his gun. *I've got to take him alive,* he kept telling himself. He raised his voice. "You'd better drop that hawg-leg, Branch. It's me—Smith."

He could see Branch stiffen, then came a pregnant moment of silence before Branch said, "Christ Almighty!"

Tucson sensed the movement even before it came, and swung sidewise, flattening himself against one of the cell doors. Flame and smoke exploded from Branch's gun, and a leaden slug flattened itself against the rear end of the building. Tucson had drawn and fired at almost the same moment, aiming low, but he was moving too fast for accurate shooting. He judged the bullet had passed between Branch's legs, and he raised his gun for a second try, then lowered the weapon. Branch had already vanished around the edge of the doorjamb and was out of sight in the sheriff's office. Tucson sprang forward to overtake him.

In the office there were the sounds of a brief struggle, and pleading gasps from the fat sheriff. The next instant, Gebhardt was flung bodily into the passageway, to go sprawling at Tucson's feet. Tucson tried to spring over him, but the sheriff caught him by the legs, pleading frantically, "Don't kill me, Smith. Don't kill me——"

"Dammit, let go!" Tucson raged, trying to shake off the sheriff's grasping hands. He had a brief glimpse of Branch pausing in the doorway, again raising his gun. Tucson dropped suddenly on the squirming figure of the sheriff and heard a bullet whine over his head. Again he fired, but the sheriff was gripping his arm, jerking it off range.

And then Branch had disappeared into the street. Tucson swore, jerked his gun arm loose and snapped the heavy barrel against Gebhardt's head. The sheriff moaned and relaxed. Tucson shook him off and, gaining his feet, leaped across the sheriff's unconscious form.

Excited yells were heard along Main Street and the sound of running feet, though in an instant the thoroughfare was cleared as though by magic. By this time Tucson had gained the porch of the office, his eyes seeking Branch. It took but an instant to spot the man. Branch was sprinting diagonally across the road, headed, probably, for the Brown Bottle Bar and such security as Trax Whitlock might give him.

"Better halt, Branch, or I'm letting you have it!" Tucson called after the fleeing man.

Branch stopped momentarily, swung around and released another shot, which buried itself in the porch roof. Then he pounded on.

Muttering exasperatedly something that had to do with "damn stubborn jackasses," Tucson grimly raised his gun and triggered a single shot. He saw dust spurt from the back of the running man's vest, and then Branch, spun halfway around by the terrific impact of the forty-five bullet, went sprawling headlong to the dust of the road, where he lay without movement.

Methodically, Tucson plugged out his empty shells, reloaded, and shoved his gun back into holster before stepping grim-faced out to the center of the roadway. Men poured from doorways and from between buildings. Powder smoke drifted lazily along the street, then lifted and dissolved in the faint breeze blowing along the thoroughfare. There was considerable yelling and excited conversation. A crowd had already formed about the stricken Branch.

Tucson pushed through the cluster of men and knelt by Branch's side. After a moment he turned the unconscious man on his back and felt his pulse. All the blood was drained from Branch's face and his eyes were closed. Tucson raised his head and looked around. "Any of you men got a flask of liquor handy?" he asked.

A dozen hands thrust bottles toward him. The corners of Tucson's lips twitched. "Looks like this town believes in toting plenty of reinforcements," he commented. Accepting one of the flasks, he drew the cork and held the mouth of the bottle to Branch's lips. The man swallowed a few drops of the liquor, moaned, and twisted away. Tucson removed the bottle and waited for Branch's eyes to open.

At that moment he heard Trax Whitlock's cold voice at his rear: "Smith, lift your arms in the air and make it fast! You dirty bustard! One thing we don't stand for in this town is shooting men in the back. Now I aim to square Art's account!"

16. A HIDDEN GUNMAN

Tucson slowly got to his feet and turned around, though he didn't lift his arms in the air. Trax Whitlock stood facing him, six-shooter gripped in one fist. "God damn it!" Whitlock rasped. "Get those arms up."

"Don't talk like a fool, Whitlock," Tucson snapped. "And if I shot Branch in the back, he had it coming. He laid a plot to ambush me. Take a look at his gun there in the road. It's been fired three times——"

"To hell with that palaver," Whitlock snarled. "Get those hands high before I bore you." Tucson gave a sigh of resignation and lifted his arms in the air. It seemed the wisest thing to do, in view of the murderous light gleaming in Whitlock's eyes. Whitlock went on, "You acted smart, Smith, though I'd just as soon you'd put up a fight."

"If I acted smart," Tucson said quietly, "that's more than you can say for yourself. Branch is wanted for murder. Have you forgotten that?"

"It makes no difference," Whitlock raged. "You got no business taking the law in your own hands. And there's no actual proof that Art killed Folsom. I was aiming to see that he got a fair trial, if he could be found. Now you've murdered him——"

Tucson's sarcastic laugh interrupted the words. "Every time you open your mouth, Whitlock, your ears grow a little longer. Branch isn't hurt bad. I aimed high on purpose. He just took one of my slugs in his right shoulder. Murder! Cripes A'mighty. He just fainted from shock. I was bringing him around when you cut in with your fool actions."

The crowd stood around, gaping open-mouthed at Tucson and Whitlock. No one, apparently, had the courage to intervene between the two, even though Whitlock's finger was already quivering on the trigger. And then quite suddenly Tucson smiled, but before Whitlock could even guess at the reason, he heard Lullaby Joslin's voice at his back:

"Take my advice and drop that hawg-leg, you lousy son of a buzzard, if you don't want a chunk of forty-five lead ripping through your gizzard!"

The words, though spoken in Lullaby's lazy, indolent tones, carried a definite threat. Whitlock's mouth dropped open. His face went a shade paler. Abruptly, he released the grip on his gun and let it fall to earth. Tucson nodded, smiling thinly. "Whitlock, you're commencing to show a glimmer of sense." And then to Lullaby, "Thanks, pard. I figured you might be due to arrive. If you'll just keep an eye on Whitlock, I'll get back to Branch."

"Damn it!" Whitlock's voice shook with anger. "You can't ride roughshod over us this way, Smith. I'll get Sheriff Gebhardt and we'll have some law enforcement here."

"Go ahead," Tucson said quietly. "Get him if you can. Last I saw of Ducky, he was sprawled in his office—unconscious. And he's going to have something to answer for too. Do me a favor, Whitlock, and drag him out here——"

And that was as far as Tucson got before he was interrupted by Luke Steed's vicious tones. "Drop that six-shooter, Joslin! You and Smith are both covered now."

Tucson glanced beyond Whitlock and saw that the four Hatchet punchers—Luke Steed, Bert Yost, Hump Pelton, and Gus Wolf—had closed in behind Lullaby. All held guns in their hands, guns that covered either Lullaby or Tucson. Tucson had already lowered his arms; now he raised them in the air again. Instead of dropping his gun, Lullaby quickly shoved it into holster.

Whitlock scooped up his own weapon, and rose, grinning nastily. "Good work, boys. I reckon I was smart to have you stay on the rim of this crowd until things were settled. I thought Smith's pards might be someplace in the vicinity——" He paused, struck by a sudden thought and glanced anxiously around. "Hey! There's a third hombre—named Brooke. Have you seen him——"

And at that moment Stony's voice entered the conversation: "Whitlock, if you're plumb eager to see me, just look this way."

Again the tables were turned. The crowd parted and there, standing behind the four Hatchet punchers, was Stony Brooke, grinning wickedly, six-shooter in hand. The muzzle of the gun was moving in a slow arc that effectually covered the men before him. Gasps of amazement ran through the crowd. A man exclaimed:

"Dam'd if that ain't teamwork!"

"Smart as hell!" from a second. "Brooke just waited until them Hatchet hands was concentrated behind Joslin——"

And from another bystander: "Smith and his pards sure move united-like."

Lullaby laughed softly and drew his gun again. Looks of dismay had crossed the faces of the Hatchet men as they glanced over shoulders and saw Stony's moving gun barrel bearing on them.

"Now, you sneaking sons-of-witches," Stony challenged them, "just start something! I'm not telling you to drop your guns. I'm asking—no, I'm practically begging—you to grip 'em hard and start pumping lead—if you've the guts to try it! Go ahead, take a chance! You can't die more'n once. Maybe I'll get some *real* excitement out of this town yet. Come on, you cheap, flea-bitten excuses for gunmen! Show some guts and start firing!"

None of the Hatchet men answered him. They shuffled about nervously, then one by one they reholstered their six-shooters. Stony said disappointedly, "Hasn't even one of you got a mite of fighting spirit? You licked already? Come on, show some life!"

And from the opposite side of the crowd came Lee Cantrell's scornful laughter. Cantrell hadn't drawn his gun. He was taking no part in the dispute. "Them cow nurses can't show any life, Brooke," he said contemptuously. "A man has to have some sense to show life—even a little—and those hombres just ain't got any sense. If I told 'em once, I told 'em a dozen times not to get smart and try to outfox Smith and his pards. But would they listen to me? No! They knew it all. They were too smart to listen to me. And now it looks like they got their rear ends in a sling——"

"Damn you, Lee——" Whitlock began, his face convulsed with rage.

"Now don't you start picking a ruckus with me, Trax," Cantrell advised mockingly. "You already got your hands full. You'd best commence squaring yourself with Smith before you take on a bigger fight. That's the trouble with you and your cow nurses. You spend so much time talking about what you're going to do that the other feller does it first, while you're still talking. And you lack the guts to back up your talk."

Cantrell was still laughing when he turned and walked away.

Stony was saying scornfully, "There's not an ounce of fight in the whole bunch. Look here, Whitlock, what do you say you and I decide this, man to man and gun to gun? Surely, *you've* got some nerve left?"

Whitlock didn't reply. Perspiration was beading his forehead. "Look here, Smith," he said nervously, "maybe there's been a bad mistake made——"

"And you made it," Lullaby drawled.

"I'm hoping he'll make another," Stony said hopefully. "Come on, Whitlock! Let's us two finish this."

Whitlock swallowed hard. He said to Tucson, "Like I was saying, Smith, a mistake was made. I shouldn't have gone off half cocked, the way I did. We can talk this over, if you'll just get Brooke to quiet down. He sounds just plain murderous."

"Maybe he is," Tucson said dryly. "Stony has to have a pint of raw blood for breakfast every day or he gets mighty mean. And the hotel was plumb out of blood this morning, Whitlock. Could be Stony wants yours. Don't appeal to me to settle things. You started this. Now it's up to you to finish it—if you can."

"Whitlock," Lullaby put in, "either you and your outfit put your irons to work, or get out of here. We're sick of the sight of you."

"And make it *pronto!*"—from Stony.

Whitlock swore, turned away and started to push through the crowd, followed by his downcast punchers. "We'll settle this some other time," Whitlock called back over his shoulder.

Tucson didn't bother to make a reply. He spoke to his pardners, "Keep an eye on those hombres and see that they don't return. I'll look to Branch."

He turned back to the wounded man on the earth. Branch was moaning, but his eyes were still closed, his face white. Tucson requested someone in the crowd to fetch Dr. Graham. He borrowed the flask of whisky again and poured a few drops down the unconscious man's throat. Branch's eyelids fluttered a trifle, and he drew a long, shuddering breath. His features twisted with pain.

Tucson raised his head and looked at the crowd gathered around. "How about you hombres moving back so Branch can get some air?" he requested. The circle around him and Branch widened instantly. Tucson said, "Much obliged." He took

Branch's hat, rolled it up and made a sort of pillow for the man's head. Again he placed the bottle to Branch's lips.

This time Branch took a healthy drink. After a moment his eyes opened. For a few seconds he gazed vacantly about, then a look of fear came into his white features as he recognized Tucson. "Am—am I going to—to die?" he asked faintly.

Tucson bowed his head. His voice was grave. "We all have to die some time, Branch. All a fellow can do when his time comes is to meet it like a man, and go out with a clear conscience. There's a few things you'll want to confess, I reckon, Branch."

"I—I guess so," Branch said weakly. A shiver ran through his body.

Tucson gave him another drink. "Look here, Branch," he said, "you might as well tell what you know. First, it was you killed Joe Folsom, wasn't it?"

Branch hesitated. His eyes searched Tucson's face, then he turned his head slightly to one side. "It was me killed Folsom," he admitted in a whisper. "I never meant to kill him, but—but—well, it was him or—well everything would have been spoiled."

"What do you mean?" Tucson asked. "You mean some sort of plan would have been wrecked if Folsom had lived?"

"That's it." Again Branch closed his eyes.

Tucson persisted. "What plan, Branch? Tell me what that metal drum and those rubber balls are used for."

"It was me took them from the sheriff's office," Branch confessed confusedly. "I took that packet of bills too——"

"What was that metal drum used for?" Tucson asked again.

"We had to have it. Everything was held up until we——"

"Why? Who's back of this? What's your game?"

Branch didn't reply. He had already spoken his last word, and his eyes went wide and staring as life faded from them. Tucson had heard the impact of the bullet even before the sound of the gun reached his ears. He saw blood welling from the ugly hole on Branch's head, high above the left temple.

The crowd scattered wildly. Tucson was on his feet, drawn gun in hand, glancing quickly about. There were no other guns in sight except those held by Lullaby and Stony. They, too, were trying to determine the source of the shot, alert for the first sign of the hidden gunman. Excited cries carried along the street. Tucson growled, "Oh, damn! Another minute and I'd have learned things. Branch thought he was dying. He'd have told everything. Who in hell fired that shot?"

"Whoever it was," Lullaby said grimly, "you're lucky he didn't get you. Branch is finished, I suppose."

"Deader'n a plugged rattler," Tucson said disgustedly.

All three men were searching the street, trying to locate the direction from which the shot had been fired. Tucson studied the wound in the dead man's head, endeavoring to gauge the angle along which the leaden missile of death had traveled. Previous to the firing of the shot, he and Branch had been completely surrounded by the crowd. That meant the shot had come from above their heads. Tucson raised his eyes. A couple of doors away, adjoining the Brown Bottle Bar, stood the Cowmen's Rest Hotel, also owned by Whitlock. The nearest window, on the second floor, of the hotel, stood open, and just beyond it a faint wisp of powder smoke drifted in the slowly moving air.

Tucson jerked out, "Come on, pards!" and started at a run toward the Cowmen's Rest Hotel. He heard Stony behind him saying:

"Whitlock owns that flea nest."

And from Lullaby, "And it adjoins his Brown Bottle too."

The clerk of the hotel was standing in the doorway of the shabby, paint-blistered building when Tucson and his pardners arrived. The clerk said in surly tones, "Where you think you bustards are headed for?" He made no move to step aside.

Tucson didn't bother to answer. Placing his hand against the clerk's face, he shoved hard, then stepped on through as the clerk went hurtling halfway across the lobby to end up against his rough board desk. There came a splintering sound of pine boards as clerk and desk collapsed in a heap on the floor. Three other men standing in the lobby made no attempt to interfere as Tucson, followed by Stony and Lullaby, raced for the stairway that stretched before them.

Reaching the second floor, they found themselves in a long hall with closed doors on either side, except for one door that stood open at the southeast corner of the building. The three men rushed into the room. It showed no sign of recent occupancy, though a faint smell of burned gunpowder lingered in the air.

"This is it, all right," Tucson growled. He looked around. There was a bed, made up; a bureau, a straight-back wooden chair. A mirror hung above the bureau. He went to the window that was raised halfway to the top and looked out. Down in the street he could see the crowd again clustered about Art Branch's dead body.

Tucson's pardners crowded close, also looking down into the street. Lullaby nodded. "This is where the shot came from, all right. You're sure lucky that bustard hit Branch instead of you, Tucson."

"He must've been a lousy shot," Stony put in.

"I figure he was a good shot," Tucson said grimly. "It was Branch he was after. Whoever fired the shot was afraid Branch would tell things. He took the quickest way of closing Branch's mouth. He couldn't get all three of us, and if he had got me there was still you two to talk to. Hang the luck! And I wanted Branch alive."

"Maybe," Stony said hopefully, "we could bust down some of these hotel doors and catch the coyote who fired the shot."

Tucson shook his head. "The fact he fired only one shot and left this door open behind him shows he got away in a hurry. He's got too much start on us, and if we did locate him in one of these rooms we'd have a hard time proving anything."

All was quiet on the lower floor of the hotel. "Anyway," Lullaby chuckled, "we threw enough of a scare into somebody so they didn't get curious as to what we're doing up here."

Stony asked what the sheriff had wanted to see Tucson about. Tucson told them what had happened. "I was so anxious to take Branch alive that I held my fire—held it almost too long. Branch was waiting to kill me when I came in, I figure——" He broke off. "How come you fellers got on the job so soon? I knew you'd come when you heard the shots, but——"

"Shortly after you left the Goldfinch," Stony explained, "Pat remembered Cantrell had given you some sort of warning about staying away from the sheriff's office today. What was that all about, and why should *Cantrell* warn *you?*"

Tucson shook his head. "It's all a mystery to me. Come on, there's nothing more we can do here. Let's go down to the end of the hall. There's probably a back stairway where Branch's killer made his getaway. We'll see where it leads, anyway."

They walked rapidly down the hall, with its closed doors on either side. At the end was a turn in the corridor and they saw a flight of uncarpeted steps leading to a closed door at the bottom. With Tucson in the lead, they descended the stairway. Tucson reached the closed door, turned the knob—and found himself entering the Brown Bottle barroom.

Stony said, "I'll be damned! A connecting door between the two buildings."

Tucson glanced quickly about the interior of the saloon. Trax Whitlock lounged at the bar. With him were Steed, Yost, Pelton, and Wolf. A doorway at the rear of the barroom opened on an alley. By this time Whitlock had regained his composure.

"Welcome to the Brown Bottle, gentlemen," he said mockingly. "After our little differences of a short time ago I never expected to see you in here. What will you have to drink? Kosky"—to the bartender—"see what the gentlemen will have."

"You know damn well we'll not be drinking with you, Whitlock," Tucson said coldly. "I want to see your guns. Lullaby—Stony! Keep an eye on these hombres."

Whitlock made no resistance. His men stood in a sullen silence. Tucson jerked Whitlock's six-shooter from its holster and sniffed the muzzle, then, somewhat disappointedly, replaced the weapon. He did the same with the guns of the Hatchet punchers and with the same results. "All right," he said, "you can relax. I don't figure any of you has fired his gun and then cleaned it since Branch was shot."

"Ah yes." Whitlock smiled. "I understand poor Art took one in the head. That's sad. But it will save the county taxpayers the expense of a trial."

"I want to know what you can tell me about the shooting that finished Branch, Whitlock. The shot came from your hotel."

"Is that so?" Whitlock's features assumed a look of surprise, and he tugged thoughtfully at the ends of his mustaches. "That's serious! My hotel will be getting a bad name."

"Don't try to act funny, Whitlock," Tucson snapped. "Branch's murderer fired the shot from the hotel's second floor. He could have escaped down those back stairs and out through the rear doorway here."

"You don't say," Whitlock said calmly. "I should think you'd get on his trail. Oh yes, I forgot, you haven't any authority to take anybody's trail, have you, Smith? And that being the case, I resent like the devil your highhanded actions in coming here and subjecting our guns to an examination. I ought to kick you out."

"Don't try it," Tucson said grimly. "Authority or no, I'm trying to find out a few things around here, and you'd better co-operate or I'm going to know the reason why. That shot was fired from the room on the southeast corner, Whitlock. Who generally occupies it?"

"I do, when I stay in town," Whitlock replied, sneering. "And you haven't a ghost of a chance tying that shooting on me. I don't know who was in there, or how he got in. Probably the door was left unlocked——"

"Who has the other rooms?" Tucson interrupted.

"None of the second floor rooms is occupied at present," Whitlock said. "Matter of fact, this is a dull season. Three of the lower-floor rooms are taken, but you don't know the occupants. You can get the names from my clerk if you want 'em. Offhand I don't remember them myself. And by the way, my clerk tells me you knocked him down and smashed his desk. More roughshod methods, Smith. If you aim to run this town, you'd better get some legal authority for your actions. Because if you don't, by God! I'm going to take steps to have you and your pards arrested. I'm sick of this business and of you three. Now get out of my saloon and stay out until you can show a legal right to be here."

Tucson smiled at his pardners. Stony looked about ready to take the Brown Bottle Bar apart, but he held his temper in check. Lullaby said softly, "It's up to you, pard. Say the word."

"I reckon we'd better be law-abiding," Tucson chuckled. "We'll get out." He turned back to Whitlock. "But don't let that make you overconfident, Whitlock. So help me, I'm aiming to have your skin—and that before many more days pass."

He was still smiling, at Whitlock now, but there was no smile in his eyes. Swinging around, and followed by Stony and Lullaby, he pushed through the swinging doors to the street.

Outside, there was still a crowd around Branch's body, and among the crowd stood Dr. Graham and Stow Whitlock.

Graham said quietly, "Looks as though I got here too late, Tucson."

Tucson nodded. "I'm commencing to think I'm not so early as I thought I was, either."

17. DEPUTIES THREE

Branch's body had been removed to the undertaker's and Tucson and his pardners stood talking, at the edge of the sidewalk, to Dr. Graham and Banker Stowell Whitlock. ". . . so that's the story," Tucson concluded. "We don't know who fired the shot that killed Branch. Also, I actually had no legal right to inspect the guns of those hombres in the Brown Bottle. There's not much can be done until you get an efficient law officer in here. I'm sure Gebhardt was in on the plan to ambush me, but I've no doubt he'll deny it. You haven't seen him, have you?"

Graham shook his head and drew a long sigh. "And now there'll be another inquest to hold, and my coroner's jury will be able to do no more than has been done previously. It's a hell of a situation we have here. Anyway, Folsom's murder is cleared up—to some extent. We haven't any idea why Branch killed him, of course."

Tucson asked, "How do I stand regarding Branch?"

Graham laughed shortly. "Your bullet entered his shoulder. You gave him plenty of chance, and fired only in self-defense. Gebhardt won't be fool enough to try and arrest you. Anyway, I don't think he will."

"Surely," Stow Whitlock put in, "the sheriff wouldn't be that stupid. I'll admit he hasn't much sense, but——"

"You never know." Graham frowned. "Ducky can be awfully dumb at times." He changed the subject: "Look here, Tucson, Stow and I were discussing something that might interest you, just before you and your pards came out of the Brown Bottle." Tucson asked for information. Graham went on, "I suggested to Stow, and he agrees with me, that we need more law authority here. To be brief, Tucson, would you be willing to accept a position as Gebhardt's deputy? You could be installed as town marshal, but a wider field of activity needs to be covered. As deputy of Carbonero County——"

"You should know better than to ask me to work under Gebhardt, Doc." Tucson smiled.

"And I couldn't blame you for refusing, Mr. Smith," the banker put in quickly. "Dr. Graham had an idea you might be able to help us for a short time, but I didn't think you'd want to stay here any longer than necessary. And the county couldn't pay much, of course." He sighed. "I guess there's nothing to it but to put up with Gebhardt until election time, then we can get a good man ——"

"Wait a minute," Tucson cut in thoughtfully, "maybe we can work something out. Trax Whitlock was——"

"Damn Trax!" the banker snapped. "If I don't settle with that brother of mine some day——"

Tucson interrupted, smiling. "Maybe I can settle with him for you, Mr. Whitlock. What I started to say, Trax Whitlock was throwing it into me, when we were in the Brown Bottle, because I was acting without legal authority—which was true. Maybe it would be a good idea for me to have some authority. So far as concerns taking orders from the sheriff is concerned, I think I might be able to persuade him not to issue any orders that didn't make sense——"

"You mean," Stow Whitlock said dubiously, "that you'd really consider serving as a deputy of Carbonero County? Why, that would mean a great financial sacrifice, not to mention your time ——"

"Good God, Stow!" Dr. Graham was beaming. "You're acting as if you didn't like the idea. I'd say Morral City was lucky if it could get Tucson."

"Of course. I agree with you," the banker said. "Only I'm so greatly surprised that Mr. Smith would consent to serve."

"I'll serve on one condition," Tucson said, "and that is that you arrange to have Lullaby and Stony sworn in as deputies too. I have a hunch they may need some authority as well as I."

Stow Whitlock looked at Stony and Lullaby. "And do you agree with Mr. Smith?" Both replied that they did. "In that case," the banker continued, "there's nothing more for me to say, except that I'm dumfounded—and very pleased." He shook hands with Tucson and his pardners. "Now, maybe we'll see Trax get his come-uppance!"

"Let's get across to the sheriff's office right now," Dr. Graham proposed. "He's sure to object, of course, but I think I can handle him. Come on, Tucson, let's get this business settled before you and your pards change your minds."

Stow Whitlock said, "I'll not go along with you. The sheriff and I never did get along very well, and perhaps things will move smoother without my presence. I'll leave it to you, Doctor. Just make sure that everything is done legally." The doctor said he'd take care of it. Whitlock nodded to the others, said good-by and good luck, and headed off in the direction of his bank.

The doctor looked after him, smiling. "I'll bet Stow can hardly wait to spread the news among the decent people of this town that we're going to have some law and order around here at last. Come on, let's go see Gebhardt."

They crossed the street to the sheriff's office and found that overweight individual slumped in a chair at his desk, bathing a red welt on the side of his head with cold water.

"I'm surprised to see you active so soon, Ducky," Tucson said dryly. "Maybe I should have hit you harder. I suppose you know Art Branch is dead and there's another mystery to be cleared up."

Gebhardt nodded. "Some fellers come and told me. I been trying to get up strength to go out and 'vestigate. I wanted to see you too, Mr. Smith. I never dreamed that Art would make trouble when I sent you that note."

"And what did you expect him to do?" Tucson said coldly.

"He come to me and said he wanted to explain things to you. Asked me to send that note——" The sheriff paused and mopped his face. "I never dreamed he intended trouble."

"In that case," Tucson asked, "why were you standing in your doorway keeping him posted on my movements? And why didn't you arrest him when he first showed up?"

"I—I thought we could talk it over with you first," the sheriff said weakly. "And then when you came and the shooting started, and he shoved me in front of you—— Good Gawd, Mr. Smith, I hope you don't think *I* was plotting your death."

"Yeah, I do," Tucson said flatly. "The way it looks to me, Ducky, Branch thought he could regain his prestige by rubbing me out, and he got you to help. He probably came to town during the night and you kept him here in the jail. His horse—or Trax Whitlock's horse—is out back in your corral. We'd just better forget the whole matter, Ducky. Just don't try to lie to me any more. You will, of course, but when I catch you in a lie I aim to skin you alive. Is that clear?" He smiled suddenly. "What a way to be talking to my new boss."

"Boss?" Gebhardt looked puzzled. "What do you mean?"

"It's this way, Ducky," Dr. Graham said, "you've never had a deputy here in Morral City——"

"Didn't need one," the sheriff interrupted. "I'm saving the taxpayers money by not——"

"It's been decided you need some help in your job," Graham continued. "Mr. Smith, Mr. Joslin, and Mr. Brooke have consented to act as deputies. You will please swear them in at once."

Gebhardt's jaw dropped, his eyes widened. For a minute he couldn't speak. "No—oh no," he said faintly. "I—I—I couldn't do it. Trax wouldn't"—he fumbled—"a lot of people might not like it. I couldn't——"

"To hell with Trax and anybody else who objects," Graham snapped. "I've talked things over with Stow Whitlock and if necessary I'll go to the city council for further permission if you act stubborn. And if that isn't enough, I'll telegraph the governor that the situation here demands more law officers."

"Let me do the telegraming to the governor," Tucson put in. "I know exactly the sort of message that will get quick action——"

"Oh Gawd no," Gebhardt moaned.

"What's your objection, Ducky?" Graham demanded.

"Th-Th-Think of all that extra money to be paid out for deputies," Gebhardt quavered. "I couldn't condone that——"

"We'll be acting without pay," Tucson interrupted, "and we'll only hold office as deputies until we've cleared up some skulduggery in these parts."

Gebhardt gathered a few remnants of fleeting courage. "I refuse," he stated. "I won't do it. I'll resign first."

"No you won't," Tucson said sternly. "I want you right here on the job where I can watch you. You try running out, and the governor will get a message that will have every law officer in this country after you. Don't forget, Gebhardt, that you're guilty—guilty as hell—of conspiring in attempted murder with Art Branch, but I'm willing to let that pass if you'll show some co-operation."

The sheriff drew a long sigh. "All right," he whined at last, "I aim to co-operate, but you got me all wrong, Mr. Smith——"

"Hell! I could get you any other way but *wrong,*" Tucson

snapped. "And furthermore, when we're sworn in as your deputies, I want it distinctly understood that we're to have a free hand, and we don't have to follow your orders."

"That don't seem scarcely legal," Gebhardt protested in a quaking voice.

"It isn't," Tucson agreed coldly, "but since when have you acted legally in this office? Now make up your mind, Gebhardt. Either swear us in, or take the consequences."

"Better swear Tucson and his pards in, Ducky," Dr. Graham urged. "You won't get anyplace by refusing."

The sheriff rose from his chair. "All right, Doc, I'll do as you say," he quavered. He turned to Tucson and his pardners. "Hold up your right hands and take the oath of office." He called them each by name, then, "I, Duckworth Gebhardt, duly and legally elected sheriff of Carbonero County, do hereby appoint you to act as deputies in my jurisdiction of said county. Do you solemnly swear, promise, and state that you will uphold the law to the best of your ability and—and——" His words stumbled, but he finally concluded the administration of the oath, ending, with some help from Tucson, ". . . of said county, to have full authority to act in any way you see fit in enforcing the law." He looked uncertainly at the other men. "Is that all right?"

"It'll do, I reckon," Tucson smiled. "But you sure garbled up the wording of that oath some. I doubt you'd got through it if I hadn't helped."

"Maybe you're right," Gebhardt said unhappily. "I ain't swore in nobody for a long spell."

"And now you'd better give your deputies their badges, Ducky," Dr. Graham prompted.

The sheriff looked dubious. "Gosh A'mighty, I don't reckon I got three badges——"

"Nonsense!" Graham interrupted. "I happen to know there must be badges around here someplace. I remember one time when a posse was sworn in. There was a badge for every man."

"I'll look and see." Panting and fumbling, the fat sheriff began to go through his desk. In a bottom drawer a cardboard box was found with some tarnished deputies' badges. Gebhardt placed three of the badges on the desk and closed his drawer. "There you are." A trace of belligerence crept into his tones. "Much good may they do you."

"We'll pick those badges up later," Tucson said, "after you've polished 'em up for us, Ducky."

"Me polish 'em up?" the sheriff said indignantly.

"Yes, *you,*" Tucson replied crisply. "You should do something to earn your pay. Of course, if you refuse——"

"I'll polish 'em—I'll polish 'em," Gebhardt said hurriedly. "I just didn't understand what you meant at first."

"Well, you know now," Tucson said. "And from now on we'll take care of the law and order. All you'll have to do, Ducky, is sit here and do the desk work and feed the prisoners we bring in."

Graham said, "Well, I've some calls to make. I'll spread the word around town, Tucson, that Morral City has three new deputies, and they'll have the backing of the better element in this county." He nodded and hurried out of the doorway.

Five minutes later Tucson and his pardners were also strolling along the sidewalk. Tucson and Lullaby were grinning. Lullaby said, "You sure got that fathead scared, Tucson."

"I thought I'd choke," Stony snickered, "when you told him he should get busy and mop the jail. To hear you talk, you'd think you were the sheriff, instead of Gebhardt. Do you think he'll do it?"

"I'll lay you ten dollars against a plugged peso he does." Tucson smiled.

"You know," Lullaby suggested, "I think if you'd put a mite more pressure on Gebhardt, he'd tell what he knows about things."

Tucson nodded. "Yeah, I don't doubt it. At the same time, I don't figure he knows much. I just think he's a tool of Whitlock's—but isn't sure exactly what is going on. Oh, if necessary, we could settle his hash right now, but he's a weak link in the Whitlock chain, and I want to keep him there. Once a showdown comes, he'll tell what he knows without much urging."

Stony glanced back toward the sheriff's office. "There's Ducky now, waddling over to the Brown Bottle. I'll bet he's heading to tell Whitlock the bad news."

"And he'll probably catch some more hell," Tucson said.

"I just thought of something," Lullaby said suddenly. "Tucson, you mentioned hash a moment ago. I'm hungry. And look, we can eat at county expense now that we're deputies."

"God help the taxpayers on a day like this," Stony said piously.

18. CHALLENGE

A week passed with nothing untoward taking place. The three new deputies made their rounds of the town, but found little to do. As Stony remarked, there didn't seem to be even any drunken cowhands or citizens to discourage. Everything continued very peaceful. Ducky Gebhardt appeared completely subdued, and sat in his office most of the time, a hangdog look in his eyes. Trax Whitlock and his punchers seemed to be avoiding the town; even Lee Cantrell, the lone wolf of the outfit, hadn't put in an appearance. The Hatchet cook had driven in once for supplies, but had no comments to make regarding activities at the Hatchet Ranch. It was noticed, however, that he picked up a plentiful supply of liquor at the Brown Bottle, which seemed to indicate that Trax Whitlock and his men had no intention of coming to Morral City for a while.

Tucson had made a couple of night rides to Gridley Marden's house in the Apparition foothills, once with Stony and the second time with Lullaby, in the hope of again seeing the galloping ghost, but the ghost had, apparently, become discouraged and given up its nocturnal riding. Nor was anyone to be found at the house when they entered. Riley Comstock had either left for good, or was away prospecting.

Tucson and his pardners were seated at breakfast in the hotel dining room, one morning, polishing off platters of ham and eggs. "Jeepers! Time's beginning to drag," Tucson commented. "This town is just too dang peaceful. I've been hoping that Trax Whitlock would do something to tip his hand, but he must have gone gun shy. Well, I'm trying to start something. I sent a rider with a message to the Hatchet——"

He broke off as Jeff Daulton entered the dining room, crossed the floor, and dropped into a vacant chair at Tucson's side. He refused to order food, saying he'd already breakfasted. Tucson said, "Anything special on your mind, Jeff?"

"I can answer that." Stony grinned. "Sure there's something special on his mind. It—she, rather—lives at the Bar-BH."

"Yeah," Lullaby put in, "I should think that girl Laure would get tired of seeing your mug, Jeff. You've been out there every day, or evening, for the past week."

Daulton blushed. "Maybe Laure does get tired of seeing me, but she hasn't said so yet. After all, I have been making regular rides, anyway—in the course of duty, of course—and if I drop in at the Bar-BH, it's only natural."

"Huh!" Stony grunted. "What duty?"

"Maybe we'll go into that one of these days," Daulton replied. He turned to Tucson. "I was just down to the railroad depot and got a telegram from my uncle."

"That so?" Tucson said quietly. "What's Uncle got to offer?"

"He was mighty interested in Denver of San Francisco, and Francisco, of Denver," Daulton said. "So he made their acquaintance. They admit to receiving book-sized packages from Grid Marden, and claim they contained small samples of silver ore. Both Francisco and Denver say they are interested in mine promotion. However, my uncle isn't convinced of their integrity and has offered them a couple of small apartments to stay in until he can check a little further."

"Very interesting," Tucson said quietly. "It's too bad, Jeff, that we don't know exactly what your uncle sent you out here for. Perhaps we'd know what to look for."

"My uncle," Daulton said gravely, "is a very secretive man, and he doesn't like me to talk too much. However, I've a hunch that before long I'll be able to take you hombres into his confidence."

"Whenever you say, Jeff." Tucson nodded and dropped the subject. "I was just telling Stony and Lullaby, when you showed up, that I'd sent a rider with a message to the Hatchet—to Lee Cantrell, in particular. I'm trying to get a little action started around here."

"What was the message, Tucson?" Lullaby asked.

"I sent word to Cantrell that I wanted to see him—*muy pronto,*" Tucson replied. "And I wrote that if he didn't show up in town *muy pronto* I'll know he lacks nerve. If I've read Cantrell right, that should fetch him damn fast."

Stony drained his coffee cup, set it down, and whistled softly.

"Jeepers! You're really taking the bull by the horns, aren't you?"

"Exactly," Tucson stated. "We can't stay here forever. I've a hunch whoever is promoting the skulduggery around here has decided to stall for a while until we get tired of waiting and pull out. This way, I may be able to bring something into the open—let certain people know that we're still after them and that we intend to keep the pressure on."

Daulton looked thoughtful. "If Cantrell comes in, I figure the Hatchet outfit will be with him. They'll be curious."

"That's possible." Tucson nodded.

"Damn you, Tucson," Daulton said genially, "I wanted to ride out and visit Laure today. Now I reckon I'll stick around."

Lullaby said mockingly, "Why, Jeff, you wouldn't figure the Hatchet gang might start trouble of some sort, would you?"

"Hell, no." Daulton laughed. "But once before when I was away I came back to find you three wearing deputy badges. This time I aim to stick around. You might get promoted to sheriffing, and I'd like to get in on one of these easy-money political jobs."

Tucson's messenger arrived back in town about one o'clock in the afternoon. He had delivered the word to Cantrell, but Cantrell had refused to state whether or not he would come to town. He had merely told the messenger to tell Tucson to "Go to hell!" and the messenger had deemed it wise not to stay for further conversation.

Lullaby said, "You may have to go after him, Tucson."

"I can do that too," Tucson replied quietly, "but we'll wait awhile and see. Cantrell probably wants a chance to think things over and try to figure out what I've got in mind."

They hadn't long to wait: it was about three in the afternoon when Trax Whitlock, accompanied by Wolf, Steed, Yost, Pelton, and Lee Cantrell, came loping into Morral City. The first five halted at the Brown Bottle and entered. Cantrell came on alone to dismount before the Goldfinch Bar.

Tucson, with Lullaby, Stony, and Jeff Daulton, were in the Goldfinch when Cantrell entered. They stood in a group at one end of the bar. A couple of punchers from the Bench-R outfit were drinking at the other end, and there were a sprinkling of townsmen scattered in between. Cantrell halted just within the swinging-doored entrance, trying to adjust his vision to the sudden half-light of the saloon, after the hot glare of the street. He asked coldly, "Is Tucson Smith in here?"

"Down here, Cantrell," Tucson answered instantly.

Cantrell crossed the floor without further speech and took a position at the bar next to Tucson and his group. Without a word Pat Finch placed a bottle and glass before Cantrell. Cantrell poured two fingers of whisky, slopping the liquor over the edge of the glass as he did so, then downed his drink. When he finally faced Tucson his flat opaque eyes looked more vicious than ever.

He said abruptly, "I'm not in the habit of being ordered to come to town, Smith."

"The fact remains," Tucson replied quietly, "that you came."

Cantrell nodded. "I'm not in the habit of refusing challenges, either. Now, is there anything else on your mind?"

Tucson lowered his voice so it didn't carry beyond his own group. "A week or so back," he stated, "you warned me not to go near the sheriff's office. You knew it had been planned for Branch to ambush me there. I owe you some thanks for that, Cantrell."

Cantrell snarled, "To hell with that."

"Why did you give me that warning?"

Cantrell's cold laughter was scornful. "I didn't want to see you bumped off by a tramp like Branch. That was an idea he cooked up by his ownself. You maybe won't believe it, but Trax didn't know about it either. You see, Trax is counting on *me* doing that job. And I wanted you saved for me." There was a certain ominous assurance in the words.

"I figured it might be something like that," Tucson said easily. "Nevertheless, Cantrell, your warning may have saved my life. I'm saying much obliged."

Cantrell sneered. "To hell with you and your thanks both."

"Take it that way if you want to," Tucson said with a nod, "but I'm going to give you a chance."

"*You* are going to give *me* a chance?" Cantrell asked contemptuously. "Don't talk in riddles, Smith. What exactly do you want?"

"I want to know what Whitlock's game is around here."

Cantrell didn't reply at once. Stony, Lullaby, and Daulton watched him, wondering how he'd react. The man's face flooded with crimson for a moment, then paled again. "Where in hell," he demanded, "did you ever get an idea I was a rat?"

"Rat or no," Tucson persisted, "I'm trying to give you a chance."

"Look here, Smith," Cantrell said coldly, "I was hired by Whitlock for certain purposes, and they didn't have anything to do with his game, as you called it. Let's say I don't know what his game is, and that I wouldn't tell you if I did. And you're a damn fool if you think I'd do any talking."

"Maybe I am," Tucson replied in the same easy tones. "To tell the truth, Cantrell, I didn't expect you to squeal. But there's always the chance you might. So there's only one thing left for me to do. Cantrell, get out of Morral City or I'm placing you under arrest."

"Yeah?" There was a sneer in the surprised tones. "On what charge?"

"Considering your past reputation, I've decided you're an undesirable. The town doesn't want such as you."

"And suppose I refuse to leave?"

"I'll give you one hour to think it over, Cantrell. If you're still in Morral City then, I'm coming after you—regardless whether you're here or down with your pals in the Brown Bottle."

"Damn you, Smith!" Cantrell's voice rose. "Don't call those bustards my pals. And you can't scare me out of the Goldfinch. I'm staying!" He concluded by calling Tucson a name.

In a lightning-like movement, Tucson raised one hand and slapped Cantrell across the face, leaving the imprint of white finger marks against the sudden rush of color. For a brief instant Cantrell tensed and the others thought he was going to reach for the six-shooter at his side, then he held his fiery emotions in check and relaxed. "Smith," he said, his tones quivering with rage, "you're forcing matters."

"I'm forcing matters." Tucson nodded. "If you mean that I'm looking for trouble, I'll admit that too. I am looking for trouble. And I'm going to keep on looking for trouble until every bustard in these parts is either dead or out of town."

"You're biting off more than you can chew, Smith," Cantrell snarled, "when you talk that way to me."

Tucson ignored the words. He removed the watch from his pocket, studied it a moment, and then put it back. "The time," he said in a level voice, "is exactly three thirty-two, Cantrell. At four thirty-two, I'll be coming after you." He swung away from the bar and started for the sidewalk. "C'mon, pards."

Cantrell squinted after them a moment, then raised his voice. "By God, Smith, I'll be waiting right here at four thirty-two, and you'd better come in with your gun smoking——" He paused, then, "No, God damn it, I'll be looking for you when the time comes. You won't have to come in here for me."

But Tucson and his friends were already outside. Cantrell swung, cursing, back to the bar and ordered whisky. The other men in the saloon quickly swallowed their drinks and hastened off to spread the news of the impending meeting between Tucson and Lee Cantrell.

19. ROARING GUNS!

Lullaby and Stony found Tucson, a half hour later, seated on the hotel porch, his feet propped on the railing. Tucson said, "Did you learn anything?"

Lullaby nodded. "I don't think there's any chance of Trax Whitlock and his gang taking a hand. They're too sure that Cantrell will down you. And when he downs you, they figure he's a sure bet to get Stony and me—one at a time."

Tucson smiled gravely. "You know, they could be overestimating Cantrell's skill with a six-shooter."

"Don't you underestimate him," Stony said swiftly. "You already know his rep. Cantrell's bad medicine. Whitlock and his hands are taking bets—giving good odds—that Cantrell will get you."

"They getting many takers?" Tucson asked.

"More than I like to see," Stony said a trifle glumly. "I talked to various men around town. They don't know you; they do know Cantrell. At the odds offered, they figure anything they bet is a good risk——"

"Damn it!" Lullaby broke in. "Why don't you let me take this business off your hands, pard——"

"Or me," Stony interrupted. "There's no use you running risks, Tucson. I can go down to the Goldfinch and just arrest him, throw him in a cell——"

"And what charge are you going to hold him on?" Tucson asked. "We'd just have the whole business to go through the minute he got out." He shook his head. "No, this is my job, pards. I made my play and I've got to back it up——"

"But one of us could handle it as well," Lullaby pointed out.

"It's my job," Tucson said again. "I've got a special reason for handling it."

Lullaby and Stony lapsed into a gloomy silence. Jeff Daulton came along the street, mounted to the hotel porch. He leaned against one of the porch uprights and rolled a cigarette. "The news is all over town, Tucson, that you're crossing guns with Cantrell. There's even fellers laying bets on the outcome." Tucson cut in to say he'd heard something to that effect. Daulton went on, "Cantrell's still standing at the bar in the Goldfinch."

Tucson said, "Drinking?"

Daulton shook his head. "Pat Finch slipped me the word that Cantrell hadn't taken a drink since we left. There was nobody but Pat and Cantrell in the bar when I went in. Cantrell is just standing there at the bar sort of looking off into blank space with those cold flat eyes of his. If he saw me, he didn't let on."

No one spoke for a time. Finally, Tucson rose to his feet, took his gun from the holster, spun the cylinder, and replaced it. Daulton said awkwardly, "Look here, Tucson, why not let me make this arrest? We all know, of course, Cantrell won't be taken without a fight."

Tucson replied gravely, "You hombres must be losing faith in my ability. Stony and Lullaby have already tried to talk me out of my job. Anyway, Jeff, you've no authority to make arrests."

Daulton frowned. He appeared to be pondering something. Then, "I've got the authority, Tucson. I think you've already figured out I'm an agent of the U. S. Treasury Department——"

"You mean the Secret Service, Jeff?" Stony interrupted.

Daulton replied, "You're on the right track, anyway, Stony."

"It's no surprise to me," Tucson said.

"So you see," Daulton continued, "I've got the authority if I see fit to use it."

Tucson shook his head, smiling, and said once more, "Thanks—but it's my job. I've got a special reason for handling it."

"You take my advice," Stony growled, "and you won't try to make an arrest. You'll never take Cantrell alive. You should start pumping lead the instant you see him."

Tucson said, "I've got a hunch I can work best close up——"

"Tucson!" Lullaby exclaimed. "That's just plain suicidal against a man like Cantrell, I'd figure. With his rep——"

"Let's not talk about it," Tucson cut in. "I've got my plans all laid. If they work out, we'll have no more trouble with Cantrell. If they don't—well, we won't talk about that, either."

He settled his Stetson more firmly on his head. The other three came close and gripped his hand hard. Then without another word, he descended the steps from the hotel porch and started west along Main Street.

"Cripes!" Stony muttered. "What's Tucson going that way for? The Goldfinch is east of here."

"He's got something in mind," Lullaby said. "Maybe he just wants to take a short walk first, to sort of loosen up his muscles." He took out his watch and glanced at it. "It's only four-fifteen now."

Daulton said, "I don't know what you hombres think of the idea, but I went over to Doc Graham's and told him what was coming up. He won't be very far off—when it happens." The other two nodded approval.

Leaning out from the porch railing, they saw Tucson cross over at the corner of Main and Kearney Streets and continue his walk on the opposite side. "For a minute," Stony said, "I thought he was heading for the Brown Bottle, but he's crossed over. Maybe the sheriff's office—no, he's passed the sheriff's office too. What in the devil has Tucson got in mind?"

"He'll be due to come back to the Goldfinch before long now," Lullaby commented. "Well, I think it's about time I sloped down toward the Brown Bottle. I aim to keep an eye on Trax Whitlock and his men."

"We'll go with you," Stony said. The three descended to the sidewalk and started west. They noticed now that the street had become strangely quiet. There were only a few people on the sidewalks, though faces could be seen in every doorway and window. A large number of horses and wagons had been removed from the hitch racks along Main Street. Valuable property could sometimes be damaged by stray bullets. A sort of ominous hush seemed to settle over Morral City as the sun swung farther west. . . .

Within the Goldfinch Bar, Lee Cantrell glanced at the old clock ticking on the wall. Pat stood motionless behind the bar. There was no one else in the room. The clock said four twenty-two. Cantrell laughed harshly. "You're getting a break, Pat. I'm not waiting for Smith to come here. I'm going after him. That will mebbe save your place getting shot up."

"If you had the sense that God give you," Finch said morosely, "you'd get on your horse and leave here as fast as it could carry you."

"Hell!" Cantrell said with a sneer, "you're like a lot of hombres, making a tin god of Smith. He scares most men with his rep. Me, I don't scare. You'll see, Smith ain't as good as he's cracked up to be——"

"He's downed a lot of men," Finch pointed out.

"He hasn't met Lee Cantrell yet. You're due for a surprise, Pat, when you see Smith dead a short time from now."

"If that happens," Finch said coldly, "I don't want to see you come in here again."

The flat opaque eyes rested balefully on Finch a minute. "*When* that happens," Cantrell stated viciously, "I'm going to come back here and take the Goldfinch apart. Oh hell, I've talked enough." He withdrew his six-shooter from holster, took out the empty shell on which his hammer had been resting, and shoved a cartridge into the chamber. Now the gun was fully loaded. Then, without another word, he pushed through the entrance and stepped to the sidewalk.

There was nothing in particular to see, though Cantrell noticed that the street appeared unusually quiet. Then, as he came into view on the sidewalk, he could hear the hushed murmur of voices run along the thoroughfare. A certain pride swelled Cantrell's breast. People were watching him, all right. That was the way he wanted it. He'd show folks a real gunman at work this day. He felt good; not much headache today, either, and his hand was steady. Yeah, damn 'em, folks would see Smith dropped at a distance that other men never thought of shooting, let alone hitting a target—not with a six-shooter. Six-shooter work at rifle range! Well, maybe not that exactly, but a damn smart distance, just the same.

Cantrell squinted both ways along the sidewalk. Some distance down the street he saw Joslin, Brooke, and Daulton, nearing the Brown Bottle Bar. Smith wasn't with them. Had he waited at the hotel? Quickly Cantrell's gaze shifted. No, there didn't seem to be anyone on the hotel porch. He started along the sidewalk, heading west, then at the corner of Main and Las Cruces streets, he stepped out to the center of the roadway and continued walking. That move should bring Smith into view.

And then, over a block away, Cantrell spied Tucson moving out to the center of the road. Cantrell's maneuver had worked: he'd drawn Smith off the sidewalk. Tucson was striding slowly along, arms swinging easily at his sides, the fingers of his right hand brushing his holster as he walked.

Cantrell swore suddenly. Abruptly he realized that Smith possessed certain advantages too. He had practically talked Cantrell into remaining at the Goldfinch Bar until almost the last moment. Cantrell mused bitterly, "And I thought I was so goddam smart, boasting how I'd stay right at the Goldfinch, and refusing to go to the Brown Bottle. Geez! Smith was planning it that way all the time, and I fell for his talk. Now he's got me walking toward the west, with the sun in my eyes. The sun is at his back!" Cantrell cursed again, something of reluctant admiration tinging the tones. "That damn fox! He's smart!" And then a sudden premonition ran through Cantrell's mind. "I wonder if he knows—if he's guessed." He laughed harshly. "Even supposing he has. At this distance, it won't make any difference."

The intervening length of street between the two men had lessened by this time. Cantrell thought, "Another half-dozen strides nearer, then I'll draw and let him have it."

That thought had scarcely passed through Cantrell's mind when he saw an abrupt burst of white fire patterned against the darker orange of setting sun and the silhouette of Tucson's advancing figure.

"He's crazy!" Cantrell exclaimed. "Nobody—not even Lee Cantrell!—does accurate shooting at this distance——"

But even as the words were being torn from his lips, Cantrell felt his body whirled half around, felt something like red-hot steel sear his shoulder as Tucson's forty-five slug ripped through bone and muscle.

Cantrell righted himself and, lips tightened against the pain, groped in the roadway for the gun that had dropped from his grasp. He straightened up after a few moments, right arm dangling helplessly at his side, the gun lifted in his left hand. He was shaken, trembling, his eyes squinting against that damned setting sun. He raised the gun, fired once—and missed. Through the blur of smoke and pain he could hear voices passing swiftly from open windows and doorways, and the words of one man reached him clearly: "By Gawd! Smith is goin' to down Cantrell!"

"You're a liar!" Cantrell half screamed. "I'll show you bustards!"

Tucson was nearer now, just coming into the range that Cantrell liked best. A second time Cantrell raised his gun, fired—and again missed.

Tucson had again done the unexpected: just as Cantrell had lifted his weapon, Tucson had broken into a queer, eccentric zigzagging sprint that carried him swiftly toward Cantrell. Cantrell fired a third time and missed that running, dodging figure closing in before his blurred gaze. His fourth bullet flew even wider of the mark. Smoke from burned black powder drifted along the street.

Everything was a wavering confusion before Cantrell's eyes now. The street seemed to swim drunkenly as that devil Smith drew nearer at every step, though Tucson's form was indistinct now, just a swiftly moving shapeless mass that drew ever closer. Cantrell's fifth shot struck the earth two full yards in front of Tucson.

And then Tucson released his second bullet. A paralyzing pain smashed into Cantrell's left arm, just above the elbow. Again he felt himself lifted and thrown to one side, and his senses whirled. By the time his mind cleared a trifle he found himself seated on the earth. Somebody—he guessed it was Tucson—was holding a flask of liquor to his lips, and Tucson had one arm around him, holding him up.

There was considerable yelling along the street and many men were crowded close. Cantrell recognized the voices of Joslin, Brooke, and Daulton, and caught odd snatches of their triumphant tones. And then he heard Tucson's impatient voice wanting to know where in hell Doc Graham was, and saying something about a tourniquet for the left arm.

Cantrell could feel something warm and sticky seeping down his shirt sleeves, and then Tucson made him lie flat and gave him another drink of whisky.

After a minute his senses cleared further, but not his vision. He found his voice, and couldn't keep a certain admiration from his tones: "Damn you, Smith, you outfoxed me."

"Maybe I was lucky, Cantrell," Tucson said quietly. "In fact, I know I was lucky. My first shot was mostly a gamble, and I won. Your second shot came too close for comfort. It whined past my ——"

"But you closed in on me then," Cantrell said puzzledly. "How did you know I was no longer any good at close-up shooting?"

"It was plain to anybody who took pains to read the signs," Tucson explained. "Your eyesight has gone bad, Cantrell. Oh, you see well at a distance. That first day we met I saw you spot Ducky

Gebhardt nearly three blocks away. But objects near to you I've a hunch are just a blur. You've been going by feel and hearing. There were the headaches you have. I've seen you fumble for a glass of whisky and knock it over. You slop liquor over your glass when you pour. You stumbled over the sidewalk at the hotel, and made a mess of rolling cigarettes. I held a light for your cigarette one day, and noticed your eyes didn't focus on the flame. A mite over an hour back, you couldn't even place me, in the Goldfinch, until you'd heard my voice——" Tucson broke off, lifted his head. "What in hell is keeping Doc Graham?"

"I see him coming along the street now," Lullaby answered.

Cantrell swore through his pain. "Why didn't you kill me, Smith, and be done with it? Do you have to rub it in? I'll kill myself before I serve a prison term. Why in hell couldn't you kill me, outright?"

Compassion showed in Tucson's face. "Remember a certain warning you gave me, Cantrell? I owed you something for that ——"

"Oh, damn you, damn you, damn you!" Cantrell moaned his frustration through clenched teeth. He tried to raise his arms in protest, but a sudden agony gripped him and he fainted away as Dr. Graham arrived on the scene.

20. TRICKY MONEY

Lullaby, Stony, and Daulton were still at breakfast in the hotel dining room, the following morning when Tucson left them and headed in the direction of the Goldfinch Bar. Dr. Graham was the only patron of the saloon when Tucson entered. Pat Finch and the doctor said good morning, and Finch asked for Tucson's order. "It's a mite early for me to take my first drink of the day, Pat," Tucson said. He turned to Graham. "I thought I might find you here."

Graham smiled and held his tumbler of bourbon to the light. "It's an old habit of mine, this early morning drink. Bad habit, no doubt, but it seems to help me start my day—particularly after a hard night with a patient. I'll likely end in a drunkard's grave."

Tucson laughed. "Yeah, or the gutter—fifty or sixty years from now."

"No doubt." Graham chuckled. "What was it Rabelais said? Something about there being more old drunks than old doctors in the world, no matter how much doctors preached against an over-indulgence in alcohol. Maybe I can be an old drunk and old doctor both."

"You'll never be an old drunk on the amount of liquor you drink," Tucson scoffed. He changed the subject: "How's Cantrell this morning?"

"Physically, he's getting along all right," Graham replied. "Otherwise, he's just as mean and ornery as ever. I kept him under an opiate until this morning, to assist recovery from the shock of your bullets, but he's feeling mighty savage. I don't foresee any trouble in his healing. If he weren't helpless, I'd expect him to try suicide, but it will be some time before he can move his arms." Tucson asked a question. Graham shook his head. "No, he refuses to even talk about Trax Whitlock. Says he's no squealer. I think he knows who killed Art Branch from that hotel window, but he refuses to talk about it, aside from denying he did it. And somehow I feel he's speaking truth. No, when Cantrell's time comes, I think he'll go to jail, or the gallows, without 'peaching' on the Hatchet gang."

"I've an idea," Tucson said, "that Branch was killed to keep him from talking. I wouldn't want anything like that to happen to Cantrell."

"I don't think it will. I've placed his bed well away from any windows where he could be killed from a distance. I've a Mexican couple at my house who are thoroughly reliable. I'm training them both to help me in my work. I've told them not to let anyone near Cantrell without my say-so. So I think we're safe on that score, Tucson, as they can both handle a gun if necessary." He put down his empty glass and lighted a cigar. "I've not yet told you that I think you were damn rash, risking your own life in order to just wound Cantrell. You should have killed him and not run such a chance. It's my idea he'd be better off dead. He won't last long in the penitentiary, and no matter how much of a killer he is, I don't believe in the torture of a prison. So why in the devil you wanted him alive is more than I can understand."

"I had my reasons for that too," Tucson replied quietly. "Maybe I owed him something. It's like this, as I see it . . ." He talked steadily to the doctor for some minutes, while Pat Finch retired to the far end of the bar to polish glasses.

The swinging doors at the entrance swung open to admit Lullaby, Stony, and Jeff Daulton. They were all laughing as they entered the barroom.

Dr. Graham was saying to Tucson, ". . . and I certainly do think it worth trying, but it's going to cost you a pile of money."

Tucson said he understood that, when Stony interrupted, "If you're talking about a poker game, Doc, don't plan too much on getting Tucson's money. He's plenty tricky when it comes to cards."

"We weren't talking about poker games." Tucson smiled. "What were you hombres grinning about when you came in?"

"Riley Comstock," Lullaby said. Tucson asked what about Riley Comstock. Lullaby explained, "He's drunker'n a hoot owl. Come in early so he could have a full day, I reckon. He's been standing down in front of the Brown Bottle inviting all of Morral City to come in and have a drink on him."

"Maybe as legally appointed deputies," Tucson said dryly, "you should have put him under arrest."

"He's not doing any harm," Stony said. "He's just feeling plumb good-natured and getting his skin soaked. I'll bet he doesn't get to Morral City once in a coon's age. If he gets out of hand, it's a job we can turn over to Ducky Gebhardt. Ducky hasn't done anything to earn his salt lately."

"Maybe Ducky's already got on the job," Lullaby said. "That Brown Bottle bartender, Kosky, looked plenty worried at the way Comstock was cutting up. He left his bar unattended and cut across the street to the sheriff's office."

Daulton laughed. "And then Ducky went scurrying from his office to the bank. Probably heading to see Stow Whitlock. You know how Ducky is. Hates to take orders from Tucson, and is afraid to act without orders. Likely he thinks he'll get a leading citizen to give him permission to make an arrest."

Tucson asked, "Where's Riley Comstock now?"

"Staggering along the sidewalk, headed this way," Stony said. "I wouldn't be surprised if he'd decided to spread his patronage some."

The words were scarcely out of Stony's mouth when the Goldfinch's swinging doors flew violently apart and Riley Comstock came lurching into the barroom. He paused just within the entrance, looking owlishly over the gathering, then made a deep bow that nearly toppled him on his face. With an effort he staggered erect. "Sheashon's greetingsh, gents," he said, waving one hand airily, and started to chart a wavering course toward the bar.

"Season's greetings!" Finch exclaimed. "What season are you talking about, Riley? This ain't Christmas or Fourth of July or New Year's."

"Sheashon of good will," Comstock returned thickly. He giggled inanely, reached out and gripped the bar. "Shet 'em up for ev'body, Pat. Ol' Riley's got money t'pay."

"Cripes, Riley," Finch said. "Looks like your prospecting has paid off. You must have struck it rich."

"T'hell with proshpectin'," Comstock said maudlinly. "But I shtruck 'er rich, all righ', all righ'. Looksh thish." He struggled with one pants pocket and produced a roll of bills large enough to choke the proverbial horse. "All through proshpectin'. I'm aimin' to catch a train and go to Denver and see some legsh shows. Thatsh life. Wine, women an' shong! . . ."

Of the men in the barroom, only Tucson was unsmiling. He said softly to Stony, "There may be more to this than meets the eye. Slip out and see what Ducky Gebhardt is doing. If he'd planned to arrest Comstock, he'd have been here by this time."

"I'll go with Stony," Lullaby said. "Something may be up."

Daulton said, "I'll head down to the Brown Bottle and see what's doing, if anything."

The three men passed swiftly from the saloon. Dr. Graham said he had to see his patients, and he, too, departed. Riley Comstock was pounding on the bar now, demanding service in a befuddled voice. He paused a moment and looked vacantly around. "Wheresh ev'body? Big crowd when I come in. Now, nobody lef', 'cept Misher Smish." He waggled one impish finger in Tucson's face. "Lotsh men don't like you, Smish. Don't think I like you, neither. Ain' goin' buy you no drinksh."

"What you got against me, Riley?" Tucson asked.

Comstock studied Tucson a moment with bloodshot eyes. "Lotsh things I don't like 'bout you," he said belligerently. "You an' yore pardsh—ain' done nothin' 'cept make trouble sence you come here."

"I've never hurt you," Tucson protested.

"Oh, is zat so!" Comstock wavered at the bar, trying to meet Tucson's gaze. "You should be 'shamed yoreshelf—goin' round shootin' at—hic!—pore ghost what nev' harmsh nobody——"

"When was this?" Tucson asked quickly.

But Comstock had apparently already forgotten the subject. He was again demanding service. "No"—to Finch—"I don' wanna bosher with—hic!—no lil' drink. Want whole bottle—hic!—Old Crow whisky—hic!—righ' now."

Tucson motioned to Finch to give the man what he asked for. Pat pulled a cork on a bottle and set it on the bar. Comstock fumbled with his roll of bills, finally managed to peel one off and toss it on the bar. Tucson glanced at the denomination of the bill and saw that it was a ten. Finch was about to pick it up when Tucson said, "Pat, let me have a cigar, will you?—that two-bit brand."

Finch turned to his back bar to get a box of cigars. Comstock was already making gurgling sounds with his bottle of Old Crow. Finch proffered the box of cigars to Tucson. Tucson chose one and dropped a twenty-dollar gold piece on the bar, saying, "I hope I don't take all your change, Pat."

"I've got plenty," Finch said. He shoved Comstock's ten-dollar bill over to Tucson, then completed the process of making change for Tucson and Comstock with some silver and one-dollar bills. Tucson stuck the money in his pocket, lighted his cigar and strolled out, with a "See you later, Pat."

Half an hour later Stony, Lullaby, and Daulton found Tucson sitting on the hotel porch, feet propped on the railing. A stub of cigar in his mouth had long since gone cold. He was frowning, as though deep in thought, and looked up without smiling as they approached. "Learn anything?" he asked tersely.

"There's something stirring," Lullaby said, "though I don't know what. We saw Stow Whitlock talking to Ducky, and a few minutes later Ducky got on his horse and headed hell-for-breakfast out of town. I never saw that fat windbag move so fast."

"I figure he's riding to see Trax Whitlock," Daulton said, "but I'm damned if I can reconcile the idea of Stow sending Trax a message. I didn't think that pair even spoke to each other."

"Something else," Stony put in. "After Stow got Ducky started, he commenced making a round of the saloons. He located Riley Comstock in the Goldfinch. We were across the street, standing in shadow, and Stow didn't see us when he came out with Comstock. Stow looked madder'n a wet hen. He slapped hell out of Comstock, but we couldn't hear what was being said. Whatever it was, Comstock sobered up plenty. He looked scared, and took something from his pocket and gave it to Stow."

"Could it have been a roll of bills?" Tucson asked.

"Cripes!" Daulton said. "I'll bet that was it—a roll of money. And then Stow gave Comstock more hell, it looked like."

"After that," Lullaby took up the story, "Stow grabbed Comstock by the arm and practically ran him all the way to the Brown Bottle tie rail, boosted Comstock into his saddle and headed him out of town. Comstock lit out like all the devils in hell were on his tail."

Tucson smiled thinly. "Stow Whitlock should get a job as a starter at some race track." Stony interjected a question. Tucson scowled. "I'm damned if I know what's afoot. But give me a mite more time to think and I believe I can dovetail all the pieces into this puzzle yet." He hesitated, then, "What's the quickest way do you hombres figure a man can double his money?"

The others looked uncertain at the abrupt change of subject. Then Stony said, "You take a bill and fold it a couple of times. Then you unfold it and you find your money increases." He snickered. "Get it, pards? You find it in creases."

Lullaby groaned. "What a God-awful pun! It has a bad odor."

"I've got a better idea." Tucson smiled. He took from a pocket a bill that looked brand-new, and held it out for the others' inspection. "What would you call this?"

Stony and Lullaby eyed the engraving of Alexander Hamilton on the bill but remained silent, fearing that Tucson was sucking them in on some joke. Daulton said promptly, "That's a ten-dollar bill."

"Don't be too sure of that," Tucson said dryly. He turned the bill over. "This is what is known as a quick turnover on your money. Now what is this bill worth with the dandy engraving of Andy Jackson on it?"

Daulton's eyes widened. Stony and Lullaby looked amazed. Lullaby said, "Neatest bit of sleight-of-hand I ever saw, Tucson. How did you do it?"

Daulton snatched the bill from Tucson's hand and examined it. It was of twenty-dollar denomination on one side, and ten-dollar denomination on the other. Tucson asked lazily, "Jeff, do you think your uncle might be interested in that bill?"

"My God, yes! Where did you get this, Tucson?"

"Riley Comstock spent it on a bottle of whisky. I thought I spotted something wrong with his bills when he was fumbling with his roll. I managed it so I got hold of this bill." Tucson added details regarding the acquiring of the bill, and concluded, "Hang on to it if you like, Jeff. I've a hunch you're more interested in it than I am."

Jeff said thanks and started to rise from his seat on the porch railing. "I'm going to find Riley Comstock, plenty *pronto*."

"Better take it easy, Jeff," Tucson advised. "Stow Whitlock sent him someplace. You won't know where to look for him. Let me mull things over a mite and perhaps I can come up with an answer."

Reluctantly, Daulton returned to his seat.

But the morning passed, as did dinner time, and the day was

into the afternoon before Tucson reached a definite conclusion. The four men were again seated on the hotel porch, Tucson buried in deep thought, the others not talking to any extent. Abruptly, Tucson got to his feet, swearing softly. "I've got something, I think," he said tersely. "Lord, what a thick-headed idiot I've been. I should have guessed long ago. Four missing Mexicans. Diggers! It's coming clearer now. C'mon, Jeff, get your horse. We're going to find Riley Comstock——"

"Hey!" Lullaby protested. "Don't Stony and I get to go?"

Tucson shook his head. "We've got to leave some law here in town. Now, wait"—as Stony started to disagree—"don't start griping. There's a job for you two, too. When we've pulled out, keep an eye on Stow Whitlock, see that he doesn't send any more men riding with his messages, or warnings, or whatever they are——"

"*Stow* Whitlock?" Lullaby looked surprised.

"Yes, Stow. The banker. I want him arrested and placed in a cell. Put some pressure on him. Make him talk——"

"I'll be damned!" Stony exclaimed. "But on what charge, Tucson?"

"Charge him with the murder of Art Branch." He held up one hand to forestall the surprised questions. "Look, I feel sure it wasn't Cantrell killed Branch. I examined the guns of Trax Whitlock and his punchers in the Brown Bottle. It couldn't have been them. Who else is left but Stow? You'll remember he was there when we came out of the Brown Bottle. Likely he fired that shot from the hotel window, escaped down the back stairs of the hotel into the Brown Bottle, then out the rear door. Then he came around the block—— Oh hell, I've sort of been suspecting him. Now today he sends Ducky Gebhardt riding someplace—where else but the Hatchet Ranch? On top of that he takes a hand in breaking up Riley Comstock's spree and sends him riding."

"But what's the connection," Lullaby asked, "between Comstock and the Hatchet outfit?"

"That's something I don't know yet," Tucson snapped, "but I aim to find out."

"Look here, Tucson," Daulton said, "I didn't think Stow Whitlock ever carried a gun."

"I know damn well he did," Tucson said tersely. "He toted his gun in an underarm holster. I've seen the bulge under his coat.

Don't forget, Stow Whitlock was a cowman before he ever got into banking. He'd be sure to know how to shoot straight."

Stony still looked a trifle dubious. "You're probably right, Tucson, but him being Branch's killer doesn't quite tally in my mind with him favoring our being appointed deputies here."

"He just pretended to favor it," Tucson pointed out. "I could read it in his face that he didn't take to the idea when Doc Graham proposed it, but he put on an act to make us think he agreed. What else could he do? If he'd bucked the idea, a lot of people might have begun to suspect he didn't want law and order here. And if he didn't fall in with Graham's plan, Graham was ready to have Ducky Gebhardt recalled from office. Stow made the best of a bad setup. So long as Gebhardt was allowed to retain his sheriff's star, there was always a chance that us deputies could be got rid of some way and then Ducky could go on taking Whitlock orders as usual."

"By cripes!" Stony exclaimed. "I think you're right."

"I know I am," Tucson responded. He was already moving along the porch toward the steps that led to the street. "So you two throw Stow in a cell. I'll see you later. Come on, Jeff! Shake a leg. We've got a ride ahead of us. So long, pards!"

He and Daulton went hurrying toward the livery stable, with Lullaby and Stony, still on the hotel porch, gazing after them. "That Tucson"—Stony shook his head in admiration—"he sure throws a shock into a man when he makes up his mind to move."

Lullaby nodded. "He sure does. He'll sit around for a long spell, thinking hard, then all of a sudden he just sort of explodes into action. Like you say, he gives you a sort of shock."

But a further shock awaited both men later that same afternoon, when the much-worried foreman of the Bar-BH finally located them in the sheriff's office. It required a little time for Stony and Lullaby to get Jed Carrick's story straightened out, so excited was the foreman, but the upshot of his story was that he had expected to meet Laure Hampton in town that afternoon and accompany her back to the ranch. And now it appeared that Laure hadn't even arrived in Morral City, though she'd left the Bar-BH hours previously. Laure Hampton had disappeared.

21. STEED GOES DOWN

The sun was touching the lower peaks of the Apparition Mountains when Tucson and Daulton pulled to a halt in a grassy hollow to rest their tired horses a few minutes. They'd been pushing hard ever since they left Morral City, and the brief rest proved as welcome to the men as it did to the animals.

"And you feel certain Riley Comstock will be at the Marden house, Tucson?" Jeff asked as the two stepped from saddles.

"If we don't find more than Comstock there, I'll be a heap surprised," Tucson replied. He threw himself on the earth and started to roll a cigarette. Daulton followed suit. Matches were lighted. Blue smoke spiraled in the evening air.

Jeff said, "I'm going to have some explaining to do to Laure when I see her. She was going to ride in and have dinner with me —come to think of it, she was late——"

"There's your chance." Tucson grinned. "You can claim you thought she wasn't going to show up. Always put a woman on the defensive when you can. She'll probably have you on the defensive the rest of your life, anyway."

Jeff grinned happily. "I'm not kicking."

"Have you told Laure of your government connections?"

Jeff shook his head. "I think she knows, though, that I'm not just a cowpoke looking for a job. When I'm not in town to meet her, she'll know something important called me away. Everything will be all right. Anyway, Jed Carrick was coming in to order a new saddle, and he'll be there to ride home with her. I don't like her riding alone at night."

"You have any special fears in mind?" Tucson asked.

"Nothing I can put a finger on. But there's been too much trouble hereabouts to suit me. Not mentioning the four Mexicans who disappeared, Laure's father was murdered, then Joe Folsom. Next Grid Marden. I don't like what's going on. It certainly was a shock to me that day I found Joe Folsom and recognized him. He was a good operative."

"Did Folsom work for your uncle too?"

Daulton nodded. "He was sent out here first, but reported that he wasn't making much headway. I was sent out to help him. You can see how finding him murdered would throw a jolt into me. Then when Gebhardt arrested me, I didn't dare tell my real identity, or I'd have destroyed any usefulness I might have—— Cripes! it's a good thing you and Lullaby and Stony arrived when you did."

The two men talked awhile longer, then Tucson got to his feet. The sun was completely gone by this time, and only a faint after-glow colored the western sky. Daulton and Tucson tightened cinches and climbed back into saddles. Tucson said as they mounted, "We'll not ride direct to the house. We'll leave the ponies a short distance off and approach the house on foot."

The light was completely gone by the time Tucson and Daulton stepped from their ponies' backs and left them tethered in the brush a short distance from the house. Stars were starting to wink into being in the eastern sky. Tucson and his companion moved cautiously forward, their steps making scarcely a sound. Then, rounding a huge outcropping of stratified rock, they saw the house, with light shining from the windows. The front door was closed.

"Comstock's there, I reckon," Daulton whispered. "What do we do, knock at the door or just barge right in?"

He stopped abruptly, his form tensing. From the house had come the sounds of two six-shooter reports, closely spaced. A third shot came a few moments later. Then silence again.

Daulton exclaimed softly, "What in the devil goes on?"

"Come on!" Tucson said. "Whatever's happened, we should be in on it."

They started at a run toward the house, dodging clumps of brush on their way until they'd come into the clear. They were nearly there when the door of the building was flung open; silhouetted in the doorway, against a background of lamp-lighted swirling powder smoke, stood a man. Tucson recognized him first. It was Luke Steed, and Steed held a six-shooter in his right hand.

Tucson spoke from the darkness. "Throw 'em high, Steed!"

Steed stiffened in surprise, then his right hand jerked up and halted in a blaze of fire and lead. Tucson, even as he drew and fired, felt the breeze of Steed's slug as it snarled past his ear.

Steed's legs were jackknifing as Tucson released his second shot. The man pitched forward from the doorway and fell, face down, to earth.

"You got him!" Daulton exclaimed. His own gun was out by this time.

Tucson didn't reply for a moment. He stood waiting, six-shooter in hand, to see if anyone else appeared. Finally, he drew a long breath. There was no further movement at the house. He said, "C'mon. I'll enter first. You keep an eye on Steed, in case he's playing possum."

He glanced at Steed's form, sprawled on the earth, then stepped over it and glanced cautiously around the doorjamb. Another step carried him within the house. He paused, glancing around. The rear door of the house was bolted. An oil lamp burned on the table. On the floor lay Riley Comstock, face down, the back of his shirt stained with blood, one outstretched hand still clutching his six-shooter.

Jeff Daulton stepped through the doorway a minute later. "Steed's dead," he stated. "Both your shots carried enough punch to——" He broke off, noting Comstock's body. "What the hell!"

"Looks to me," Tucson said, "as though Steed and Comstock had a disagreement and Comstock lost the argument." He stooped down and turned Comstock over. The man's eyes were closed and a bloody froth bubbled from his lips and soaked into his matted beard. He was still breathing, though his respiration was far from strong. Blood showed on his shirt front too. "Hit twice," Tucson grunted. With his Barlow knife he cut away Comstock's shirt, then tore up a bandanna and did what he could to stanch the flow of blood. "He's done for, I figure," Tucson said finally. "Looks to me like he'd missed his shot and Steed didn't. Then when he went down, Steed threw in a second shot, in the back."

They lifted Comstock to one of the bunks and covered him with a blanket. "Damn it," Tucson said irritably. "I was counting on talking to him too. I think there are things he could tell us. Now he'll likely die without regaining consciousness. I wonder if there's any whisky around here. A few drops might stimulate him to life, for a short time."

They searched the house, but there was no whisky to be found. "I was afraid there wouldn't be," Tucson said. "Lack of whisky was what brought him to town today. I reckon he got thirsty and decided a celebration was long overdue. Did I hear you say Steed was dead?"

Daulton nodded. "I'll get another blanket and throw over him after I've dragged the body away from the doorway." He went out and returned within a few minutes, closing the door behind him. "Well, I guess there's nothing more for us to do but wait and see if Comstock regains consciousness. There's a chance he might. What did you expect to get out of him, Tucson?"

Tucson didn't appear to be listening. "Y'know," he said finally, "the first time we were here, that table"—motioning to the table on which the lamp stood—"was standing right where it is now, in the center of the room, on that Navajo rug. Then, when we next came back, the table was standing by the wall, but the rug was still in place. That was the night Stony shot at the galloping ghost girl. Thinking about the arrangement of the furniture, I sensed there was something different, but for a long time I couldn't figure out what it was. Then, today, it came to me. It was the difference in the way the table was placed the two times we were here."

Daulton frowned. "Is that important? I don't see——"

"You will, mighty quick now." Tucson smiled. "Things began to come clearer to me today. I was thinking about the four Mexicans who disappeared. They were hired for digging, and they were here a month. Now what digging could they do that would take a month?"

Daulton frowned. "You don't think they were mining?"

"Now you know better than that, Jeff." Tucson smiled. "What has the position of that table to do with mining?" He paused, then, "I'll give you another hint. That rug under the table is nailed down. The rug across the room isn't. Now use your head."

Light suddenly dawned for Jeff. "You mean—— By God, Tucson! You've hit it! Aces to tens there's——"

"There's a secret room been dug under this floor," Tucson finished. "And if one end of that rug isn't nailed to a trap door, I'll eat my Stet hat. Furthermore, I'll make a guess as to what happened to those four Mexicans. Whoever hired them to excavate the earth from under this floor didn't dare let them live to tell what they'd been doing. And so he had them killed——"

"Judas priest!" Jeff exclaimed. "What are we waiting for?"

Excitedly, he began to move the table. Tucson seized hold

and helped him, then stooped and felt beneath one end of the Navajo rug where it was nailed to the edge of the trap door. The next instant he had flung back the door and a square hole of darkness yawned at their feet.

"There you are." Tucson smiled. "And a very neat arrangement this is. A man can descend to this lower room, and when he pulls the door closed over his head, he pulls the rug with him and it lays flat, completely concealing the trap door."

"Come on," Daulton said. "There's stairs built in to descend. This is what I've been looking for. If we haven't hit the jackpot this time, I'm a monkey's uncle."

"Or your uncle's monkey." Tucson smiled. He glanced quickly at the bunk where Riley Comstock lay, still unconscious, though in the light from the oil lamp a slight rise and fall of Comstock's chest could be noticed. "All right, grab that lamp and we'll go down and learn what's to be seen."

Jeff picked up the lamp and was just about to take the first step on the stairway leading below, when a voice hailed them from the darkness at their feet:

"The first man to come down here gets a bullet in his body—and the next man as well. So you'd better stay where you are!"

22. THE METAL DRUM AGAIN

Tucson and Jeff tensed. Their eyes widened. Jeff's jaw dropped and he replaced the lamp on the table with a slightly unsteady hand.

"I'll be——" he commenced.

The voice from below spoke again. "And if you men have any sense you'll get out of here before Jeff Daulton and Tucson Smith start after you——"

"Laure!" Jeff yelled.

An instant's silence from below, and then the girl's voice, the tones uncertain, "J-Jeff—is that you?"

"Laure!" Jeff yelled again.

Without waiting, Jeff plunged down the stairway, tripped on the second step. There was a sudden crash from below, then Laure's wailed, "Oh, Jeff—Jeff dear! Did you hurt yourself?"

Tucson said, "Hold everything, I'll be down with the lamp."

Seizing the oil lamp from the table, he descended the short stairway to the room below. At the foot of the steps Jeff was seated on the floor, grinning sheepishly and rubbing his head. Laure was kneeling close by, her arm around him. Tucson noticed she still clutched in one hand a cheap nickel-plated revolver.

Tucson said as he reached the lower floor, "Jeff, you sure move fast when you get started. You hurt?"

Daulton climbed to his feet. "Naw!"—disgustedly. "I just fell over my own clumsy feet. It's just that I was so danged surprised to find Laure here—Laure, how did you get here?"

"That blasted Luke Steed forced me to come," the girl said angrily. "This morning when I was starting to town to meet you, Jeff, he was waiting behind some brush on the trail. He tossed his throw rope over me and threatened to yank me out of the saddle unless I headed my horse for here. Well, I don't like to be yanked from my saddle, so I——"

"Did that coyote hurt you?" Jeff demanded hotly.

"I've not been hurt at all," Laure said. "After we'd been here awhile, Riley Comstock showed up. Riley was mad as blazes to find me here. He and Steed argued, and finally Steed put me down here and closed the trap door. I found a couple of lamps and lighted them, then hours later, it seemed, I heard voices arguing above. Then shots. I didn't know what to think. I was scared silly, though. Later I heard more shooting, and steps above, and talking. I blew out my lamps, figuring I'd not make such a good mark if I had to trade shots with anybody."

"That was when we arrived," Jeff said. "Previously, Steed shot Comstock, though he's not dead yet. When we got here, Tucson finished off Steed." He added brief details for Laure's information.

"I looked around when I had my lamps lighted," Laure said, "and I found this revolver under a bench."

"Probably Marden's," Tucson said.

"Anyway, it was a gun," Laure continued. "I could hear you two talking above, but couldn't recognize words or voices. I was just plain petrified when you started down. I'm not even sure this gun will shoot. The cartridges in it are all corroded." The girl's face was flushed with excitement. She placed the gun on a bench beside a pair of oil lamps and a scattered handful of matches. "It gets mighty stuffy down here—but just imagine, a room under the floor of this old house! I never knew about it before. And, Jeff, Tucson, there are some of the oddest objects around here. There's a hand press, and money's been printed, and—and—but look for yourself."

Tucson had already lighted a second lamp and was surveying the room. Naturally there were no windows in it, but it had been floored and the walls were faced with slabs of rock. Some clothing hung on pegs on one wall; a workbench ran the length of the opposite wall. Sheets of paper were stacked at the end of the bench. Nearby were a number of engraved metal plates. There were engraving tools of fine steel, bottles of colored inks, fine pens for imitating the red and blue hair lines that appeared in the bank notes of that day, bottles of acid, a cutting board and press.

"But what does this mean?" Laure asked.

"Counterfeiting equipment," Daulton explained. "The Whitlock gang has been making its own money. Laure, I haven't told you before, but I'm an agent of the U. S. Treasury Department——" He paused at the girl's surprised exclamation, then continued, "We've known for some years now that counterfeit ten- and twenty-dollar bills were being circulated from this part of the country and from Denver and San Francisco. Such bills as we picked up showed them to be the work of one man—and mighty fine work it was, I'll admit—but we could never run down the source. Now it looks as though we'd gone a long way in breaking up the counterfeit ring—thanks to the help of Tucson and his pards——"

"Look here," Tucson said, from the far end of the room. "I've found that metal drum, Jeff." Laure and Daulton quickly moved to his side to examine the missing metal drum, which now rested, on its axle ends, between two supports; a detachable crank with handle was affixed to one end.

"But what the deuce is it for?" Jeff asked, puzzled.

Tucson chuckled. "It makes phony money look more real." He opened the door in the side of the metal cylinder, plunged one hand within, and produced a fistful of nearly new counterfeit notes and a couple of small oily-looking rubber balls. A trace of sand sifted from his hand.

"I get the idea," Jeff exclaimed. "It wouldn't do to have new counterfeit bills circulated, so this is used to make them look old. When the phony notes are printed, they are placed within the drum, with some rocks, dirt, and rubber balls. Then the drum is revolved by means of the crank, and the whole mess is tumbled together, over and over, until the bills achieve an appearance of wear. They get dirty and creased from the small rocks and sand, pick up oily smudges from the rubber balls; this makes them appear like genuine bank notes."

Tucson nodded agreement. "You've hit it."

"My grief!" Laure exclaimed. "Counterfeiters are smart, aren't they?" Jeff answered grimly that sometimes they were too smart for their own good. Tucson moved along to the clothing hanging on pegs.

"Hey," Tucson said suddenly, "look at this."

Laure put in, "Yes, I was wondering what women's clothing was doing here. And there's a wig with long white hair too. The cloth of the dress—and the wig too—feels sort of stiff, like it had been painted, or something——"

"It has." Tucson nodded. At his feet he noticed some tin cans and brushes. He picked up one of the cans and read the label pasted on the side: *Phosphorescent Paint—Guaranteed to Gleam in the Dark*. Below was printed the address of the manufacturer. Tucson said to Laure, "I'm surprised you didn't notice these clothes when you were in the dark, Laure."

"Probably I didn't happen to glance toward them at that time," Laure responded. "I would likely have noticed a great deal more than I did if I hadn't been so scared and upset. Mostly, I've kept my eyes toward that trap door, wondering what would happen next."

"Phosphorescent paint?" Jeff frowned. "But what is it used for, Tucson?"

"Mainly," Tucson explained, "it's manufactured for use in the theater, in stage plays and so on. Magicians often employ it in their tricks, so they can produce spirits and ghosts. I remember one play I saw where a skeleton danced in the dark. It was simply done by putting a man in a black suit, with a skeleton pointed on the cloth."

"Ghosts!" Jeff exclaimed. "So this explains——"

"This explains the galloping ghost." Tucson smiled. "I'll bet that old white horse I noticed in the corral when we were here before is smeared plenty with this paint. And by the time somebody got dressed in this painted dress and wig—well, there's your ghost girl. I suspected something like this was being done."

"But, Tucson," Jeff said, "you told me the ghost appeared gradually, then as gradually faded from view. How do you account for that?"

Tucson laughed. "That part's simple. The brush is cleared completely away from the front of this house, but is only thinned out on either side. When the brush is thick, you can't see the ghost at all. When we first saw it, it was through partially thinned brush. Then, where there was less brush, we saw the ghost plainer. Where there was no brush at all to obscure the view it was in full sight. That same arrangement of brush made the ghost seem to gradually dissolve to nothingness as it traveled behind thicker growths. That wide sandy stretch in front of the house deadened the sounds of hoofbeats."

Jeff shook his head. "Well, I'll be blasted!"

"But why," Laure asked, "did somebody think it was necessary to put on this ghost act in the first place? Of course, superstitious people believe the Apparition Mountains are haunted, so that made the ghost all the more believable, but I can't see why anybody should take the trouble to put on such an act."

"I think I know why," Tucson said, "but let's hold off a spell. If Riley Comstock regains consciousness, maybe he'll explain it clearer than I can. What say we go back upstairs?"

They ascended the stairway and closed the trap door. Riley Comstock lay as before, barely breathing, but still alive, though Tucson found his pulse very thready, as though it were likely to stop at any instant. "There's nothing we can do but wait, I guess," Tucson said. "Or, I'll tell you what, Jeff. You take Laure to town, or to the Bar-BH. I'll stay here until Comstock dies."

"Golly, Tucson," Jeff said dubiously. "If he does come to and makes some sort of confession, I should be here to listen. I'd offer to stay and have you take Laure home, but I'd like you for a witness if Comstock does say anything."

"Good grief!" Laure exclaimed. "There's no reason why I should be taken anyplace. I'll stay. I'm just as eager as you two are to see if Riley can tell us something. Poor old Riley. I've known him for years. I never thought to see him end like this."

Jeff looked relieved. "All right, we'll all stay. I'll have to make some arrangement, too, to move all that counterfeiting equipment to town. That's all solid evidence and I'll need it in my case when I make my report. Gosh, Tucson, this has been a real haul."

Laure said suddenly, "I'm hungry."

Tucson smiled. "You sound like Lullaby. Well, there are supplies here and coffee. Why don't you and Jeff cook up something while we're waiting? There's plenty firewood back of that stove. Meanwhile, Jeff, I'll go bring up our horses from where we left them in the brush. They'll need watering."

Jeff and Laure agreed and Tucson departed. He was back in about an hour and entered the house to smell coffee and bacon cooking. "I put the broncs in the corral out back," he said. "Your pony is out there, Laure. The scuts hadn't even troubled to unsaddle it." He laughed. "That old white horse is in the corral too. I reckon they haven't renewed his phosphorescent paint for some time. He's commencing to look sort of patchy. Shows up all right in spots, but he sure dissolves into darkness at others."

Food was eventually placed on the table and the three ate. The men rolled cigarettes and smoked while the time passed. Laure curled up in a chair and went to sleep. From time to time Tucson crossed the floor to examine Riley Comstock, but could see no change in the unconscious man. The hours dragged by.

"Must be getting along toward dawn," Tucson commented once, and again, sometime later, "I wish to cripes we had some whisky. A few drops might stimulate Comstock to a mite of life——" He broke off, then, "Coffee is a stimulant. I wonder if I brewed up a good strong potful—cripes! it's worth trying, anyway, and we'll all be needing some Java again before long."

The fire in the stove was built up and coffee put on to boil.

A half hour later Tucson trickled a few drops of strong coffee between Comstock's lips, but the effort produced no appreciable result. By this time, Laure had awakened. The girl glanced through the window, saying, "Golly, the sky is graying in the east. It's almost morning. Look here, while we're waiting for Riley to regain consciousness, why don't we start loading the counterfeiting equipment on horses? Jeff has to have it for his evidence. I'll be glad to help."

Daulton and Tucson turned back from Comstock's bunk. Tucson said, "That's a right idea, Laure. There's Steed's horse and some other broncs in the corral out back. You can saddle and bring up our mounts too, then we'll be ready to head for Morral City when Comstock is gone. He can't last much longer."

Daulton said, "Tucson, you stay here with him. Laure and I can handle the saddling and loading." Tucson nodded agreement. The trap door was reopened and Daulton and the girl started carrying up the metal drum and other equipment, not forgetting to bring the dress and white wig the "ghost girl" had worn.

23. SHOWDOWN!

Some time later, just as Daulton and Laure had finished packing and tethered the saddle horses at the side of the house, Tucson called to them: "You'd better come in. Comstock's coming to."

By the time they had entered, Comstock's eyes were open and he was looking vaguely up into Tucson's face, while Tucson held a glass of water to his lips. Recognition, and then a look of anger crept over Comstock's features. "Thet damn Luke Steed jest 'bout ruined me with his hawg-laig, didn't he? Whut ye doin' here, Smith? It looks like our game's plumb finished, when I see you here."

"It's finished," Tucson said, and asked Comstock if he were in much pain.

"Can't say thet I am," was the reply in a surprisingly strong voice. "Jest feel sorter numb and cold from the waist down. I reckon one of Steed's slugs done somethin' evil to my backbone." His eyes searched Tucson's face. "I'm near my finish, ain't I, Smith?"

"You haven't got a chance, Riley," Tucson replied. "Maybe you're better off this way. Your gang's finished. Want to tell what you know?"

Comstock nodded. "Though ye'd not git a word outten me if Whitlock had played square. But I was through with sech varmints when they started warrin' on wimmen. Shore, I'll tell ye anythin' ye wants to know."

Tucson asked, "Was Grid Marden the man who engraved the plates?"

"Ye guessed it. How did ye know?" Comstock replied.

"To me he seemed the only one capable of doing such work."

Comstock's story came slowly under Tucson's questioning, and with various promptings from Daulton, while Laure remained in an armchair near the window. Tucson told what had happened since he'd arrived at the house, and Comstock looked his gratitude at the news of Steed's death.

Years before, Comstock's story went, Stow and Trax Whitlock

had held up a train in Oregon and robbed a United States mail car of thousands of dollars. Later Stow had been captured and sent to prison, but Trax had got away with the money. During his first year in the penitentiary, Stow had escaped and rejoined Trax, but while in prison, Stow had become acquainted with Grid Marden, who was serving a term for counterfeiting. Eventually, the Whitlocks had arrived at Morral City, purchased the Hatchet Ranch, and then waited for Marden's release from the penitentiary to set up their counterfeiting plant.

"Thet Marden was yeller as egg yoke," Comstock said, "but he couldn't be beat at makin' plates for the printin' of imitation bank notes. It was decided he had to have a quiet place to work, so we come here and hired them Mexes to dig a room under this floor. They done a good job, too, but Trax was afeared they'd talk 'bout it. So he had Steed and Gus Wolf kill 'em when they were leavin' here, and bury 'em. Trouble was, their Mex pals come a-snoopin' around, suspectin' somethin' bad had been done to 'em. So the Whitlocks cooked up that ghost act." Something like a snicker escaped the bearded lips. "Betcher didn't know I took the part of thet ghost gal, did ye? I uster make rides round the house 'most every night. Some of the Mexes seed me and got skeered. They stayed away after thet. Other folks too. So we was left free to make our money."

Tucson asked a question. Comstock said, "Ben Hampton? It was Trax killed him. Ben noticed one day that this floor sounded hollow underfoot. He'd come here to visit and c'lect the rent from Marden. 'Bout thet time Trax rode in, and Ben mentioned the floor to Trax. Trax got to fearin' that Ben might get suspicious, so he yanks his gun and let Ben have it, plumb center. Then we takes the body out on the range and left it to be found, after startin' Ben's hawss for home. I was sorry 'bout thet. I allus liked Ben, but Trax said 'Business was business,' and we didn't have no time for sentiment in our job."

Daulton glanced over his shoulder at Laure, but the girl didn't appear to have heard Comstock's recital of her father's death. Tucson said, "That feud between Trax and Stow Whitlock was just an act, wasn't it? I've always felt there was something phony about it. Stow overacted. He was always too ready to accuse his brother of skulduggery."

"Shore it was an act," Comstock replied. "Just put on to fool folks. Stow's the real leader. He's been passin' out them fake bank notes for years. Can ye think of a better place than a bank to pass counterfeit money? Then we sent monthly packets of bills to a couple other fellows—Harry Denver of San Francisco and Pablo Francisco of——"

"Those two have been arrested," Daulton said. He mentioned Joe Folsom and asked further questions.

"Thet Folsom nigh upset our apple cart. He used to come visitin' a lot, and we had to keep our eyes peeled. One day Grid got careless and left the trap door open while he come to the corral to see me. When we got back, there was Folsom just leavin' with thet metal drum, which he'd grabbed, along with some packets of finished bills and rubber balls and so on, which he'd shoved inside the drum. Folsom thrun his gun on us and made a getaway on his hawss, but the drum door had come unfastened and rubber balls and bills got scattered out as he was leavin'. I reckon he discovered the door was open and closed it in time to save a coupla rubber balls and the bills you hombres found. Later, scattered out front, we picked up a lot of bills and balls he'd dropped, but I'll betcher there's still bills and balls sprinkled out in thet brush thet we missed."

Comstock rested a minute and went on, "Shortly after Folsom got away with thet drum, Branch rode in. We told Art whut had happened, and he took out after Folsom. Art downed him before he could reach town. Then Art rode in to tell the sheriff. Ducky knowed we was counterfeitin', and he got paid to take Trax's orders, but he didn't know how we worked or anythin' about thet drum. Anyways, Ducky, Art, and Trax rode out so's they could pretend to find the body. They had got to where Folsom was lyin' dead, when Trax spied Daulton some distance off. Then they hid out with the idea of framin' Daulton for the killin'. 'Bout thet time, Smith, you and yore pals arrived and sp'iled the plan."

Tucson asked, "What was Cantrell's part in the counterfeiting?"

"Lee didn't take no part," Comstock said. "Lee, he's a bad 'un, but he sorter figgered passin' queer money was beneath his dignity, or somethin' like thet. There was just me'n Grid and the Whitlocks runnin' the money game. Steed, Yost, Wolf, Pelton, and Branch was in on it too. The rest of the Hatchet crew didn't even know we was makin' fake bills."

Tucson interjected a question. Comstock replied, "I reckon it was you Mesquiteers that fired on me thet night when I was playing ghost, wa'n't it? Anyway, ye come to the house later. Thet shot missed me, but I figgered I'd best make tracks fer safety. I hid my white hawss in the deep brush, and come in the house the back way. Grid was sittin' in the dark, shiverin'. He'd plumb lost his nerve. He realized somebody was gettin' wise to us, and he was all fer rushin' outten the house and surrenderin' to ye. I tried to stop him, but he wouldn't listen. Me, bein' in my ghost-gal disguise, I didn't have no gun on, but I grabs a butcher knife from the table to sorter scare him. Somehow, while we was rasslin' in the dark, he fell back agin the knife, and he got stabbed. It was an accident, ye might say."

There was something smug in the old scoundrel's manner as he confessed to Marden's murder. "I realized t'once Grid was done fer, so I went down to our secret room and pulled the trap door after me. In a little while I could hear you fellers talkin' above my head, but ye never guessed I was hid jest below. When I told Trax 'bout it later, he was plumb upset, and he passed the word to Cantrell to git rid of you hombres, which was the kind of job Lee had been hired fer. Well, thet didn't pan out neither, and the Whitlocks kept gettin' nervouser all the time. It was then Stow got the idea 'bout Laure Hampton."

Comstock's voice had grown weaker. "I never did hold with thet plan, but it was put through 'fore I had a chance to stop it. The idea was for Laure to be kidnaped and held captive until you meddlin' Mesquiteers promised to leave. Like I say, I didn't know 'bout it till Steed got here with Laure. Me, I never yit warred again' no wimmen and I figgered I was too old to start, so me'n Steed done a heap of wranglin' about the matter. Finally I sees murder in his eye, and I went for my gun, but my rheumaticks has slowed me up some and he beat me to th' shot and my shot missed. Then he plugged me agin, damn him!"

Daulton asked for an explanation of the two-face bank note. A ghost of a smile crossed Comstock's pallid lips. "I sartain messed things up," he replied. "Y'see, after Marden was killed—by accident ye might say—Trax taught me how to print them bills. The plates was all there ready. All's I had to do was handle the inks and the press, and I done right well. I was printin' some yesterday and drinkin' a mite of whisky while I worked. I reckon I muster got confused and used the wrong plate on some of the notes. 'Bout thet time I decides to go to Morral City and get me some more whisky, my bottle havin' run empty in practically no time a-tall. So I grabs me some money I'd jest printed and forked my hawss. I got me a good start in town too, until Kosky in the Brown Bottle spots somethin' wrong with my money, and then Stow caught up with me and he give me merry hell and sent me ridin' for home——" He broke off and looked inquiringly at Tucson. "Say, my belly and chest feels right chilly. Does thet mean I ain't —got—much more time?"

"It looks that way, old-timer," Tucson said kindly. Comstock muttered something that had to do with wondering if there'd be lots of "wine, wimmen, and song" where he was going, and closed his eyes. He didn't open them again, and five minutes later he was dead. Tucson drew the blanket up over Comstock's face and came to the center of the room. He heard Laure say that the sun was almost up, and glancing through the window, he saw that day had come.

Daulton said, "Gosh, Comstock just lasted long enough to give us the information we needed."

Tucson nodded. "He was one tough old coot. Funny thing, he could view the killing of those four Mexicans without batting an eyelash. Even the murder of Laure's dad didn't hit him too hard. He could condone the killing of Joe Folsom, make and pass counterfeit money, plunge a knife into Grid Marden—all this without the slightest twinging of conscience. And yet he turned against the whole Whitlock outfit because the gang violated his own code of not warring against women. Comstock could stand anything except that matter of forcing Laure to come here. I guess even the worst of men have one streak of good left in 'em if it has a chance to come out."

Laure nodded. Daulton was looking queerly at Tucson. He said, "That's quite a speech, Tucson. Just what are you getting at?"

Tucson said, "Have my pards and I been any help to you, Jeff, in breaking up this counterfeiting ring?"

Daulton stared. "Have you been any help? Good lord, Tucson, more help than I can name. I'd been licked without you. Now I've got all the names I need to make arrests, I've got evidence that will——"

"Let's forget one name in the bunch, Jeff, as a favor to me," Tucson cut in. "You heard Comstock's confession. You heard him say Lee Cantrell never had a thing to do with the counterfeiting. When you make out your report to Uncle Sam, let's leave Cantrell's name out of it."

Daulton frowned. "Cantrell! What you trying to save his neck for, Tucson?"

"Maybe something's owing to Cantrell," Tucson said quietly, and said again, "As a favor to me, Jeff. I'd like a chance to decide Cantrell's fate, without tying him into the counterfeiting ring. Once his name got into the Government's black book, he never would have a chance. I'd like to try my own way of settling with Cantrell."

Daulton smiled suddenly. "It's a deal, Tucson. I'll forget that Lee Cantrell ever existed. And now let's get started for Morral City. Ready, Laure? Good. Let's ride! There's a showdown coming and I'm getting mighty impatient."

Laure and Daulton passed through the doorway first, with Tucson close behind. The first rays of the sun lifting above the horizon were warm on their faces as they stepped into the open and started around the corner of the house toward the horses. Abruptly, Tucson paused, listening, as the sound of pounding hoofs reached his ears.

The next instant a body of riders, with Trax Whitlock at their head, rounded a gigantic upthrust of sandstone, just beyond the wide stretch of sandy wash. The riders hadn't yet spied Tucson and his companions leaving the house.

"Back, Jeff, back!" Tucson snapped, as he seized Laure's shoulder and hurled her back through the doorway.

Even as he and Jeff followed the girl within, Trax Whitlock's sudden angry yell showed they'd been seen and recognized. A bullet smashed viciously into the doorjamb, perilously close to Tucson's head, just before he slammed the door and bolted it. A ragged volley of lead flattened itself against the house wall. One slug came through a window, shattering the glass, and buried itself in the rear wall.

Tucson drew a long breath. "Yeah, there's a showdown coming, all right, Jeff, but we've got to face the fact that we don't know now who's going down."

24. CONCLUSION

For nearly an hour now the firing had been almost continuous. The Whitlock faction was well shielded behind low rocks, and so far as they knew, Tucson and his friends hadn't managed to hit anyone. By this time there wasn't a whole pane of glass remaining in the windows of the house. Powder smoke swirled in the small room. The faces of Tucson and Jeff were powder-grimed. A ricocheting bullet had scraped skin from the back of Tucson's right hand. The shirts of the men were wet with perspiration. They had both tried to persuade Laure to keep down out of danger, but the girl had insisted on doing her part in the defense by loading guns for them. Comstock's gun and ammunition had been brought into use, but now cartridges were running low.

Tucson accepted the freshly loaded gun the girl gave him, peered around the corner of a window jamb, then fired a quick shot as he saw a man's shoulder appear at the edge of a sandrock outcropping. There came a sudden yelp of pain, and then Whitlock's angry order to his men to keep out of sight.

"Think I winged one," Tucson said grimly. By this time Laure had finished loading Tucson's empty gun and hurried across to another window where Jeff was shooting. Jeff fired once, then said ruefully, "Dang it! I missed, I reckon. Those coyotes have got us pinned to one spot, while they can duck around from rock to rock. If they'd only come out in the open, where that brush has been cut away, we might——"

Laure cut in, speaking coolly. "Better go easy on the cartridges. There aren't many rounds left. And here's something else you won't like. Our water bucket's nearly empty."

"Don't let it worry you, Laure," Tucson said. "We'll get out of this yet."

The girl smiled from her crouching position on the floor. "There's no need to lie to me, Tucson. I'm past twenty-one. We're in a mighty desperate fix, and I realize it as well as you do."

"That's my game girl!" Daulton exclaimed, a smile appearing

on his powder-begrimed features. "She knows what's what, all right, Tucson. We don't have to baby her."

"We don't have to baby her," Tucson repeated. "But we'd better start babying our cartridges, and save 'em for when they're needed worse than right now." He paused. "Those scuts saw the horses loaded with that counterfeiting equipment. They won't let us get away if they can help it. Look, supposing I take a fully loaded gun and make a dash outside for a horse. If I can get to town for help——"

"It won't work, Tucson," Laure interrupted. "They'd shoot you down the instant you appeared outside."

"I might even get one or two of 'em," Tucson persisted. "I think there was just four men beside Whitlock—Wolf, Pelton, Yost, and Ducky Gebhardt—and Ducky won't be showing his head, I'll bet."

"I don't like the idea," Daulton said stubbornly.

"I'll tell you, Tucson," Laure proposed, "we'll all make a dash for our horses and——"

"Nothing doing," Tucson said. "Whitlock and his gang are too well protected behind rocks. They'd pick you off——"

"And how did you expect to get away, then?" Laure asked coolly.

Tucson grinned wearily. "All right, you win." In his heart he knew that he and Jeff alone had a bare chance of making a get-away, once outside, but with Laure too the risk was too great to be taken.

Whitlock's voice hailed him from outside. Tuscon peered cautiously around a corner of the window, but Whitlock wasn't in view.

"What do you want?" Tucson yelled back.

"If you surrender we'll let you go," Whitlock called.

Tucson laughed scornfully. "You can prove that by going away *pronto*." He added, "I can't believe you, Whitlock."

Whitlock cursed. "How'd you like it if we rushed that door?"

"Come ahead!" Tucson invited. "That's what we're waiting for!"

Whitlock didn't answer this time. Even the firing of his gang fell off, as though they were talking things over. Tucson said, "I might be able to slip out that back door and——"

"And you'd have to come around the house to reach your

horse," Daulton said. "They'd spot you at once. Forget it, Tucson."

Again Whitlock raised his voice. "If you don't surrender, Smith, we're going to set fire to the house."

Daulton gave a short laugh. "They'd have a hard time setting fire to this rock building."

"You forget," Tucson pointed out, "that the roof is made of planks—planks and tar paper. They could sneak around to our rear and toss some burning brush on the roof. That dry wood would catch mighty easy. Once it burned through, this place would not only fill with smoke, but burning embers would start dropping. We'd be suffocated, if not burned to death. We've got to face it, they don't dare let us escape. We know too much." He paused, struck by a sudden idea. "Wait. Maybe I've an idea." He turned swiftly to the window and called to Whitlock, "You can't scare us that way, Whitlock. Go ahead, set fire to the roof if you like. We're not quitting!"

"Danged if I get what you're doing." Daulton frowned. "You practically dared them to set the roof on fire. What——"

"Look here," Tucson spoke swiftly, "if they set the place on fire, you leave me with two guns, fully loaded. Then you and Laure open the trap door and go downstairs. It would take a fire quite a while to burn through this floor. Meanwhile, I'll wait up here. I can stay close to the floor where the breathing won't be too bad. If necessary, I can take the rest of the water in the bucket and soak a blanket and lay under it. By the time the roof is burned off, Whitlock and his gang will think we're finished. When they come in, I can pick them off as they come through the doorway——"

"Do you think for one minute," Laure said indignantly, "that we'd leave you for the safety of that downstairs room?"

"Why not?" Tucson demanded. "You'd be safe, and after I've settled with those coyotes, we can all——"

"It won't work, Tucson, and you know it," Daulton said.

"Besides," Laure pointed out, "it gets too stuffy in that room when the trap door is closed. I prefer powder smoke——"

She broke off as the abrupt sound of firing was heard outside, and the sudden pounding of hoofs. Excited cries and yells filled the air. Tucson said, "What the devil!" and risked a glance from the nearest window. Then he gave a wild whoop of delight. "It's

Lullaby and Stony! And they've a dozen riders with them! C'mon, Jeff, let's get in on this!"

Together, the two men plunged outside, six-shooters in hand. Riders were plunging wildly about. The air was filled with gunfire. Then Trax Whitlock's voice was heard begging for mercy. The smashing detonation of a six-shooter cut short the plea. Lullaby came tearing up and skidded his pony in a long scattering of sand and gravel as he pulled it to a stop. Already the sound of firing had died away.

"You all right, Tucson?" he yelled. "You, Jeff?" Lifting his gaze, he saw Laure emerging from the house. "Laure!" he cried his relief. "So this is where you are." He glanced at the guns in Tucson's and Daulton's hands. "Might as well put away your irons. The fracas is over, gents."

"But how did you know we were here?" Tucson asked as Lullaby dismounted.

"Didn't for sure," Lullaby replied. "Jed Carrick hit town last evening with the news that Laure had disappeared, just after we finished giving Stow Whitlock a going-over. Hey! He really broke down and confessed to killing Branch, like you said. We put on more pressure to see what else we could learn and he started blabbing some stuff about counterfeiting. But danged if we could get him to say he knew anything about Laure. He just turned plain stubborn. We picked up a couple of punchers from the Rocking-T who were in town and then rode to the Hatchet. There was just three hands and the cook there, and they swore they didn't know where Trax and the others had gone. We wasted half the night trying to prove they were lying, and then gave up and came on to the Bar-BH. After we got riders there, this seemed like the next best place to look. We heard the firing while we were still some distance off——"

He paused as Stony came loping up, followed by Jed Carrick, who greeted Laure joyfully. Other men arrived more slowly. Stony said, in pretended disgust, "Dang it, Tucson, every time you get away alone, we have to come and pull you out of a fix."

"I reckon you're right." Tucson smiled. "What about Trax Whitlock and his men?"

"Whitlock's dead," Stony replied. "So are the others, with the exception of Ducky Gebhardt. He quit cold when he got a scratch on his arm, and now he's whining for somebody to listen to his confession. None of us felt low enough to finish him off. That no-good sheriff will end his days on bread and water in prison, or I miss my guess."

"Bread!" Lullaby exclaimed. "I just remembered, it's time for breakfast. I'm hungry!"

"There!" Stony spoke dolefully. "I've done it again. Won't I ever learn to keep my big mouth shut?"

Laure had been talking to Carrick and the other Bar-BH hands. Now she turned to Lullaby. "There's canned beans and bacon and tomatoes and coffee at the house, Lullaby. I can fix breakfast for all of us in mighty short time."

Lullaby doffed his sombrero and made a low bow. "Laure, you're a woman after my own heart—but I guess you'll have to be content with Jeff's."

"And while we're eating," Tucson said, "I'll tell you a story of a secret room and a ghost that won't ever ride again."

Laure took Jeff's arm and started for the house, while the rest followed more slowly behind. By this time, the sun had climbed higher, casting a golden light on the jagged peaks of the Apparitions.

A week later Tucson entered the bedroom in Dr. Graham's house where Lee Cantrell lay stretched beneath covers, his head propped on pillows, one arm and one shoulder swathed in bandages. The doctor was in his office, talking to a patient. A curtain fluttered in the soft breeze coming through an open window. Tucson stopped just within the entrance and stood looking at Cantrell. After a moment he drew up a chair and sat down near the bed. He said quietly, "How you feeling, Lee?"

"What's it to you?" Cantrell half snarled. He eyed Tucson defiantly, and his steady gaze seemed clearer than usual. Probably rest and the proper food had had much to do with that.

"Oh, I was just wondering," Tucson said casually. He rolled and lighted a cigarette. Blue smoke drifted through the room.

"As if you really gave a damn how I feel," Cantrell sneered. "I'm surprised your pards didn't come with you to give me the horse laugh—me, helpless as hell. Do you think I'd be here now if I had the use of my arms? Damn you, Smith, why didn't you kill me and be done with it?"

"I had a reason for that too," Tucson said quietly. "Lullaby and Stony will be in to see you and say good-by before we pull out. At present, they're still at the Bar-BH enjoying themselves. Jeff Daulton married Laure Hampton this morning, and there's dancing and lots of food. Too bad you couldn't be there, Lee."

Cantrell laughed harshly. "If I could make to get that far, I'd be gone a lot farther. And I'm not interested in marriages."

"I suppose not," Tucson agreed genially. He drew thoughtfully on his cigarette and exhaled. "Doc Graham tells me you're mending fast. Your arm and shoulder will be as good as new before you realize it, Lee, then you can be leaving."

"That's really something to look forward to," Cantrell commented sarcastically. "Sure, I'll be leaving here—with handcuffs on my wrists, and nothing ahead but the trial and a long sentence, if not worse." His voice rose on a bitter note. "I tell you one thing, I'll not last long in prison. If I can't make a getaway, I'll kill myself——"

"Prison?" Tucson's features assumed a look of surprise. "Who said anything about prison? There's no charge against you, Lee. You'll be free to do as you like."

There was a long silence. A look of incredulity crept over Cantrell's face. "You running a whizzer on me, Smith? Hell! I drew money from Trax Whitlock. Doc has told me how that counterfeiting ring was broken up. I was one of the gang."

Tucson said, "Bosh! You were contemptuous of that counterfeiting scheme. We know. Even Stow Whitlock admits that. There's only him and Gebhardt left alive now. Jeff Daulton isn't making any charges against you. I can't see where there's anything much against you at present. Sure, you've killed men, but they were the sort that deserved killing. If you hadn't killed them, they'd have killed you."

"You know a hell of a lot about me, it seems," Cantrell said in a sneering voice.

"Yeah, I do," Tucson admitted. "The past ten days or so I've made it my business to learn more. I've got a lot of friends around the country, Lee, men who know of you too. I've written letters and sent telegrams. You've been mean, hard, but I still think there's a chance for you—if you want to take it."

Some of the belligerency died from Cantrell's voice. "Look here, Smith, what's your game? Why are you giving me a break like this?"

"Maybe something's owing to you, Lee?"

Cantrell said in a weary voice. "Oh hell, because I warned you against Art Branch? I've already told you I did that so I could kill you myself——"

"Wait," Tucson interrupted, "let me do the talking for a minute. That scar on your head, Lee—I know how you got that."

"Sure," Cantrell said sullenly, "it's no secret. I got my head bashed in by a killer horse. I should've known better than to enter that corral."

"Let me tell it," Tucson said. "I read an account of it in a newspaper, at the time. You risked your life entering that corral to save a little two-year-old kid who'd crawled through the bars. The baby's life was saved, while you took one hell of a tromping from that horse. And you were only about seventeen or eighteen then, Lee."

"Aw-w-w!" Cantrell could only sputter for a moment. "So what?" he growled. "Maybe I was just showing off."

"I doubt that too," Tucson said. "Anyway, after you got out of the hospital, you started going mean. The older you grew, the meaner you got, and the more gun fights you got into. You may not realize it, but that wasn't all your fault. You had some bad luck."

"What in the devil are you talking about?" Cantrell demanded.

Tucson explained. "Doc Graham has made a mighty thorough examination of your head, Lee. He tells me your skull never healed right. There's a certain pressure on your brain that will have to be removed or you'll grow steadily worse. Now it's only headaches and bad eyes and meanness. Within another few years it may end in insanity."

"Hell! Do you expect me to believe that?"

"You're believing it right now, Lee. Don't try to bluff me. I know."

"All right"—sullenly—"I believe it. So what? So I'll get worse and end up in the booby hatch. By God, I'll shoot myself first!"

"Maybe that won't be necessary," Tucson said in the same quiet tones. "There's a doctor in the East who specializes in the sort of operation you need to relieve that pressure on your brain. He might be able to cure you."

"And charge like hell for his bone cutting," Cantrell snapped. "No—that's not for me. I don't have that much money."

"It's not a question of money, Lee. My pards and I aim to put up the cash. And if you come out cured, there'll be a job waiting for you on our 3-Bar-O spread, back in Texas. But the operation you need is a mighty dangerous one. Instead of curing, it might kill you. It's up to you to decide whether you want to take that chance. It's solely up to you, Lee."

Cantrell's head dropped on his chest. There was a long silence. Tucson took a final drag on his cigarette, stubbed out the fire on the sole of his boot, then rose and tossed the butt through the open window. When he returned to the bed, Cantrell had raised his head, but his eyes were moist. Tucson said again, "It's solely up to you, Lee."

Cantrell tried to reply, but for a moment his voice failed him. Finally he said brokenly, "God, you're a white man, Tucson Smith. I don't deserve this. You've made me realize things I never even thought of before. If I could be like you and your pards——"

"Forget it." Tucson smiled. "We're just ordinary cow folks. You can be like us, or better, if you choose. The question is, do you want to risk that operation?"

Cantrell swallowed hard. "Right now I want that operation so bad I hurt all over. The sooner I can have it, the better. It's the only decent chance left to me. . . . Damn you, Tucson Smith. You shoot me up so I can't shake hands, and I never wanted anything more in my life. But I'll do it yet. I swear it! And you won't be sorry for giving me this break. I'll—I'll—Tucson! Get out, will you, before I start bellerin' like a fool kid?"

"Go ahead and beller, Lee. I'm leaving." Tucson got to his feet and playfully gave Cantrell's head a slight push. "Get better fast, cowboy. We'll be seeing you again before we pull out."

He left the bedroom and pulled the door closed behind him. In Graham's office he answered the doctor's inquiring look with a short nod. "Lee wants the operation, Doc. You can telegraph that eastern surgeon to make arrangements, whenever you think Lee is fit to leave. I figure there's a lot of good stuff in that boy, if it's only given a chance to come out. He's never had anyone treat him decently before."

Graham slowly shook his head in perplexity. "Damned if I know how you do it, Tucson. You must have a mighty persuasive tongue to make an ornery cuss like Cantrell behave like a white man. I knew a parson once who always spoke of his converts as 'firebrands plucked from the burning.' Looks to me, Tucson, like you'd done a mite of plucking."

They talked a few minutes longer before Tucson departed for the street. On his way to the hotel the doctor's words recurred to him: "A firebrand plucked from the burning." Tucson smiled to himself. "Trouble is, there's so danged many still waiting to be plucked that it looks like an endless job." He drew a long sigh. "Oh well, all a man can do is keep trying—just keep trying. . . ."